also by Sara Daniell

THE STOCKBRIDGE NOVELS
Summer Seventeen & You
Under the Owl Tree

STAND ALONE NOVELS
A Life Unexpected
An Unfortunate Journey
Anything Goes on a Friday Night

ANTHOLOGIES
In Creeps the Night
A Winter's Romance
On the Edge of Tomorrow

A Stockbridge Novel

Falling in Reverse

Sara Daniell

LIVONIA, MICHIGAN

Edited by Wendi Temporado

Falling in Reverse

This book is a work of fiction. The characters, incidents, and dialogue are drawn from the author's imagination and are not to be construed as real. Any resemblance to actual events or persons, living or dead, is entirely coincidental.

Published by H2O
an imprint of BHC Press

Library of Congress Control Number:
2017945385

ISBN Numbers:
978-1-947727-97-7 (hardcover)
978-1-946848-57-4 (softcover)
978-1-947727-96-0 (ebook)

Visit the publisher:
www.bhcpress.com

Also available in eBook

To all the ones who need second chances.

Acknowledgments

To Katie Ivy, for being the best beta reader ever,
for reminding me to write, and for new friendship.
You're a rockstar!

Falling in Reverse

Chapter One

SADIE

Five words changed the course of my life: *He is in foster care.* Those five words made my heart stop. I couldn't imagine why the family I gave him to would give him to the system. *Is there something wrong with him?* It didn't make sense. He was perfect, and I remembered handing him over was the hardest thing I'd ever had to do in my life. But I did. I did it to protect Dane and myself. We were young, and I was scared. A day didn't go by that I didn't regret it, and now… What the fuck was I going to do?

I drove into Stockbridge, unsure of how to approach anyone after being gone for so long. New York and Juilliard were my home, and just as normal people do when they get busy, I lost touch. I'd be lying if I said I didn't work hard on losing touch, though. I put in overtime avoiding phone calls, emails, and occasional letters. Guilt since the ninth grade ate away at me. I let it fester until it created a nasty sore in my heart. I purposefully pushed everyone away, hoping one day they'd all forget about me—especially Dane.

But the things we do, and think we can somehow avoid, always come back to haunt us. They have a way of making us face our demons.

My hands gripped tighter around the steering wheel as I got closer to my dad's house. He was the only one who knew I was coming home. I didn't bother telling anyone else. That way if I chickened out and left, no one would have even known I was there to try to stop me.

I cursed when I saw the gas light come on. My old Rover sucked gas like crazy. Instead of turning to go to my dad's house, I turned toward the gas station on the corner of Main Street. I took Dane's old ball cap off the dash and put it on my head before parking and getting out.

My hands trembled as I dug through my purse, trying to find my debit card. All I could think about was the reason I was there and how to say what I had to say to Dane. He'd hate me more than he probably already did.

"Sadie? Sadie!" I turned to see Trevor getting out of an amazing GTO. I thought I might pee my pants.

I dropped my debit card and bent down to get it. When I stood, I was being wrapped in a hug.

"You're home!" he said excitedly.

I hugged him back and laughed. "Yeah. I am."

He picked me up so my feet were off the ground. "I've missed you! You have to have dinner with me tonight." He put me back down and stepped back, grinning. "I can't wait for you to meet Jason! You'll love him!"

I laughed. "Whoa. Breathe, Trev!"

He was bouncing he was so excited. "Jason's my boyfriend."

My eyes widened. "That's...that's great, Trevor." I hadn't seen him in almost eight years. He hadn't changed much, just a little taller and more filled out. "I don't know about dinner. I'm sure my dad will want to hang out. I'm probably not going to be here long."

His smile faded. "But I haven't seen you in eight years."

How did I say that I didn't contact him and tell him I was coming on purpose? I came here with one mission and that was to talk to Dane because I needed help.

"Yeah, and it's totally my fault. I got your emails and texts. I was just... busy. Ya know?" I walked over to the pump and swiped my card. I hit all the buttons I needed to before putting the pump into the car.

He moved back even more as he kept his eyes on me. "You weren't going to tell me you were home, were you?" He sounded hurt. He shook his head. "I guess I'll see you in another eight years then." He turned and headed for his car.

"Trevor," I said before he got into his car.

He turned his head so he could look at me.

"Wait." I pulled up the lever on the gas pump so it'd pump automatically. "I'll come to dinner. What time?" I did my best to smile.

I was hoping not to see anyone but Dane. The trip was hard enough, and seeing everyone would only make my heart hurt worse. I missed them.

He smiled a little. "Seven. There's a new dance studio in town. Mine and Jason's place is the apartment above it."

"What's the name of it?"

"Stockbridge Dance Academy."

I nodded. "All right. I'll see you at seven then. And sorry I didn't tell you I was coming. I didn't tell anyone except my dad."

He nodded and kissed my cheek. "You'll like Jason. He can cook."

I laughed. "Awesome."

I waved at him after he got into his car and shut the door. I let out a heavy sigh as I watched him drive away.

Why did I agree to dinner?

I needed to talk to my dad about everything that was going on and then find Dane. I didn't have time to waste.

After taking my receipt, I drove to my dad's. When I pulled into the driveway, he came out with my mom by his side. *Shit.* He must've told her I was coming home and something was wrong. I was hoping not to get Mom involved with all of this yet. I wanted to wait until I knew things for sure and had a plan.

I got out of the Rover and went around to the back where Dad met me. I opened the trunk and he started pulling my bags out. No hug, just silence. *Did he know?* I turned to face Mom who had her arms crossed in front of her. They had to know.

I followed them into the house and froze when I saw the same letter I received sitting on the kitchen counter.

Dear Mr. and Ms. Solis,

Your grandson is in foster care is in the custody of the State of Georgia.

Sincerely,
Anonymous

Tears filled my eyes as I looked at my parents. "Who is sending these letters? Do you think it's real?"

Dad set my bags down. "It's real all right; I called and confirmed it with DHS this morning. When you called and said you were coming home, I figured this is what it was about. Who is sending the letters, Sadie?"

I started to say something, but Mom beat me to it.

"We did a no-contact order eleven years ago!" Her shout made me jump.

"I don't know who is sending the letters," I said quietly. "But, I have to get him."

"And do what? Give up everything you've been working toward to raise a child?" Mom snapped.

"Yes," I said as tears fell.

Dad pinched the bridge of his nose and let out a dramatic sigh. "Talk to Dane."

"That's why I'm here."

"Did you ever tell him anything about the baby?" Mom asked.

I shook my head. "No. You both told me not to, and when I thought I might, I chickened out because I didn't want him to question why I didn't tell him about it sooner. But now I don't have a choice. I need his help."

"I'm gonna go put food on the grill. We can talk more about this over dinner," Dad said as he started pulling things out of the fridge.

"Trevor invited me to dinner. He saw me at the gas station."

Mom scoffed. "No. You're eating here and we're discussing this."

I wanted to argue, but Mom had those *don't push me* eyes.

"Yes, ma'am." I took my phone out of my back pocket and text Trevor, hoping he still had the same number.

Me: Not gonna make it.

I didn't wait for him to reply. I turned my cell off and took my bags up to my room.

Chapter Two

DANE

I wiped the sweat from my forehead after I finished packing up the work trucks with my crew. I gave them instructions for the next day and sent them home. I needed to grab some paperwork before heading home for the night, so I jumped in my truck and headed to the office. As I pulled into the parking lot, I saw Trevor's car.

"Weird," I mumbled. He should've gone home by now. I shut the truck off and went inside. When I came in, I heard Trevor muttering from his office. I pushed open his door and leaned against the frame. He was slamming a stapler into a stack of papers until it jammed. Cursing under his breath, he threw the stapler into a nearby trashcan.

"What has you here so late and pissy?" I asked. "Did you and Jason have a fight?"

"I made plans with an old friend for dinner and she canceled on me. I should have known that she would since she didn't even fuckin' tell me she was coming home or talk to me the past eight years."

I stiffened. "Sadie's back in town?" She was the only person I could think of that had been gone that long and could get to Trevor like this.

He looked at me and nodded. "I saw her at the gas station earlier."

I clenched my jaw. "Oh. Well…I'm going to grab some stuff from my office before heading to Zach and Hales'. You and Jason want to come over for dinner?"

He ran his hand down his face. "Sure. Might as well. I'll go get him then meet you there."

I nodded before going to my office. I did my best to keep my mind going from where I had tried to avoid for so long while I grabbed what I needed before heading out for the night.

I SLAMMED MY bare fists into Zach's punching bag over and over again. *How could she come back here and fuck with Trevor like that? What gave her the damn right?*

I was in the process of letting off steam when I heard Hales' voice behind me. I stopped hitting the bag and looked down at my knuckles to try and get a control on my breathing. They were bruised and bloody. She was going to kill me for not using boxing gloves.

"Yeah?" I asked without turning around.

"Dinner is ready. And you know Zach has gloves, right? I mean, it's not like I've told you a million times or anything."

I turned to face her. "I know." I grabbed the clean washcloth from her hands. She knew me too well. I started wiping off my knuckles. "How's the monkey today?"

She looked down at her stomach that was barely a pooch. "Making me puke my guts out." She looked at me. "Go get a shower and meet us outside. The boys and Millie asked to eat on the deck tonight."

"I don't have any clothes here. I took them all home."

"I'm sure Zach has something you can wear."

"Can I ask you a question before I go take a shower?" She turned back toward me and waited. "I'm a good guy, right?"

She sighed. "Dane, if this is about you leaving Millie to go to the Marines again, stop it. We all get why you went. Millie understood, too. And when she asked you to come home, you did. You have to stop worrying about that."

I looked up from my knuckles. "Trevor saw Sadie today." I ran my hand down my face and beard that I had grown out to hide the nasty scar on my chin.

"*What?*"

"She's back, Hales. Tell my brother I'm going to steal a shirt and some shorts."

Her eyebrows drew together. "Yeah…I'll tell him."

I kissed her cheek as I walked by. "You're amazing, Hales."

"Want me to make her go missing?" she called after me with a chuckle.

I shook my head. "Nah. Don't worry about it."

I went upstairs to Hailey and Zach's room to grab some clothes of Zach's but stopped when I saw a velvet box hidden under a stack of gym shorts.

"What the hell?" I mumbled as I opened the box.

"Dammit, you weren't supposed to see that. No one was." Zach came into the room. "I came into the room to hide it better."

"Are you going to ask Hales to marry you?"

"No." He took the ring and hid it deeper in the closet.

"Why not?"

"Because when I mentioned marriage a few days ago she laughed and said anyone who got married was an idiot."

I winced. "Ouch."

"Yeah." He handed me some clothes. "Go get cleaned up."

WHEN I CAME outside, I took a seat next to Millie. Everyone had started eating but stopped and stared at me awkwardly. I knew what they were doing. They were trying to gauge my feelings since finding out Sadie was in town.

I rolled my eyes. "I'm fine, guys. I'm not going anywhere."

Hailey crossed her arms and raised her eyebrows, slightly tilting her head to one side. Everyone else started eating again, except her.

Her and Zach's twins, Elliot and Jamison, started talking to her, thankfully, taking her attention off me.

Trevor looked at me apologetically. "I shouldn't have told you. Sorry," he whispered.

I shrugged. "It's fine."

I nudged Millie and smiled at her. "I'm not going anywhere. I promise." She smiled and nodded before she took another bite of food.

When I left for the Marines, I had been in a dark place. Losing Elliot hurt and then losing Sadie, I lost it. Without thinking, I enlisted into the Marines. No one said it aloud, but they all blamed Sadie.

I got out after four years because the only girl that mattered to me asked me to come home. My Millie. Zach and Hailey were growing their family, and I promised Millie that when I did come home, she could live with me and I'd raise her. We'd bonded so much after her dad passed away.

I kissed her head. Millie was twelve years old now and my whole world. The past four years Trevor and I had built a very successful construction business and it was finally time to build Millie and myself a home. Living in her and Elliot's old house had been good for a while, but the longer we stayed there, the more time we spent at Zach and Hales. While that place had good memories, it was also filled with sad ones.

"Trevor, I'm going to take the next two weeks off. I think it's time for me to start working on the house for me and Millie."

Millie gasped and grinned. "Really?"

"Yes, really." I gently tugged on one of her curls.

Trevor smiled. "Why don't we have the business do it? It will go quicker, and we have enough money put aside to use toward other projects."

"Sounds like a plan." I smiled before starting to eat.

I was excited to get started on it and it'd busy my mind instead of thinking about who was home. Just when I thought I might get over her and be able to move on, she came crashing into my world again.

Chapter Three

SADIE

I couldn't sleep. After talking to my parents, I couldn't do anything but think. Think about my son who was out there somewhere. Think about telling Dane. Think about *not* telling Dane. Think about what this meant for Juilliard and my dreams.

I pulled the pillow over my face and screamed into it.

When I pulled the pillow off my face, I stared up at the glow-in-the-dark stars on my ceiling. I remembered when Dane put those up for me because he knew how much I loved the stars.

Grabbing my phone from the nightstand, I sat up, turned it on, and held my breath as I waited for all the texts I missed to come in. I exhaled slowly as I saw a text from Trevor.

Trevor: Fine

One word. Trevor only texting one word was never a good thing. Or, at least, it wasn't in the past.

I held my thumbs over the text keys thinking about what to say. Really, I just needed my best friend. No matter how much time had passed, I couldn't deny when I needed him.

Me: I know it's late, but I need you before I completely fall apart.

Trevor knew about the pregnancy, but he had no idea I'd given the baby up for adoption. All he knew when I left for a year to go to dance school was that I had lost it.

Trevor: You need me? Since when?

I didn't really go to dance school. My parents sent me off to live with my grandparents in Duluth until I had the baby. Then I came home after I got all the baby weight off. Since I homeschooled while I was away, I was able to start back at high school and graduate on time.

Me: Since forever.

It took a little bit before he answered.

Trevor: What's wrong?

Me: Where are you?

Trevor: I'm on the couch at Coach Eliot's old house.

Me: Can I meet you somewhere?

Trevor: Meet me at the dance studio

Me: Don't tell anyone. Please.

Trevor: Let me make sure Millie and Dane are asleep. Meet me there in an hour.

Me: Okay.

I got out of bed, got dressed, threw Dane's old ball cap on, and headed out to my Rover. I'd ride around to pass time until he met me there.

I GOT OUT of the vehicle when I saw Trevor's car pulling in, locked the door, and waited for him to get out.

When he did, his eyes flicked to my hat before leaning against his car. "Do you want to talk out here or go in?"

"Inside."

He nodded and walked to the door. He unlocked it and shut off the alarm as we came inside. "We can talk in Jason's office."

"Wow," I whispered. I had the slightest urge to lace up my ballet shoes.

"Yeah. Dane designed it. He's amazing when it comes to this kind of shit. I'm good with the business side and the people."

We walked into Jason's office and Trevor motioned for me to sit. I shook my head. I was too nervous to sit.

"Tell me what's going on."

"You look great, Trev." I leaned against the desk.

"Thanks. I have to work out a lot to keep up with Dane and to keep off the weight from eating all of Jason's cooking." He smiled. "You look good, too. Now, stop putting off telling me what's going on."

"I'm not putting it off. I'm trying to figure out where to start. Honestly, I feel like I'm going to throw up right now." My throat started getting tight, and I could feel the well of tears about to spill from my eyes.

He stood and came over to me, putting his hands on my shoulders. "Tell me."

It was so hard saying the truth out loud. I'd kept it in for so long.

"Remember..." I bit my lip. "Do you remember when I got pregnant our ninth-grade year?"

"Of course I do. You've not been the same since you lost the baby."

"Remember when I went off to that dance school for a year?"

He nodded. "Your parents thought it would help you."

"You never told anyone about the baby, right?"

"Of course not. You were devastated. It was hard enough seeing one of my best friends going through that; I couldn't watch Dane go through it too. It was bad enough watching him lose you over and over again."

I looked down at my feet. "Trev, I never lost the baby."

"What do you mean?" His tone was angry and confused.

A few tears fell. "I left to stay with my grandparents in Duluth. I was homeschooled and stayed there to have the baby. To have...my son. We had a family lined up for him and everything." My whole body was shaking. I walked over to a chair and sat down.

"Son? He's alive?" he asked angrily. "And you kept it from Dane? How did you put him up for adoption without his approval?"

Tears were falling heavily. "I told them I didn't know who the father was."

It hurt he was so angry, but he had every right to be.

His fists clenched. "Why are you telling me this now? It's been eleven years."

I could barely speak through my sobs. "H-He's back i-in the system."

"Fuck." He moved quickly and wrapped his arms around me. "We need to go talk to Brink and Dane. Now."

"I don't know h-how." I couldn't stop crying.

"Then I'll help you."

"My parents and I both got anonymous letters. My dad confirmed it with Child Protective Services this morning." I wiped my eyes on the back of my hands. "Don't hate me, Trevor. I was young and stupid. I listened to my parents instead of my heart."

He sighed and gently touched my face. "Sadie, I could never hate you. I'm angry, but I don't hate you."

"What if Dane is with someone at home? I can't just show up."

"The only 'someone' he will have there is Millie. He has custody of her now."

That news shocked me a little. "Well, then I definitely can't tell him with Millie there."

He closed his eyes. "She'll be asleep. I won't put off telling him. If you want me to go alone and tell him I will." He looked at me. "This is going to hurt him a lot, Sadie."

"You don't think I know that?" I narrowed my eyes at him and wiped the tears away.

"No, you don't know. But I will tell you more about that once we go talk to him."

He pulled out his phone. "I'll text him to let him know we're on our way. And I'll text Brink."

I thought for a second about letting him go talk to him, but there was no way I could do that. I had to own up to my mistake. Dane and I had a son out there and he had every right to hear it from me.

Chapter Four

DANE

I paced the living room as I waited for Trevor to get to there. What the hell could have been so important that he had to talk to me *right now*? Whatever it was, it wasn't good. Trevor knew how much trouble I had sleeping and wouldn't have text me if it wasn't important. He wouldn't risk waking me up.

I rubbed my beard and jaw before plopping down on the couch. I wasn't seated long when I heard a key going into the front door lock. I jumped to my feet as Trevor walked in. I opened my mouth to ask what was going on when I saw three people behind him: Brink, Zach, and Sadie. My mouth stayed hanging open as my eyes landed on Sadie. My heart felt like it was going to beat out of my chest while knots formed in my gut. I hadn't seen her in eight years and there she was standing in my living room at three in the morning looking as sexy as ever.

"What the hell is going on?"

Zach shrugged. "Don't know, but I was told you'd need me."

When Sadie walked in a bit more, I noticed her eyes were swollen from crying. I always hated to see her like that. I had beaten up a lot of people over the years who made her cry. I looked away from her gaze to Brink.

He pointed to the couch. "Sit."

I did as I was told and waited.

Sadie was wearing my hat. The hat I gave her forever ago. She walked over and stood in front of me.

"Dane," she said quietly and sniffled. She struggled to make eye contact with me.

"Sadie. It's been a while," I said as I looked at her. "Why have you been crying?" *Dammit, not supposed to care, remember? You haven't seen her in eight years. Don't care.*

"Because I'm a horrible person. I came back home to talk to you." She paled, and I was afraid she might pass out.

I looked to my brother who had sat down next to me before looking to Trevor and then Brink. No one was giving away anything. *What is going on?*

"Maybe you should sit. You look like you're going to be sick."

She nodded and sat on the loveseat across from me. She finally met my eyes.

"Remember when I went off the dance school for a year?"

"Yeah. It was right after you dumped me."

She was crying more now. She nodded. "This has to do with the reason I always push you away. I've kept something from you. A big something, and now I can't anymore."

Trevor sat down next to her. I watched as he put his arm around her shoulders.

"What did you keep from me?"

"I was pregnant. I didn't go to dance school. I went to stay with Mammaw June and Papaw John in Duluth. Because..." She took a steadying breath. "My parents thought it'd be best if I go there and have the baby, put it up for adoption, and then come home as if nothing ever happened. I-I gave our son up for adoption, Dane. And now he's back in the system."

I could tell it took every ounce of energy she had to say those words to me.

"W-What?" Zach asked, voicing the words I couldn't get out. "Dane has a son and you never told him?"

She couldn't form words. Instead, she nodded and started bawling.

"Zach, this is hard enough without you losing your temper," Brink said from the other side of me.

I watched as Trevor held on to Sadie as she cried. I sat there feeling a multitude of emotions. Anger, hurt, confusion, shock, sympathy. All of the emotions were fighting to win.

I had a son. *A son.* I felt tears fill my eyes. He had to be close to twelve. He couldn't be much younger than Millie.

I felt a hand on my shoulder. "Dane," Zach said worriedly. He gave my shoulder a squeeze, but I didn't look at him. I couldn't stop staring at Sadie. She had kept the fact I had a son from me for eleven years. I missed out on eleven years!

Eleven fucking years.

"Are you wanting to get your son?" Brink asked, breaking the silence.

Sadie nodded. "Dane, if you want to press charges for me lying to the hospital and adoption agency and telling them I didn't know who the father was, I understand."

Her hands were clasped in her lap and shaking terribly.

I didn't say anything. I had a war going on inside of me. I wanted to hate her but, at the same time, I didn't. I couldn't. We had been in ninth grade. We were just kids. But that didn't mean I forgave her. She'd lied to me over and over again.

"Dane, you're worrying me." I could hear the worry and fear in Zach's voice. I couldn't blame him. The last time I was this upset, I enlisted in the military a few days later.

I hadn't spoken to anyone after Sadie left. Not until I enlisted.

Brink stood. "I'm going to go call Quinn. I'll use the office phone."

"I won't press charges," I said, finally making myself speak. My voice sounded odd to me.

Sadie stood. "I'll leave." She looked at Trevor. "Please tell Brink to let me know what he finds out."

"I'm going to follow you back to your dad's place," Trevor said as he stood.

I glared at Trevor. "Did you know I had a son?" Anger had finally won out. Sadie looked at Trevor worriedly.

Trevor shook his head. "She told me she lost the baby. I hated seeing her go through that pain so I didn't tell you. You were already hurting because she pushed you away. I didn't want to add to it."

"You knew she was pregnant?"

Trevor nodded.

"So, every time I asked you why she broke up with me and why she pushed me away, you knew it was because of the baby?"

Trevor nodded again. "Yes."

"Get the fuck out," I growled. "Both of you."

I walked to the kitchen and went out the back door. I headed straight for the Owl Tree. Before I could think better of it, I hit the tree several times. The pain it caused snapped me out of my shock. I fell to my knees and started crying.

I heard a shuffling sound beside me and then felt a hand cuff my left shoulder.

"Let it out, buddy," Zach said calmly.

"I have a son I didn't even know about, Zach! She kept it from me for eleven years!"

"It's fucked up."

I looked up at him without wiping my eyes. "What do I do?"

"I'm pretty fuckin' pissed off right now. I'm probably not the best person to ask."

I dropped my head and stared down at my hand that was starting to swell. I closed my eyes before opening them up again and standing. "You should go home."

"No way in hell I'm leaving. I'm staying with you until I know you're all right."

"Then you'll never leave. I won't ever be all right when it comes to this. But I won't go and re-enlist." I wiped at my eyes.

"Of course you won't. You have a little girl counting on you to stick around. And now a son who needs a father."

I nodded. "I have a son. I've missed out on so much, Zach. How can I ever make that up to him?"

"You didn't know. Be honest with him." When I got a good look at Zach, I saw tears in his eyes. "I have a nephew." He wiped his eyes. "All I can think about is that he's probably scared to death. Why is he in the system if Sadie had adopted him out? I need more answers."

"Me too. Let's go see what Brink found out." I grimaced when I moved my hand. It was a fucking stupid idea to hit a tree.

"And some ice."

I nodded and we headed inside. I needed to find out where my son was and how I could get him.

Chapter Five

SADIE

I woke up next to Trevor. He'd let me stay at Jason's place with him. I felt like the worst person in the entire world. It was my fault that Dane was pissed at Trev. I tried to get up quietly so I could leave without waking him.

"Hey, I'm heading home. Go back to sleep," I whispered when I saw him open his eyes.

"What time is it?"

I looked at my phone. "Nine."

He sat up quickly. "In the morning?"

"Yeah."

He jumped out of bed. "I'm so running late!"

I watched him rush around, throwing off his clothes and putting on new ones. I followed him downstairs and out to the parking lot. He hugged me quickly, got in his car, and sped off.

I looked at my Rover then got in. After making my way down the road a bit, I called Brink, hoping it was still his number.

"Hello?" Quinn's voice rang out through the speaker.

"Quinn?"

"Yes. May I ask who's calling?"

"Sadie."

"Ah. Hello, Sadie. Brink just went to bed. I can give you a rundown about what he found out or I can have him call you once he wakes up."

I quickly pulled onto the shoulder. "No, tell me. Please." I could hear my heartbeat it was thudding so loudly.

"DHS is going to come do a house study and interview of Dane on Friday. Brink has stated that Dane would like to get custody of him and they have agreed, as long as Dane takes the classes and passes everything, he will be allowed to get Tate. A test has to be done so Dane doesn't have to tell them you lied about not knowing who the father is. Once the test results come back, it should just be a matter of time. Brink is working on documents for the both of you so you can share custody. He said it could still be a couple of weeks before Tate can come live with Dane, but you both will be allowed visitation rights as soon as the test results come back. Brink will be able to tell you more once he wakes up."

"Wait…"

"Wait what?"

I felt like I was going to throw up. "I want him to live with me. Did anyone plan on discussing this with me?" I was pissed.

"You gave up all rights to him, Sadie. Dane did not. It was the quickest and easiest route to do."

I couldn't answer. I didn't know what to say. She was right.

"Besides, you're still in school. Do you even have a home or a job? You will have to have both before DHS would even consider you."

"I have a job and an apartment. But since getting the news, I planned on moving back to Stockbridge with my parents until I can get on my feet. I knew keeping him in New York wouldn't work because I want Dane to be as involved as he can." Tears filled my eyes. "Just do what you guys have to do to get him here."

"We will. I'll have Brink call you once he wakes up."

I wanted to thank her but my throat was too thick with guilt and stress. I hung up and burst into tears. I rested my head on the steering wheel as I cried. Once I finally calmed down, I drove home.

Dad was at work but Mom was on the front porch swing waiting for me. I got out of the Rover and walked up the steps. I leaned my back against the railing and ran my fingers through my tangled hair.

"I heard you told Dane."

I nodded.

"I was told he'd be fighting for custody."

I looked at her. "He is, but not how you made it sound. Quinn makes a good point. I'll be moving here and don't have a house or a job right now." I wiped my eyes. "I gave up my rights, Mom. Dane didn't. He didn't even know. Had he have known, Tate would have been with him since birth."

"Your father and I could fight for him." She raised a brow at me.

"What? You two are divorced. And you can't do that! You two are the ones who told me I should do the adoption and not tell Dane!"

Tears filled her eyes. "I know. Dammit, Sadie, I know! But do you honestly think your father and I didn't regret that decision? All we saw then was our baby girl having a baby of her own. Dane's life at home wasn't the best. We thought we were making the best decision."

"Why didn't you help us then? Why didn't you let me keep him and raise him at home?"

"You had dreams! We didn't know we were making a huge mistake then!"

We were yelling so loudly at one another we were making some of the neighborhood dogs bark.

I shook my head and ran my fingers through my hair again. "I can't do this with you right now." I went inside and slammed the door. I went to my room, locked the door behind me, and sat on the floor with my back against the bed.

My phone dinged.

Dane: We need to talk.

Me: When?

Dane: Tonight. Millie is going to spend the night with Zach and Hales.

Me: Do you want me to come to your house?

Dane: Yeah.

Me: What time?

Dane: Is eight okay?

Me: Yeah.

Dane: All right. See you tonight then.

I stared at my phone for several seconds before putting it down and getting into bed. I stayed up most of the night with Trevor, talking to him about everything and crying on his shoulder. I didn't deserve a friend like him. I did him and everyone else so wrong, but I was thankful for his comfort because, dammit, I needed it.

I kicked my shoes off onto the floor and got under the covers. I needed sleep and to let my brain rest before having to go face Dane again.

Chapter Six

DANE

I looked down at my watch for the tenth time. *Ten o'clock.* I cursed under my breath and grabbed my keys. I got into my truck and headed to Sadie's dad's house. It didn't take me too long to get there, but it seemed to take forever. I'd hoped she just stood me up and not that something had happened to her. I parked and shut off my truck before getting out and hurrying to the door. I pushed the doorbell. I knew she was home when I saw her Rover parked in the driveway.

The door opened and her dad stood there with a surprised look on his face. "Dane?"

"Is Sadie okay? She was supposed to meet me to talk but she never showed up."

He yawned. I clearly had woken him up. "She's asleep upstairs. She woke up long enough to eat dinner but then said she was going to lay back down for a little bit until she had to leave. I forgot to wake her up. She asked me to." He moved out of the way. "Come on in."

I put my hands in my pockets and shook my head. "No, don't worry about it. Let her sleep. I'll catch up with her after she's gotten some rest."

"Dane?" I heard Sadie say from inside. She was rushing over, pulling her ponytail through the back of my old ball cap. "I'm so sorry! I woke up and realized I never woke up to my alarm." She looked at her dad. "I'll be back later."

He nodded and moved so she could walk past him.

She looked up at me once she made it onto the porch. "I'm so sorry." Her dad shut the door.

I shrugged. "I'm sure you're tired or you wouldn't have slept so much."

She nodded. "I was about to call you." She drew her eyebrows together in confusion. "Why are you here?"

"It's ten and...I was worried. You were supposed to meet me at eight." I shrugged again. "Like I said. You had to be tired to sleep so much." I pulled my keys out of my pocket as I headed for my truck. "Let's just drive around."

She followed me to the truck and got in after I opened the door for her.

I let out a shaky breath as I opened my own door and got in. I hadn't been this nervous in years.

"How's Juilliard?" I asked after a few moments of silence.

"Really good. Going on my eighth year there. I work there, too. I perform in the ballets and help write plays."

I had spent all day calming myself down and reminding myself that she had been only a kid. It didn't excuse the fact she never told me, but it had calmed me down enough to start thinking.

"That's good."

She was playing with the ring on her thumb. She'd had that thing since as long as I could remember.

She nodded. "It's amazing there. It's really been a dream come true," she said quietly.

My grip on the steering wheel tightened. "When do you go back?"

She didn't say anything for several seconds. "I don't. I mean, I have to go back and get all of my things from my apartment. I also need to talk with the school and quit my job." She turned her head to face the window instead of me.

I loosened my grip. I don't know why but knowing she was going to stay calmed me down. I wasn't really paying attention to where I was going and was shocked when I realized I was heading to the lake. We remained silent until I parked. This was the spot we used to come when we were younger. It was the reason I bought it.

She looked at me and smiled a little.

I looked at what I had gotten done on my new home today. After talking to Trevor this morning and fixing things with him, the team and I had gotten a lot of work done.

"You're really doing it?"

"Doing what?"

She used her eyes to follow the frame of the house. "Building on the lake. You always said you would."

"Yes. I bought this place a few years back. It connects to Zach and Hales' place." I kept my eyes on the frame. "Millie loves it out here."

"How is she?"

Music was softly playing on the radio, and I noticed her fingers tapping to the rhythm on her thigh. Sadie always felt music so deeply. I guarantee she was choreographing in her head.

"She's good. Smart. Like scary smart, but she's good. She still has bad days, but I don't think that will ever change."

She nodded. "Yeah, she's been through a lot." She looked at the house again. "Can you show me?"

I nodded. "I changed some things throughout the day. As I calmed down some."

As I said the last part, her eyes fell, and I could see she was ashamed. She got out of the truck.

I killed the engine and got out. I walked over to her and pointed at the main part.

"This part will be the living room and kitchen area. The house will be separated into two parts. I've added a second section to the plans earlier today. It will have a bedroom, bathroom, small kitchen, and a small living room." I put my hands in my pockets. "Just in case you don't want to eat with us or something," I said the last part quietly. "The main house is connected to the small one by a hallway.

She looked at me in shock. "W-What?"

"Yeah, if you want to move in or stay here some." I shrugged. "You don't have to, but I figured you'd want to be near Tate."

Her breath caught in her throat. She closed her mouth but kept her eyes on me. I couldn't tell if she was happy, pissed, or just nervous.

I looked away from her and out at the frame. "We have to work together to make the best of this. I don't want to put Millie or Tate in a home that is filled with tension."

She leaned against a steel beam. "I'm so sorry I kept it from you."

"I know you are. But it may take me a while to forgive you."

"I'm not asking you to forgive me, Dane. I don't think I'll ever forgive myself."

I leaned against one of the beams. "I'm going to push for the house to be done as quickly as possible. Anything you want added to your part, you need to let me know." I straightened up. I couldn't slouch for long; it wasn't in my nature anymore.

"Dane, don't. You don't have to do this. Not for me."

"I'm not doing this for you. I'm doing this for our son."

She flinched a little at the words *our son*. She swallowed hard and nodded.

"I'm shocked they kept the name I gave him. I figured they would have changed it." She wiped her eyes. "I want to know why he's in the system." She struggled to get the words out. "Has Brink said anything about that?"

"His adoptive parents were killed in a car wreck."

"He wasn't hurt, was he?" She pushed off the frame and stood straighter.

I rubbed the back of my neck. "He's physically fine. Emotionally, he's struggling." I looked at her and met her eyes. "Millie and I are going to meet him this weekend. Do you want to go?"

She looked at me like she was shocked I'd even ask. Of course she wanted to. She smiled and nodded.

"But, do you think maybe we should just go? Bring Millie another time? I think it's going to be a big enough shock that he's meeting his birth parents for the first time. He's eleven. I'm sure he's going to hate me for giving him up." Tears filled her eyes. "He's going to hate me, Dane."

"You won't know until you talk to him and he knows Millie and I are coming. They're close to the same age and Brink and I both thought he might respond better to her."

She glared back at me with her jaw clenched.

"Is there a reason you're looking at me like that?"

She scoffed. "Sounds like you guys have it all figured out." She walked toward the truck.

"So, you're pissed because I'm actively trying to get my son?" I was trying not to snap. "Isn't that why you came to tell me? I'm confused, Sadie. What the fuck did you expect out of all of us?" I was furious. "The poor kid has been through hell and you're angry because we're trying to make it easier on him?"

She turned on her heels to face me. "To include me, Dane! Instead, you're making plans and treating me like I don't have an active say in how we handle all of this! Instead, you're just inviting me like it's a fucking birthday party!" Her whole body was shaking as she yelled at me.

"I was fuckin' pissed at you last night and didn't want to talk to you. So, yes, I made plans without you. I've been doing that for eight years now. But at least I'm trying to include you. I'm trying to work on including you in every-thing! That's more than you've ever done for me."

She kept her eyes on me and I watched her walls crumbling down. Her once square shoulders fell and she hung her head.

I cursed and punched one of the beams. Then I cursed again at my own stupidity. After punching the tree the other night, I knew I probably fucked my hand up good this time. "I'm not trying to make you feel bad." I looked down at my hand and then back at Sadie.

The frightened look on her face killed me. She glanced at my hand and then at me. Her voice shook as she said, "Take me home."

I tossed her my keys. "Just take the truck." I looked out at the water. Tears were filling my eyes. I felt like I was about to fall apart right in front of her. I'd lost the grip on my emotions and anger and acted like a damn fool punching that beam.

She tossed them right back at me. "I'll call Trevor."

The emotions regarding having a son were too raw. I wasn't thinking straight. "Do what you want," I said, my voice breaking.

She took her cellphone from her back pocket and walked off.

I walked to the beach and sat. *That* was not how the evening was supposed to go. We were supposed to come to an agreement and work together civilly. Instead, I'd lost my temper and she ran—what she seemed to do best when things got hard.

Chapter Seven

SADIE

I couldn't get ahold of Trev. I cursed when I realized I was going to have to go back and work this out with Dane. He was right, we had to do what was best for Tate. Me being dramatic and getting pissed wasn't the right way to go about any of it. With a defeated sigh, I put my phone in my back pocket and walked back toward the house. Thankfully, there were no walls so I could see right through it to the lake. I saw him standing near the water. The closer I got, I could see his shoulders moving. Then I heard him.

He was crying.

My heart shattered inside my chest as I picked up my pace. Once I made it to him, I wrapped him in my arms and cried with him. We were in this together. We had to be. There was no other way.

His arms wrapped around me as he buried his face in my hair. "I'm sorry. I didn't mean to lose my temper," he said as he slowly started gaining control.

I rubbed his back. "Shhh," I said, trying to soothe him. He had every right to lose it, and I'd be lying if I said I hadn't lost my temper over all of this, too.

When he pulled back from me, his eyes were red and swollen. "I never intended to yell. I wanted us to talk and figure things out."

I reached up and wiped under his eyes with my thumbs. I kept my hands on his face and made sure his eyes stayed on mine.

"I know. We're in a mess, Dane. We need to work together and not against each other. I'll move into the house with you. I'll do anything I can to make life for Tate as easy as possible. Whatever it takes."

"And I will do my best not to be so angry. That's not good for anyone." He looked down at his hand, and my eyes followed.

I wanted to comment on his anger. I had never seen him act like that. It was scary. But the sight of his hand had me worried.

"Dane…" I barely touched it, and he winced.

"I'm an idiot for punching the stupid beam."

It was super swollen. "I pushed you. I'm sorry." I looked at him. "You need to get that checked out."

"Sadie, there's a lot that has changed about both of us. We need to take this week before we get Tate to learn about each other again. We don't need any surprises when he gets here." He looked back at his hand. "I guess I should go get it checked. Dammit."

"Can I have your keys? I'll drive you to the ER."

He pulled the keys out of his pocket and handed them to me.

I made sure he was in and helped him buckle so he wouldn't have to use his hand. He didn't like that I had to do that, but he'd get over it. Dane hated when his man card got fucked with.

I walked around the truck and got into the driver's side. I was about to stick the key in the ignition but stopped. I swear my heart did too. A picture of me was on his dash, next to the fuel gauge. Next to mine was a picture of Millie. I was shocked to be in such an important spot. Anyone next to Millie had to mean something. She was his entire world.

"What's wrong?" he asked when I still didn't start the truck.

Before I left, I sneaked the picture into his truck with a note. The note was short and simple. I'd intended on writing more, but I couldn't see through my tears. He'd kept it. That meant it meant something to him. That *I* meant something to him.

"It's been eight years, and you kept it," I said quietly.

He looked at his dashboard before looking out the window. "Yeah…I did."

I smiled a little and cranked the truck. "I figured you would've burned it." I pulled onto the road and drove toward town.

"I would never burn it. No matter what's gone on, I still love you," he admitted quietly.

There was a lot I could say in response to that, but I wasn't prepared to spill my heart out in that way. Not yet. Like he had pointed out, we both had changed. Before we addressed our relationship, we had to learn to co-parent.

I couldn't not respond at all, though. So, I reached over and held his left hand that wasn't hurt. When his thumb moved across my knuckles, a surge of emotions filled me. Little gestures like that made me a hot mess. It was gestures like that and when he buried his face in my hair and held me that made me remember when our love was unstoppable.

Those little moments that he and I only shared when no one else was around. *Don't go there, Sadie,* I reminded myself. *Not yet.*

Dane's phone started ringing so he let go of my hand to answer it. He looked at it before accepting the call. "Hey, Hales. What's up?"

He listened for a second before talking. "I will be over after I go get my hand checked out." He groaned. "No, I'm fine. I was an idiot and hit something I shouldn't have. I'll be there later. It will be late but I will be over. No don't come. Hales, don't—" He slammed the phone down on the seat. "Great."

"She's coming, isn't she?"

"Yeeess," he said, exasperated.

"Well, is everything okay? I mean, why did she need you to go there?"

"Her and Zach wanted to check on me and for me to stay with them tonight. They're paranoid," he muttered.

"Paranoid?" I stopped at a red light when we came into town and turned my head toward him.

He shrugged. "I might have left eight years ago, and ever since then, whenever I get overly upset, everyone worries I'll disappear."

"You left? Where did you go?" The light turned green, and I started driving again.

He looked back out the window. "Does it really matter?"

"Apparently it does if Hailey and Zach want to keep an eye on you tonight." He sighed. "I joined the Marines."

I knew something was different about him and not just that eight years had been good to him. Age looked good—I shook my head to stop my mind from going there. But yeah, different.

"Oh," I breathed out. "Ummm. Wow."

"I was in there for four years. I was thinking about re-enlisting when Millie called and wanted me to come home. I've felt guilty about leaving Millie ever since. I won't be joining again."

I pulled into the hospital entrance and found a parking spot. I turned off the truck and looked at Dane.

"Did you go to war?" I looked at his hand. "Sorry, we can talk about this later. Let's get you inside."

"Yes, I did," he said before getting out of the truck.

I had so many questions, and although I saw him standing here and was fine—well, sort of—I still worried like he was leaving for war tomorrow.

I got out of the truck, locked it, and walked with him inside.

Chapter Eight

DANE

I rolled my eyes when I heard Hales' voice from where I was in a room.

"Hales has such loud voice," I said with a chuckle. "You may want to go save whoever she's yelling at." I winced as the doctor worked on my hand but I kept my eyes on Sadie.

She shook her head. "Nope. I'm good."

I clenched my jaw as the doctor finished putting my hand and wrist in a brace. I felt sweat forming on my brow.

"I'll get some medicine for you to take. You won't need surgery, but the brace will need to stay on for several weeks.

Sadie chuckled. When the doctor gave her a disapproving stare, she covered her mouth. The doctor shook his head and left the room. Just as he shut the door, Hales barged into the room.

"Did you scare the hell out of a poor nurse?" I asked with a frown.

Hailey's eyes went to Sadie after she saw that I was okay.

"Why are you smiling?" she snapped.

Sadie's mouth opened but closed again. She glanced at me and then at Hales. "The doctor was giving Dane orders, and I thought it was funny. Dane is stubborn."

"And how the hell would you know that? You've been gone for eight years!"

"Hailey, don't," I said through a clenched jaw.

Sadie looked at me. "I'll be waiting outside." She kissed the top of my head before walking out.

Hailey's mouth fell open. "Tell me you're not back together!"

"We're not together, but we are working on getting along." I was trying to keep my voice lowered but needed her to hear how serious I was on the matter. "I won't have Millie or Tate in a home filled with tension."

"Why is she going to be involved at all? She gave up those rights, Dane!"

"She was fourteen, Hales. Only a little older than Millie. She was being pushed by her parents to give him up. No, I don't agree with it and, yes, I'm still pissed she didn't tell me. But she's his mom."

"And your dad is your dad, but he isn't fit to be," she retorted.

"My dad is an abusive asshole. Sadie was young and stupid. Besides, if we deny her rights, she'll fight us, and that's not something I want to put Tate or me through."

That calmed her down. *Some.* She pointed to my hand. "Did she piss you off?"

"Does it matter? I was an idiot and broke my hand. I shouldn't have let my temper control me. I know better."

"Yes, it matters, Dane. It matters a whole helluva lot. I'm not letting her destroy you again."

A nurse came in and kept a safe distance between Hailey and her as she handed me discharge papers. "Mr. Shaw, you're free to go." She backed away and waited near the door, keeping her eyes on Hailey.

Hailey rolled her eyes. "Okay, so I came in a little dramatic."

"A little? You terrified the poor girl."

She smiled a little when I raised a brow. "They weren't going to let me back. They said the room was at capacity."

I chuckled and shook my head, standing. "Hales, no matter what happens, I'm not going to leave again. I made a promise to all of you and to Millie. I'm not going anywhere." I knew that was what she was afraid of. She was scared I'd get hurt and leave her again.

"It's not just that, Dane. You deserve to be happy. This curveball Sadie threw… It's worse than any curveball I've ever thrown. And I've thrown some really badass ones." She leaned in closer. "I have every right to not like her. I'm going to try. For you and for your son. But right now, this is hard to forgive. It's almost unforgivable. And I can't keep my crazy-pregnant self quiet. You know that."

"I know. It's going to be hard on everyone. Zach wants to kick her ass, and if she wasn't a woman, he probably would."

She watched me sign the discharge papers.

"Well, if I wasn't pregnant, I would."

I took the prescription from the nurse and the medicine that I probably wouldn't take. Sadie was right; I was stubborn as a damn mule. "Do you still want me to come to your house tonight?"

"Yes. I want to make sure you don't bring that bitch into your bed."

The nurse stood by the door unsure of her next move.

I rolled my eyes. "I wasn't planning on it." I looked at the nurse and smiled. "Ignore her. She's pregnant and cranky." I winked at her.

She opened the door to let us out.

Sadie was in the waiting room chewing on her nails, a habit that hadn't changed over all the years. She stopped when she saw Hailey and me.

"I'll see ya at your house soon," I said to Hales as I nudged her toward the door. After she left, I turned to Sadie. "You ready? I can drive you home."

She put my keys behind her back and shook her head. "You took a pain pill. The nurse told me."

I blinked a few times. "Only one. It won't do much to me. Besides, I'm going to have to drive once I leave your place anyway."

"I don't like that idea. How about you leave your truck at my house, and I drop you off at Zach and Hailey's?" Her tone didn't leave much room for argument.

"All right. But you can just take me home and drive my truck. I'll get Trevor to pick me up from work and swing me by to get it."

She thought about it for a second and then nodded.

Sensing her tension, I attempted some small talk. "Have you met Jason yet?"

"Briefly," she said, acting like she didn't really want to elaborate.

"Did you not like him?"

"It was in passing, on my way to the guest bedroom above the studio." She cranked the engine.

"And?" I asked with a raised eyebrow. We all loved Jason.

"I can't say if I like him or not yet. He literally handed me a blanket from a closet and said goodnight. That was it."

"You'll like him once you get to know him. We all love him. He makes Trev very happy."

"I know he does. I'm just… I don't expect many people to like me here, Dane. I really fucked up." She shrugged. "Are you and Trevor okay?" she asked as she started driving. "I put him in a hard place asking him to keep that from you."

"We're fine. After I calmed down some I was able to talk to him."

She smiled, but it faded a little as she got lost in her thoughts. "I wonder who he looks like. I hope he has your red hair and freckles."

I stared out the window. "I honestly hope he's nothing like me."

"Oh stop." She laughed a little. "I hope he gets my olive skin so the sun doesn't hate him like it hates you."

"Yeah, it does hate me. And working in construction doesn't keep me out of the sun much."

"The sun makes your freckles play connect the dots." She snorted when she laughed harder. "Remember that time Trevor and I connected your freckles on your face with a Sharpie in the fourth grade? They sort of resembled a really weird butterfly." She was laughing so hard that I worried she might not be paying attention to the road.

"I remember. It took me forever to get it off." I smiled. "Now pay attention to the road, Daisy."

Her laughter faded and she held the steering wheel with both hands.

When we got to Zach and Hales' house, she parked in the driveway and got out to open the door for me before I could do it myself.

"Sadie, I'm fine." I got out and looked toward the front of the house. Zach and Hales were waiting on the porch. "Looks like Mom and Dad waited up," I said sarcastically.

"Wonder if they'd freak out if I kissed you goodnight." She bit her lip, fighting a smirk. She stopped just as we started walking. She looked at me in awe.

"Why are you looking at me like that? It's weird."

"You called me Daisy."

I felt my cheeks turning red. "I guess I did. Goodnight, Sadie." I kissed the top of her head before turning and headed toward Zach and Hales, who were waiting to hear about my entire night in detail. All I wanted to do was go curl up next to Millie and go to sleep.

Chapter Nine

SADIE

The expression on Dane's face was priceless when he saw me getting out of Trevor's car. He stumbled and almost fell over a bucket. Everyone was busy working on Dane's new home, and I was there to help. Or more like make sure he was following doctor's orders. Plus, Dane and I had a week to get to know each other again, and we had zero time to waste.

Trevor handed me a hard hat, and I replaced Dane's old ball cap with it. I was hesitant to set it down on a workbench, but I knew I couldn't carry it around with me.

"What are you doing here?" Dane asked as he came over with a large board propped on his shoulder.

"I'm here to help." My eyes went to his hand that wasn't in the brace. "Where's the brace?" I put my hands on my hips.

"Umm…in the truck." He smiled guiltily. "I couldn't work with it on."

"I tried to reason with him earlier, but he's being stubborn," Trevor added with a grin.

"Going to get more tools, eh?" Dane raised a brow at Trev.

Trevor shrugged. "She is a tool." He snorted. "I mean, the good kind."

Dane smiled and shook his head. *Damn. That smile.*

I cleared my throat. "Go put it back on." I reached up and took the board from him. When he had it, it looked like he held it with ease. I had no idea it was so heavy until I stumbled a little and Trevor had to take it from me.

"Easy now. Dane is a lot stronger than you are."

Dane pouted as he went to his truck to get the brace.

I took the hard hat off, set it on a workbench, and walked over to help him. I needed to make sure he put it on right. I took it from him and helped him, making sure it was secure and wouldn't slip off.

"Maybe you should let Trevor and the rest of the guys work without you today."

"Where would the fun be in doing that?"

"I'd make it fun." I immediately regretted saying that. I blushed when he laughed. "I totally didn't mean that like it sounded."

"By the shocked look on your face when it came out of your mouth, I figured you didn't. You still don't have a filter, I see.

"And you're still stubborn."

"Yeah. Actually, I'm probably more stubborn than I used to be. The Marines added to it."

"Take off for the day. I came to help, but now I think you need to leave or you're going to be tempted to work."

He peered at the house being worked on then to me. "I. . . I haven't taken a day off in a long time."

"Well, me either, but here I am. You said yourself we need to get to know each other again before we meet our son. We only have five days, and if you work every day, we don't have much time left." I smiled hopefully.

He ran his good hand through his hair. "Fine. I guess I can take time off."

I waved at Trevor who was cutting a board. He laughed and shook his head when he saw Dane getting into the truck. I got in and watched Dane as he backed the truck up and then pulled onto the driveway.

"Where do you want to go?"

"I guess Coach's old house. We could order pizza and talk."

"All right."

"What time did you take your pain meds this morning?"

He stayed quiet for a second. "I didn't. I don't like how pain medicine makes me feel. I haven't taken one since they forced that one on me last night."

"Dane, baby, you…" I frowned. I shouldn't have called him that.

Who was I kidding, though? I couldn't deny my feelings for him. Little things would continue to slip out without me even meaning to. I loved him. I'd always love him. Eight years was a long time, but in that time, I wasn't *with* anyone else. I had occasionally dated, but it never worked out. No one was ever *my* Dane. Instead of my heart growing distant, it only ached for him more. I always thought maybe I could fix things with him, but not in this way. Not because we had to, but because we wanted to.

I stared out the window. I didn't know how to speak after letting that slip.

"I what?" he asked, his voice breaking some. He cleared his throat.

"You should take your meds." I ran my fingers through my hair and my heart stopped. "Turn around!"

He slammed on the brakes and I planted my hands firmly on the dash to steady myself. He looked over at me. "What's wrong?" he asked in a panic.

"My hat. I mean, your hat! I left it. Dane, we have to go get it!"

Okay, so yeah, I was completely having a panic attack over a hat. But it was the only thing I had that was something of Dane and myself before things went bad. Before I ruined everything. He wrote our names on the bill, and I put a heart around it. It was ours, and I wore it every single day. What if it accidentally got thrown away or something?

He shook his head and made a U-turn. "Shit, Daisy, you scared the hell out of me."

"Okay, so we've learned a few things about each other already. You're still stubborn, look sexy carrying a large board, you still call me Daisy, and I still call you baby, I'm obsessed with your hat, and I need to weight lift because I couldn't even hold a damn board." I laughed. "And I still don't have a filter." Oh, and I still love you, but I'd save that for another day.

He chuckled. "I've become stronger than I used to be. I work out a lot. And I like you not having a filter."

My eyes went to his arms, and I smiled in appreciation. "I can tell."

When he pulled onto the graveled parking area at the house, I got out as soon as soon as he came to a stop. I hurried over to the workbench where I had left it. My heartbeat slowed to a normal pace as soon as I put my hands on it. I put it on my head and winked at Trevor when he saw me. He was nailing a board in on the second floor.

I hurried back over to the truck and got in. "All right, I'm good now."

"Promise me you won't scare me like that again if it's just a hat you left behind."

I put my seatbelt on. "That hat being left here is an emergency to me. It's silly, I know. But it's special to me."

"What am I going to do with you?" he asked as he drove toward the road.

Both of my eyebrows shot up as my imagination went wild.

He *tsked* me which made me laugh.

"Daisy's mind, always in the gutter," he teased.

I bit my lip and then smiled a little.

Chapter Ten

DANE

I sat at the table for a "family meeting." Which meant I was about to get jumped on by everyone. The kids were all asleep, and instead of getting a few more hours of work in on my house, I was in Zach and Hales' kitchen. Brink, Quinn, Jason, and Trevor were even there.

I picked at my brace as I waited. I looked up and made eye contact with Hales just as she started speaking.

"Okay, someone say something besides me. Every time I open my mouth lately, I'm a bitch." Hales glared at Zach. When he didn't say anything, she made eye contact with everyone else in the room before sighing in frustration. "Fine," she growled, turning her attention back to me. "Dane, we all think you're being too nice to Sadie. Trev let it slip that you were adding a small living area for her onto the house. Are you insane? Listen, we understand she was young and scared, but that doesn't mean shit to us. Your son is scared to death and lost the only parents he's ever known with no living family except you and Sadie. You have Millie to protect, too."

Hailey held up her hand when I went to say something. "Sadie has a life back in New York. I know she's said she's giving it up and moving here, but what happens when she decides to go back and takes Tate with her? How do we know she's not playing you just so you can help get him out of the system?"

I looked at Brink for help.

"Dane has already thought of that. Which is why he will have complete custody. We will be making a separate document with Sadie that states she has certain rights, but in the end, Dane will have complete guardianship. At least until we know if she plans on staying or running off."

I nodded. "I'm not an idiot, Hales. Give me some credit."

"Okay, so back to the reason we're all worried. You being too nice to Sadie." Hailey glanced around at everyone who was nodding. Everyone except Trevor. He was stuck in the middle.

I sighed. "I love her. Nothing will ever change that. Yes, I'm extremely angry, but I still love her. But I know to be careful. If you remember, I'm the one who asked her to marry me and instead of talking to me she ran off in the middle of the night leaving me with nothing but a note. I won't let Millie or Tate be hurt by her, but I can't not let her see him. And the easiest way is to build a place for her to stay."

"If you're stuck on that, then build her her own little house. Don't connect it with yours. You have ten acres. Build it somewhere else," Zach said, getting angry. "I won't watch you get hurt again then shut down! You nearly died the last time! Have you even told her what happened?"

I rubbed my jaw through my beard absentmindedly. "She knows I joined the Marines."

"She ran because of the guilt of keeping Tate from him. She let the guilt push him away. But she's back! Give her some damn credit," Trev said, getting angry himself.

I saw Jason put his arm on the back of Trevor's chair.

I smiled a little at Trevor. "We are going to give her a chance. It took a lot for her to come to us for help, and that's what we're going to do. We're going to focus on Tate and helping him."

My phone dinged, and I saw Sadie's name. I smiled a little and looked down at it.

> Sadie: I know I'm pushing my luck here, but I need you right now. I'm freaking out, Dane. I'm not fit to be a mom. How do I look our son in

the eyes and answer the question we all know he's going to ask, why I gave him up.

Hailey groaned. "Let me guess, it's her," she snarled. "I'm going to check on the twins and Charlie and go to bed." She walked out of the room and shot Zach "the eyes," and he followed.

Brink and Quinn stood. They both hugged me before leaving to go home. I looked at Trevor and Jason.

"Go home and get some sleep. I need to go check on Sadie."

"Is she okay?" Trevor asked.

I peered down at the message. "She's freaking out about Tate."

"Is Millie staying here with Zach and Hales?" he asked. "She can stay with us if she needs to."

"Can you take her to our house? I will be home as soon as I talk to Sadie."

"Yeah, we can. We'll just stay there tonight. Don't rush," Trev said as they both headed down the hall where Millie was sleeping.

My phone dinged again.

> Sadie: Forget I texted that. I'm okay. I know you have Millie to take care of. I'll be fine.
>
> Me: I'm on my way.
>
> Sadie: I'm not at home.
>
> Me: where are you?
>
> Sadie: Our thinking spot.

The daisy field.

> Me: I will be there soon.

I PULLED UP to the daisy field and parked. I got out and walked over to where Sadie was lying in the flowers. I nudged her foot.

"Hey, Daisy." I sat down next to her.

She sat up and pulled her long hair into a messy bun. My old ball cap was beside her.

"Sorry, I smell like bug spray. I had to douse myself in it." She laughed. "Mosquitoes love me."

"I remember," I said with a chuckle. "The sun hates me and so do bugs, while the sun loves you and so do bugs," I teased.

Sadie's Latino roots she got from her mom always made her tan easily and never burn. We used to tease her about being like Heinz 57 sauce. None of us really knew what Sadie's ethnicity was. I'll never forget when she raised her hand during the ACT in second grade and didn't know what bubble to fill in then ended up filling them all in.

I watched her cross her legs so she was sitting Indian-style. She started picking at a blade of grass.

"Sadie, you'll never know if he will like you or not until you try. Tate is going to need time to get to know both of us and to become comfortable."

"I know," she answered quietly. "I'm just inside my head..." She looked at me. "And I miss you. When you're around, I feel better." Her phone started ringing from under my hat. She picked it up and silenced it. "My friends in New York are worried about me. All they know is that I had an urgent matter that had me come back here." She wiped her eyes.

"When do you go back to get your stuff?"

She shrugged. "Haven't thought that far ahead. My roommate is keeping it all safe." She leaned back on her hands and brought her eyes to mine. "What are you thinking right this second?"

"I'm thinking about our son and how scared he must be. And I'm thinking about whether he'll like me or not." I smiled a little. "And I'm thinking about you."

"Me?"

"I always think about you," I admitted.

She stared up at the moon and smiled. "I always think about you, too."

I laid back and looked up at the stars. "It seems we do a lot of thinking and not much talking or acting." I turned my head to face her. "I love you, Sadie. A lot. But I'm worried. I've been hurt by you before. Several times."

"Well, you're wrong. You did a lot of acting out your feelings, and I never gave you anything in return. Well, I did, but then I didn't." She laid next to me and turned on her side, folding her left arm under her head. She reached over and took my good hand that was lying on my chest. "I know I've made a lot of mistakes when it comes to you, but I've grown up a lot over the past eight years."

"So have I. A lot has happened."

She played with my fingers.

I turned my attention back to the night sky as I thought about my time in Afghanistan.

"Tell me about it. I want to know everything."

I turned my head toward at her. "All right, but I need you to come home with me."

"Now?"

I nodded and stood. I held my hand out to her. "It's a show-and-tell thing."

"Will you be shirtless?" She laughed and took my hand.

I chuckled. "Actually, yes."

"I'm so in," she said as I pulled her to her feet.

Chapter Eleven

SADIE

W hen we walked into Coach's old house, a plethora of memories came flooding in. It was so overwhelming, I had to remind myself to breathe. When we came into the living room, I saw Jason and Trevor on the couch watching a movie.

The last time I was in this living room I was telling Dane he had a son. I also remembered when I was hanging out with everyone and knew I was leaving to go to New York but they didn't. Dane asked me to marry him, despite all the bullshit I put him through. I think he knew I was about to tell them all I was leaving Stockbridge, so he panicked. He'd probably never admit to it, but I felt it in his plea for me to marry him. This room held so much tension.

"Give me a second. The guys can keep you company."

Trevor patted the spot next to him. He put an arm around my shoulders when I sat down. "What are you guys doing here?"

"I'm not really sure. Something about show-and-tell." I looked at Jason. "Hey."

Trevor scrunched his forehead in confusion.

Jason smiled. "Hey. What are you showing and telling?" he asked as he wiggled his eyebrows.

"Sadly, not that kind of show-and-tell. But, he did say he'd be shirtless, so, I'm not complaining." I laughed.

Trevor's smile faded and so did Jason's. "What were you guys talking about before he mentioned a show-and-tell?"

"The Marines."

I swear Trevor paled some. He turned to Jason. "Please go—"

Jason was already up and hurrying toward where Dane had disappeared.

I scrunched my eyes. "Ummm."

Trevor patted the seat next to him. "I'm sure Jason can't talk him out of it, so I'm going to warn you. Dane was injured in Afghanistan."

"How bad?"

He pulled out his phone. "I keep a picture of what he looked like when we saw him, and that was a few weeks after his injury. It's a reminder that I need to make the most of life and look out for him." He pushed on a picture before turning it and showing me. It was Dane unconscious with tubes in his nose and mouth. He had a large bandage on his face covering a section of what his beard covered.

"He doesn't know I still have this. We almost lost him."

I felt sick. I turned away from the phone and at brought my eyes to Trev. "That's my fault, isn't it?"

He put his phone away. "Well, you weren't the one who shot him but... but you leaving is why he joined the Marines. Well, most of it anyway. He just...lost it. I think he wants you to know why everyone is angry with you, plus he sees himself as a monster. That's why he grew the beard out." He gave me a weak smile. "It was a nightmare seeing him like that."

He's no monster, I am.

I felt...unworthy. I'd lied to him over and over again, I kept his son from him, I broke his heart so many times that I pushed him to put his life on the line. No, I may not have been the only reason, but I was a huge part of the puzzle that broke him.

"I didn't tell you this to make you feel bad. Just to prepare you. If he's wanting to show you, then that's something big."

"And me staying here and not running is something big." I put my trembling hands under my thighs to steady them. "We have to face our demons. It's the only way to get past it all."

"That's what I believe, too." He looked away from me as Jason came back into the living room.

"Dane didn't change his mind," Jason said to me. "He's in the bathroom upstairs at the end of the hallway."

I nodded and stood. I took a steadying breath as I walked up the stairs. When I made it to the bathroom, I knocked on the door. The door opened slowly, and he looked down at me. The scar was on the left side of his face on his jawline.

"I was shot" —he touched his chest— "several times." He kept his face tilted from me some. "I know it looks bad, but the beard covers it up."

I walked in and shut the door behind me. It was crazy how love gone wrong could push you to the point of insanity. My leap over the edge was running away to New York. Dane's was joining the Marines and almost getting killed.

I reached up slowly and touched his scars. I studied every bullet hole and the thick scar on his jaw where he trimmed his beard so I could see. I'm sure they were painful reminders of me and how I hurt him.

"I'm so sorry," I said quietly, my fingers stopping on a bullet wound only a few inches away from his heart. It was covered by a black and white daisy tattoo.

He covered my hand gently with his own. "I wanted to show you this so we can leave the past in the past and to show you why everyone is so overprotective. I tried telling them it was my fault. I'm the one who signed up, but they're being stubborn."

"They have every reason to hate me, Dane." I leaned forward and kissed the top of his hand that held mine.

He gave my hand a squeeze. "We still have a lot to work on, Sadie. Tomorrow, do you want to help me design your part of the house?"

"About that… My parents think it's a bad idea for me to move in."

He dropped his hand. "Oh. Okay."

"That doesn't mean I'm not. We just have a lot of things to take into consideration."

He nodded. "I know." He picked up his shirt and started putting it on. "I'll just make a little house on the property. That way I can use it as a guest house or for you."

"Dane, I—" I stopped, trying to think of the best way to put what I needed to say. Our focus needed to be 100% on Tate, but I knew if I was close to Dane every single day, I'd start focusing on him and me. We had this undeniable connection, like a force between us that made us forget how to think logically. Or, at least, it was still that way for me.

"I don't know how to be around you and not want you," I admitted. "And I know that's not where our focus needs to be right now."

He shrugged. "It's fine. We should focus on Tate."

I nodded.

"We should head downstairs. I have to be up at four and I'm sure you could use some sleep."

I tucked some hair that had fallen out of my bun behind my ear. "Yeah, you're probably right." I was confused. I had just admitted that I still wanted him, and while he had the appropriate response by blowing it off and agreeing we need to focus on our son, I couldn't help but wish he would've given me some confirmation that he struggled with wanting me too. I was selfish for thinking that at all.

I walked out of the bathroom, Dane following close behind me.

"I'm going to check on Millie. I'll be down in a second."

"I'll just have Trevor take me home." I put on my best smile.

He gawked at me for a moment. He opened his mouth like he wanted to say something, but he ended up just nodding before disappearing into a room.

Chapter Twelve

DANE

I sat in my office working on the blueprints for my house and a few other projects. Since I couldn't use my hand to work, I decided... No, that's a lie. I was hiding away until my beard grew back. I shouldn't have trimmed it. I was a complete moron. I thought maybe if I showed Sadie and we talked, we could work on us along with helping Tate, but I had been wrong. She didn't want that. Yeah, she said she wanted me, but lust and love were two different things.

We had always had a connection. If she had wanted us to work, she wouldn't be pushing me away again. My shoulders sagged, and I rubbed my head. *Why couldn't I have a normal life?* I didn't look up when my office door opened, I knew it was Trevor. He was the only one who had a key to my door.

"How are the sites coming?" I asked, keeping my eyes focused on the paperwork on my desk.

"Good, boss."

I rolled my eyes. "Don't be a smart ass. You know I'm not the boss. You are."

He sat down in the chair across from my desk. "Do you really want me to go into the logistics of this company?"

I looked at him in confusion. "What the hell are you talking about?"

"How you are technically the boss, not me?" He raised a brow. "Someone is a grumpy ass."

I sighed. "Sorry, and your name is on the company, remember? People don't like dealing with me."

"What's your deal? I mean, not that you don't have a lot on your mind or anything."

"I'm sorry I'm being a jerk. I don't mean to be."

"It's fine, man. I get it. So, want to know why I'm here?"

"Sure." I stopped drawing and gave him my complete attention.

"I helped Sadie pick a moving company earlier. She said she doesn't want to have to leave with everything going on. Her roommate is getting her things packed up for her. She also quit her job and school. She's really staying. It's official."

I smiled a little before turning back to the plans. "Pay for it all out of my account."

"But she already paid for it."

"Oh. Okay. Trev, what if I suck at being a dad?"

He laughed. "Are you insane? Dane, you've been such a great father figure to Millie. You stepped up to the plate so Zach and Hailey could raise their own family. You have nothing to worry about. Tate is going to adore you."

I played with the button on my pen. "Thanks. I'm nervous about meeting him."

"It's tomorrow. I know you are. Have you heard from Sadie today?"

I shook my head. "She wants us to focus on Tate. Which I get."

"Wait, what? But you two should be talking, right?" He sounded so confused. "I mean, didn't you guys have like a moment or something when you showed her the truth about you?"

I relayed to him everything that was said, and by the end of it I was feeling even more depressed.

"Oh. Damn."

I ran my hand absentmindedly over my shirt where the bullet holes laid underneath.

He rubbed his jaw and leaned back in the chair. "So, basically, she wants to fuck you." He laughed a little. "What's wrong with that?"

He stopped laughing when I glared at him.

"How would you feel if that's all Jason wanted you for?"

"Dane, Sadie loves you. You know that."

"You didn't answer my question. How would you feel?"

"Like a toy, I guess."

"Something to play with when the mood suits then put aside until later. That's not what I want. It's never been what I wanted, but it's all I've ever gotten. I won't do it again."

"But she loves you." He furrowed his brow. "I don't understand. You two have always done this shit. I know it's mainly her issues that cause her to pull away, but what's stopping you two now? She's back for good." Poor Trev was such a hopeless romantic.

My phone dinged.

> **Sadie: What are you wearing tomorrow? Why the fuck is it so hard to pick out something to wear? I don't want to come off as like some Betty Crocker bullshit mom, but I also don't want to look like I'm too young to have my shit together.**

I handed my phone to Trevor. "You better answer this question. I don't have a clue how to answer her."

Trevor burst out laughing. "Betty Crocker bullshit Mom."

I leaned back in my chair. "And I don't know what's stopping us. You'd have to ask her." I closed my eyes.

"Oh, I will." When I opened my eyes, I saw him texting her. "I'm telling her to calm her ass down and just be herself."

"I've already tried that. It doesn't seem to work."

When he handed me back my phone, I instantly wanted to punch him. He didn't text her about what she was wearing at all. Instead, it said:

> **Why the fuck are you being so difficult? We can work on us and be parents. Married people do it all the time. Stop waiting for the perfect opportunity, you fucking idiot.**

"Well, gotta go, boss!" Trevor hurried out of the room.

"What the hell?" I asked in a shout.

I heard him laugh and then the main door shut. A few moments later, I heard his car start up and, glancing out the window, I saw him drive off.

"Asshole," I said in a growl. I looked down at my phone.

> **Me: That wasn't me. Trevor was supposed to be sending you clothing advice.**
>
> **Sadie: Oh.**

After staring at the text for a few moments, I text back.

> **Me: But that doesn't mean I don't feel that way.**

My phone started ringing. It was Sadie.

"Hey."

"A text. You tell me that in a damn text?"

"Technically, Trevor said it through a text."

"And then you proceeded to tell me that you felt the same way. In a text, Dane."

Is she seriously mad at me right now?

"You're angry with me because I told you how I felt through a text?"

"Yes! I need to be looking at you right now. I need to see you when you when you say something like that!"

I pinched the bridge of my nose. "I'm so fuckin' confused right now."

She hung up on me.

What. The. Hell?

I looked at my phone in shock, then I slammed it down in frustration and went back to my work.

Chapter Thirteen

SADIE

I stared out the window as Dane drove. Millie was in the back so I couldn't address the whole text situation that happened yesterday. Not that I would have anyway. We were on our way to meet our son. *Our son.* Nothing else mattered to me. It couldn't, and it shouldn't.

I was so scared I was going to cry as soon as I saw him. I'd even practiced what I might say to him. But the reality was that nothing could prepare you for something of this magnitude. Seeing your own flesh and blood, the one you dreamt about since the day you gave him away—was surreal. I was a mix of emotions.

Millie didn't speak to me at all, which Trevor and Dane both warned me was normal for her. She didn't speak to people she didn't have to interact with on a daily basis.

I looked down at my navy skinny jeans and brown-suede ankle boots. I adjusted my white tunic-style shirt and ran my fingers through my loose curls. I should've gotten a haircut. Having hair down to my stomach wasn't very motherly. Or was it? I dropped the strand of hair I was holding when I noticed Dane gawking at me.

"What?" I was definitely regretting doing the whole blonde ombre thing now. DHS was going to take one look at me and laugh.

"Just trying to figure out why you're examining your hair so closely."

I shrugged and looked out the window again. "How close are we?" I wiped my sweaty palms on my pants.

"We're almost there." He looked in the rearview mirror at Millie. He gave her a small smile. "You okay, munchkin?"

I turned in my seat so I could see her. I gave her a warm smile. Millie nodded before looking out the window. Dane's smile faded as he focused back on the road. He had been extremely quiet. We both had. But what we really wanted to say was probably safer staying in our heads.

When we pulled up, I thought I might puke from the nerves.

"You have our I.D. and everything?" I asked Dane, my voice shaking.

"Millie and I do. And I have the documents. You were supposed to have your I.D."

"Shit," I mumbled and grabbed my purse. I let out a relieved breath when I saw I had everything. "I'm good. Sorry, I should've said crap."

He parked and turned the car off. He got out and opened the door for Millie before coming over and doing the same for me.

"Thanks," I said as I got out. I put my purse over my shoulder and shut the door.

Dane took the folder from Millie then took her hand. Millie was bouncing a little. He smiled softly at her.

Millie smiled at him. "Do we get to bring Tate home today?"

"No. We're just meeting him today. I have to finish the classes and pass the home exam."

Millie frowned. "Oh."

I kept taking deep breaths. *What if I pass out? Or what if I throw up?*

"Mr. Shaw?" a woman asked with a smile as we entered the building.

"Yes, ma'am. And this is my niece, Millie."

She shook his hand. She turned to me. "And you must be Miss Solis." She held her hand out to me.

I shook it and smiled a little. "Hi."

"Mr. Shaw, the blood work came back, and you are definitely Tate's biological father."

Dane smiled. I smiled too. Of course he was.

After we handed over all of our documents and filled out some paperwork, we were instructed to go wait in the waiting room. I started chewing on my nails, but Dane grabbed my hand to stop me.

"We'll get to see him soon."

I nodded, willing back my tears.

Every time I closed my eyes last night, all I could see was me handing a little crying Tate over to the nurse who took him away forever. I remembered crying for weeks straight, begging my parents to let me go get him. And now, he was in the same building as me. I was only separated from my son by a few walls.

I admired my hand that was still being held by Dane. I only looked up when I heard our names being called. We stood, and I was thankful when Dane let go of my hand and put a steadying hand on my back. He must've sensed I was having trouble standing. I felt Dane's hand tremble.

As we followed the caseworker, everything seemed to move in slow motion. It was like I lost control of all of my senses. I wasn't even sure how I was concentrating enough to walk.

We walked into a tiny room that had chairs and a round table. As soon as we were seated, they brought him in.

Tears filled my eyes, but the biggest smile spread across my lips. It was like seeing Dane when he was that age. Red hair, freckles, and the biggest blue eyes. He got his height, too. Definitely not a shorty like me. His crooked smile was his daddy 100%.

Millie waved a little at him and gave him a small smile as Dane stood slowly. His eyes never left Tate's.

"I'm Dane," his voice broke some.

"And I'm Tate, but you already know that." He chuckled. His voice was the sweetest thing I had ever heard. I wanted to scoop him in my arms and never let go of him.

Dane smiled a little. "This is your cousin, Millie."

His eyes moved to Millie, and he waved. "Hi, Millie."

"Hi," she said quietly as her face turned red.

"Millie's really shy," Dane said as he slowly sat back down.

Tate nodded. "Me too." His eyes found me and his smile faltered some before returning.

"I'm Sadie Solis."

He nodded and looked up at the caseworker who motioned for him to sit down. He sat in the chair across from us.

"I'll leave you four alone, but if you need me, just wave at that mirror near the door. I'll be in there watching to make sure everything is okay." The caseworker left the room.

Tate stood. "I don't want to sit, is that okay?"

Dane smiled. "Of course."

Millie watched Tate with a bright smile. "You look like Uncle Dane."

Tate smiled proudly and nodded.

His hair was cut so cutely. Short on the sides and longer on the top, all messy and hip. He had my style. Skinny jeans with a few holes and a Rolling Stones T-shirt. I smiled when I saw his shoes.

"Converse are my favorite," I said, hoping to break the tension.

Tate looked down at his shoes and then back at me. His eyes then went to Dane's boots.

"My caseworker got me these, but I like boots like his," he said motioning toward Dane's feet.

"Well, we will get you some then. You need to make a list of things you like and dislike. Millie and Sadie want to go shopping for you. I'd go, but I suck at shopping. I'm better with my hands."

"What do you like to do for fun?" Millie asked in almost a whisper. Dane smiled proudly at her.

"Before my parents…" he stopped and frowned a little. "Before they died, I was on a traveling baseball team. I like basketball, too. What about you?"

"I like to dance. Uncle Dane played baseball. He could have gone pro."

Dane's face turned red.

"What's your favorite team?" Tate asked, showing some excitement. He even took the chair near him and moved it over so he was closer to Dane and sat down.

"The Braves. What about you?"

"The Mets. They're gonna squash the Braves next season." Tate smiled when Dane laughed.

"We'll see about that."

Millie giggled. "Uncle Zach coaches the baseball team in Stockbridge."

"And he owns the best pizza place in town. We'll have to take you there," I added.

Tate looked at me. "Do you do stuff for fun?"

I smiled. "I dance. I went to Juilliard, a big dance school."

His eyebrows scrunched together. "Is that why you gave me away?"

My breath caught in my throat. "No," I said quietly. I was shocked he'd asked that.

His expression turned apologetic. "I'm sorry for asking. I was told not to ask about it." He glanced at the see-through mirror worriedly.

A few tears fell down my cheeks. "It's okay. You can ask those questions if you want."

Dane gave him a gentle smile. "It's okay to ask whatever questions you want. We'll answer them the best we can."

Tate nodded and kept his eyes on me. "I kind of... I..."

"What is it?" I asked. "I won't be mad at anything you ask or say, I swear. This is hard for you."

"I don't want to see you right now," he said quietly and looked down at the floor.

My heart was ripped from my chest and stomped on.

I looked at Dane, at Tate, and then stood. "I understand." I left the room before I completely broke down.

I made it to the bathroom before allowing myself to lose it.

Chapter Fourteen

DANE

I knew I would have a lot to talk about with Sadie later, but right now I was
going to focus on my son.

"What all do you want to know from Millie and me?"

He kept his eyes on the door she walked out of for several seconds. "I
didn't mean to make her cry."

"Tate, right now we both want to make sure you feel comfortable. And if
you're not comfortable with her right now, then she will understand. You're
angry at her, aren't you?"

He peeled his eyes away from the door and looked at me. He nodded.
"They told me you didn't know about me."

"No, I didn't. She only told me a week ago. That's when I started fighting to see you."

"If she gave me away, why is she here?"

The hard part of all this was that Tate was eleven, almost twelve. This
wasn't a child who didn't understand. He understood the situation entirely,
making this all harder.

"I can only tell you what she has told me. She was in ninth grade, just a little older than you, and she was scared. She told me her parents were pushing her to put you up for adoption, but she's never stopped thinking about you. I know that isn't the best answer, but it's all I have to give you. I wish I had known about you. I feel like I've missed out on so much."

"I have pictures. I'll bring them with me when I move in with you."

"I can't wait. And give it time. Sadie is a great woman, she was just a scared kid. I won't make you have a relationship with her, but she'll be around. Right now, I want to focus on us getting to know each other and get you home with me."

Millie smiled. "Do you like dogs?" she asked quietly. She was good at changing the topic when she knew it was getting too tense.

Tate smiled. "I love dogs."

"Do you have one?" she asked in a cheerful tone.

He shook his head. "My mom was allergic."

Millie grinned at me, and I nodded. She was practically bouncing. "Uncle Dane is going to get us both a puppy if you want. I've been asking for one, and he finally gave in."

I laughed. "She tends to talk me into a lot of things. I'm sure you probably will as well."

Tate smiled. He favored Sadie some. The shape of his eyes and when he smiled all the way, he looked like her.

"They said it will be a little longer before I can come live with you—" He was going to say something else when the caseworker walked into the room.

"I'm sorry, but time is up." Ms. Shepard smiled warmly. "The door is always open, Mr. Shaw. Come back whenever you'd like but call before to make sure you can bring Sadie. Tate said he wanted to see her, but that proved to be too hard."

I nodded. "I will." I stood. "We'll see you again soon. Get that list of things you like and don't like together. Give it to Ms. Shepard. She'll get it to me." I smiled at her. "Thank you, Ms. Shepard. For everything."

She shook my hand. "Of course."

Millie smiled at Tate. "I'll see you soon too."

He put his hands in his pockets and nodded with a smile.

She walked closer to him. "I lost my parents, too. Uncle Dane will look out for you like he does me."

Tate teared up a little and hugged her. She hugged him back and kissed his cheek.

Tears filled my own eyes. Not only was my son right here in front of me, but Millie was talking more to him than she had to anyone outside the family. When she pulled back, I smiled at him.

"Am I allowed to hug you or would you rather me wait?"

He wiped his eyes and launched himself into my arms.

I wrapped my arms around him as tightly as I could without hurting him. I kissed the top of his head. "We'll see ya soon."

After he let go, Ms. Shepard walked us out.

I said bye to her again before finding Sadie in the waiting room.

"Hey," I said as we walked over to her.

She stood. "Hey."

We headed outside to the truck and, after I let Millie into the truck and gave her the keys to start it, I shut the door and pulled Sadie into my arms.

"I'm sorry."

She pulled back and wiped her eyes quickly. "Don't feel sorry for me."

I didn't know what to say to that. "Sadie, give him time."

I opened the door for her. She got in without a word.

My heart broke for her, but that was not something I could fix.

I SAT AT the kitchen table with Zach and Hales.

"He looks exactly like Uncle Dane, Uncle Zach!" Millie said excitedly.

Zach smiled. "Does he?"

"Yes. He has red hair and freckles and everything!"

I chuckled. "Him and Millie hit it off, and guess what, Hales?"

"What?" she asked before taking a drink of her water.

"He likes baseball."

Hailey's eyes lit up and she smiled. "Really? Yes!"

Zach burst out laughing. "We finally got a baseball player."

I smiled. "I can't wait for you guys to meet him. He's amazing."

Millie giggled. "Ms. Shepherd is getting us a list of his likes and dislikes so we can get him stuff."

I handed Millie my phone. "Go start a search for puppies." She hugged my neck and kissed my cheek. "I have to go to adoption classes soon, so behave."

She nodded and ran off.

"You're getting a puppy?" Zach asked with a raised eyebrow.

I nodded and held up two fingers. "Two. One for Millie, and one for Tate." I couldn't stop smiling. "He's perfect, guys. And you should have seen Millie with him. She talked to him and even hugged him."

"Wow, that's awesome. This will be great for Millie," Hailey said and then looked at Zach. "I'm never getting a puppy, am I?"

Zach shook his head. "We have three boys and a baby on the way. I think not."

Hailey stuck her lip out and laughed when Zach kissed her.

"You can have a dog when you let me get a motorcycle."

I loved watching those two. They were so cute and perfect for each other. Why the hell didn't Hales want to marry him?

"Argument over." She made a face at him and turned back to me. "Where's Sadie?"

"I dropped her off with Trevor. Things didn't go so well for her," I said as my smile faded.

"Let me guess, she freaked out and hid?" Hailey rolled her eyes.

"No, Tate said he wasn't ready to see her, so she left and waited in the waiting area."

Hailey's mouth fell open. "Seriously? Damn. Smart kid." Hailey threw her hands up when Zach glared at her. "What? He's a smart kid."

Zach shook his head and looked at me. "I need to go get the kids from Hailey's parents. You and Millie staying for dinner?"

"Just Millie is if that's okay. I have adoption class tonight. They're trying to get them all in as soon as possible."

"Sure, she can just stay the night." Zach smiled. "I'm proud of you, Dane."

"I'm so nervous. I'm afraid I'm going to screw up somehow. I'm just ready for him to be with all of us."

"We are all ready, too." Zach stood and held his hand out to Hailey.

"Give me a minute with Hales, Zach."

He took his hand back and Hailey looked at me. Zach cuffed my shoulder on his way out.

"First, can you please stop making low blows at Sadie? I don't want Millie or Tate to hear them once he's here. I know you are angry at her, but so is he, and I don't want anything to fuel his anger."

"I won't do it around the kids."

I raised an eyebrow at her skeptically. "She's trying to do better. She's moving here officially. And today really broke her heart."

"As it should," she mumbled, staring at the floor.

"Please just try for me and Tate."

She slowly moved her eyes until they were on mine. "Okay."

"The other thing involves you. I want to ask you something but don't get mad." When she nodded, I smiled. "Why don't you want to marry Zach?"

"Because, we're almost married by common law. Why would we spend unnecessary money to prove to people that we're in love?"

"You could go to the courthouse."

"I'd do that. Elliot did ask me the other day why my last name isn't Shaw like his brothers' and Daddy."

"Think about it." I stood and kissed the top of her head. "And while you think about it, take a peek in Zach's sock drawer."

"Why?" Her eyes widened when I looked at her and smiled. "No way."

I grinned. "Go look and let him know you love him."

"I adore him." She stood and smiled at me before walking out.

I chuckled before going to find Millie to get my phone back and see what puppies she had picked out.

Chapter Fifteen

SADIE

I walked into the house close to midnight.

I'd stayed with Trevor and he brought me to the studio so I could dance and clear my head. After that, I'd worked out since I hadn't in a week. It felt good to blow off some steam, and the last thing I wanted to do was go to my parents' house and have to see the two people who made me give Tate away.

They were the reason he hated me.

They were the reason for everything.

It wasn't my fault. I was a minor. I was confused and scared. I thought I was doing what was right because it was what I was told to do.

I walked into the house, trying to be quiet so I didn't wake anyone. I set my purse and keys down on the counter and jumped when I heard a cup slam down on the kitchen table.

That's when I noticed Mom was sitting there.

"I have been worried sick, Sadie!" She stood. "Where have you been? We've been waiting to hear how the visit went."

"I wasn't ready to talk about it," I said quietly. I couldn't look at her. Right then, the sight of her made me sick.

"Not ready to talk about it?" she scoffed.

Hot tears fell down my cheeks. "No, Mom, not ready to talk about it," I said through clenched teeth.

"Well, too bad because you're going to have to at some point! We are his grandparents and your mother!"

I was at my breaking point. I glared at Mom, my eyes full of fire. "You're nothing to him! You gave him up, not me! This is all your fault! You selfish woman, you took him from me! You plagued me with years of guilt, you are the cause of me pushing away the only man I will ever love!" I was crying so hard and screaming at her I wasn't sure if anything I was saying made sense. "You took my baby away from me!" I screamed again. "He hates me! My son hates me!"

I felt arms wrap around me and knew it was Dad by how much he towered over me.

"Breathe, baby girl," he said calmly as he held me. He was the only thing keeping me standing. If he hadn't come in, I would have crumbled to pieces on the floor.

"He hates me, Daddy," I cried softly against his chest.

"Shhh, stop trying to talk. Just breathe and cry it out. It's going to be okay. It's all going to get better with time."

"You weren't there, Daddy. He told me to get out of the room. He looked at me like I was nothing."

Dad didn't say anything as I talked and cried. He sat down on the floor with me and held me in his arms, leaning against the oven.

I WOKE UP in my bed, vaguely remembering Dad carrying me in the night before. My throat was sore and my eyes were puffy. When I rolled over to grab my phone from the nightstand, I stopped. There was a vase full of fresh white daisies and a cute little brown teddy bear in a pink tutu.

I stretched and sat up. I swung my legs over the side of the bed and leaned forward to dig through the flowers to see if there was a card. *Nothing.*

I yawned and picked up my phone. I scrolled through all the messages from friends back home and replied to a few. I then took a picture of the bear and flowers and sent it to Dane.

> **Me: Do I have you to thank for brightening my morning?**

He's the only one who had ever bought me daisies.

> **Dane: I thought you could use something to make you smile. Don't give up, Sadie.**
>
> **Me: I'm not. I'll never give up. I'm just kind of...broken right now.**
>
> **Dane: I understand that feeling. The good thing about being broken is you can be fixed.**

I smiled.

> **Me: What are you doing today?**
>
> **Dane: Ummm...I don't want to tell you. You'll call me a stubborn ass and be mad.**
>
> **Me: You're working.**
>
> **Dane:** ☺
>
> **Me: Well, I could really use your company later. You should take me on a date. You know, since you still need to tell me in person that you think I'm a stupid fucking idiot and need to work on shit with you.**
>
> **Dane: You could always come and actually help me. And I'd like that but I have classes tonight. It would have to be after that if we wait until tonight. Of course we could do lunch.**
>
> **Me: I will come help after I go talk to Jason about a job. And I know they told me I didn't need the classes, but maybe I could go with you.**
>
> **Dane: Sounds like a plan.**
>
> **Me: I love you.**

And that's how I rolled. Since he dropped some crazy shit in a text, I dropped some crazy shit in a text. *Bam. Take that, Dane Shaw.*

> **Dane: I love you, too. Always have. Always will.**

Me: Oh yeah? Well, I love you past the moon and stars, around Jupiter and Saturn, bigger than life itself. SO THERE!

Dane: Lol. See ya soon

I laughed and felt like some tension had been lifted off my shoulders. I grabbed clothes from my closet and headed down the hall to take a shower.

Chapter Sixteen

DANE

I yawned for the hundredth time. I was exhausted. I hadn't been able to sleep knowing both Tate and Sadie were unhappy. Tate wanted out of the system and Sadie was upset because of how Tate had responded to her. I blinked a few times and looked at the house. We had two teams working on the house to get it up quickly. I wanted to bring Tate there. I heard Trevor's car as he pulled into the drive. He got out, walked over and handed me a piece of paper.

"Ms. Shepherd faxed this to the office."

I eyeballed the list and nodded. "It's Tate's likes and dislikes." I folded the paper gently and put it in my pocket. "Do you think we'll have this place done in two weeks?"

Trevor nodded. "Probably before then."

I relaxed some. "Good."

I looked away from Trevor as the Rover pulled in. I smiled some when I saw Sadie get out.

Trevor walked over and hugged her before whispering something in her ear. She laughed before he headed back to his car and to the next work site.

"Hey, how did the job thing go with Jason?"

"You're looking at the newest ballet instructor," she said and then did the perfect plié. And the only reason I knew what that was from years of watching Sadie practice and her quizzing me to see if I knew what the dance move was called.

"Millie will be excited. She loves ballet."

"I can't wait." She was beaming. She turned her attention to the house. "Wow! It's really coming together, Dane. It looks great."

"The guys are doing great. They're trying to finish it quickly." I smiled before pulling out the piece of paper. I handed it over to Sadie. "Do you think you and Millie could get stuff for his room and for hers? I don't have a damn clue."

She looked at the list and smiled. "Of course."

I relaxed. "Good, because the idea of shopping scares the hell out of me. Jason is the one decorating my house."

I pulled my wallet out and pulled out my extra debit card. "I had the bank make me an extra card. Now, what do you want for lunch?"

She took it with a little hesitation but proceeded to put it into her purse.

She put her hands on her hips. "Don't you have something urgent to tell me first?"

I liked seeing Sadie get some of her sass back.

I tapped my chin with my finger. "Do I?"

She raised a brow and tapped her left foot.

I laughed. "Okay. Stop being a fucking idiot and work on things with me."

The smile Tate shared with her spread across her face. She kissed my cheek. "Since you asked so nicely."

I tilted her chin up so I could see her smile. "He shares your smile, Sadie."

She teared up. "He does?"

"Yes. And with time you'll have his heart. He won't be able to not give it to you."

For a moment, it felt like only Sadie and I existed, but that feeling was interrupted when some of my workers started whistling and making comments about Sadie and me getting a room.

My face turned red and I cut my eyes at them to pierce them with a glare. They all laughed and went back to work.

I looked back at Sadie and smiled. "Let's go get lunch."

After I let my hand fall from her chin, she took it in her own as we walked to her Rover.

When I raised a brow at the old junker, she laughed.

"Oh come on, you know you miss riding in her."

"I spent more time fixing the thing than actually riding in it."

I immediately recognized that mischievous glint in her eyes and knew her mind totally went there.

I laughed. "That's not what I meant."

"I'm pretty sure that's where Tate was conceived." She chuckled and opened the passenger door for me.

I got in and watched her every move until she did then I took her hand in mine. "Promise me something."

She cranked the engine and looked at me. "All right. What?"

"If you decide to leave me again, tell me to my face, not in a letter."

"Dane, I'm not leaving again."

"Then promise not to leave me again."

She turned in her seat, staring me straight in the eyes, and smiled. "I promise not to leave you again. Stockbridge is my home now."

I put my forehead to hers. "Good."

I LAID ON the floor of the newly-finished home. The guys finished it in a week. I owed them a shit load of overtime but it was finished. I sat up and looked at the door as it opened and Millie and Sadie came in with tons of bags.

"Did you guys get everything for yours and Tate's rooms?"

Millie nodded. "And the bathrooms." She inspected the empty room. "What about your room and the rest of the house?"

I laid back onto the floor. "Jason is taking care of the furniture and decorating for the house."

They set everything down and both laid down on the floor with me.

"Jason will have everything set up before DHS shows up Thursday." I turned to look at Sadie. "You're sure you're okay with me going to see Tate?"

"Yeah, just please be sure you tell him I said hi. And don't forget to give him the letter I wrote him if he seems like he wants it."

"I will." I looked back up at the ceiling. "The guys are going back to their other jobs and only a few are staying to work on the guest house. It will take a little bit longer to be finished."

I sat up. "Sadie, do you want to go with us to pick out some puppies?"

I knew Sadie didn't want to stay with her parents much longer. She and her mom still weren't talking since their fight. She thought her mom was going back, but now her parents were actually thinking about getting back together.

"It's okay, I can always crash at Jason and Trev's place if I have to."

She sat up and smiled. "I'd love to. As long as it's okay with Millie."

Millie smiled. "I'd like that."

I smiled at her. Millie was getting attached to Sadie. I was excited about that but also worried. I know Sadie said she wouldn't leave but I still had this fear she would.

"You like dogs, right?"

"Yup!"

"Good, because this family is about to get a bunch of puppies."

Sadie laughed.

"Let's get the rest of the bags out of the junker and go get those puppies." I stood and stretched. I helped both of the girls up. "Can you hang out here this afternoon to wait on Jason? If not, we can stop and drop the key off with him."

"I don't mind." Sadie took my hand in hers.

"You're going to love these puppies." I held the door open for my girls and started bringing everything into the house.

Chapter Seventeen

SADIE

Trevor, Zach, and I all took orders from Jason when everything arrived. We moved everything into its place, fixed up the kids' rooms, and cleaned up so everything was perfect for when Dane and Millie brought Tate home.

Hailey would be there as soon she picked up a few pizzas from Quinn's.

It killed me that I couldn't be there to bring him home, but Tate was nervous and asked that only Dane and Millie bring him. We weren't supposed to get him for another few weeks, but Brink and Quinn got it moved up sooner.

"Ummm...we have a problem," Jason said with a frown.

"What?" I asked, wiping sweat from my forehead.

"Well, the house looks great." He grabbed my hand and dragged me to the master bedroom that was at the back of the house on the first floor. "Except this room." The room was empty. Completely. "I forgot to get furniture for Dane's room."

I heard the barking of the four puppies from the fenced-in backyard through the open window. We all got one. Dane's and Tate's were boys while Millie's and mine were girls.

"Know anyone who can deliver on demand?" I laughed.

"I may be able to make a few calls. If not, I can go get an air mattress for him. It will at least get him through tonight."

"Or he could sleep on the couch." When I turned to look at him, he was gone. "Or not," I mumbled.

Zach came into the room. "I'm guessing my brother forgot about himself again."

I walked away from the window and nodded. "Yeah. It seems so."

"He does that. Are you going to hurt my little brother, Sadie?"

I hated that he even had to ask, but I hadn't given him a reason not to. "No."

He nodded. "Good. I haven't seen him this happy in a long time."

"We're not even really a thing right now. We're in this weird limbo. Friends, but holding hands, telling each other we love each other, but zero physical contact. We're being careful not to rush it because we know our focus needs to be on Tate. But no, Zach, I won't hurt Dane. Not again."

And that was the truth. We hadn't even kissed yet. Everything with us right now was baby steps.

"So, you guys got four damn puppies. Why? They're going to be huge ass dogs."

"Because Millie couldn't say no to all of them. And yeah, Newfies are massive." I laughed. "We'll be busy, that's for sure."

He laughed. "I'm guessing the people only had four puppies. How much did my brother drop on those things?"

I laughed. "No clue. He wouldn't tell me."

My smile faded when I saw Hailey in the doorway.

She frowned. "Why is Dane's room empty?"

"He forgot about himself. Again," Zach said with a smile. "Jason is trying to fix it. But you should see the rest of the house. It's amazing."

She smiled. "Yeah, I saw the living room and Millie's room. I was heading down to Tate's." She looked at me. "Hi, Sadie."

I smiled. "Hey, Hailey." I motioned toward her growing belly. "Congrats on baby number four."

Hailey rubbed her stomach and smiled at Zach. "What can I say, my man knows how to do his job."

I laughed.

"That and no birth control seems to work."

Zach smiled. He walked over and put his hand on her belly.

"Pizza is downstairs. What time did they say they'd be here?" she asked him.

Zach glanced at his watch. "Should be in a few minutes."

Hailey squealed. "I can't wait to meet my nephew!"

She grabbed Zach's arm and they walked out of the room.

I followed out of the room and out to the front porch.

I sat on the front steps and waited. Dane was bringing our son home.

I didn't tell my parents about him coming home early. I was still so angry with my mom.

I didn't want to overwhelm Tate, either. This was all going to be a lot to take in.

His room was decorated in baseball gear. It was easy since Zach, Trevor, and Hailey were obsessed.

I left my journal in his sock drawer. It was where I wrote down every dream, every regret, and the pain of losing him. One day, maybe he'd read it. I'd hoped it could say everything I wanted to, but may not get the chance for a while.

I wanted to be an open book with him, but on his terms, when he was ready.

I stood when I saw Dane's truck pulling in.

Dane parked and got out. He opened the back door for Millie and Tate to get out. Tate was dressed almost identical to Dane in his blue jeans, t-shirt, and boots.

I wished I'd had my camera with me, but it was in a box and in a moving truck on its way there.

Millie was smiling at me. She looked back at Tate and whispered to him. Tate smiled at her.

Dane put his hand on Tate's shoulder. He had the biggest smile on his face.

I looked behind me and saw Zach, Hailey, and Trevor coming out onto the porch.

Zach had sent the kids to Hailey's parents so they wouldn't destroy the house while we got everything ready.

They came to a stop in front of us. "Tate, this is your Uncle Zach and Aunt Hales. They have three boys that aren't here. This is my business partner and may as well be your uncle, Trevor."

Zach grinned. "You look just like your dad."

Tate looked up at Dane and then at Zach. "Thanks, I've heard that a lot."

"Hey, Tate," I said with a smile.

He smiled. "Hey, Sadie."

"You ready to go see your new room?" Dane nodded toward Trevor who hurried back inside. "And we all have a surprise for you."

I wanted to pick him up and squeeze him, but, of course, I didn't. Besides, he was almost taller than me already.

It wasn't long and then Trevor was coming back out with Tate's puppy in his arms. "This is for you," he said as he came over to Tate and handed him the puppy.

Tate's mouth fell open as he reached out to take him. He laughed when the puppy started licking his face.

That laugh. The best sound in the entire world.

"You'll have to give him a name." Dane smiled down at him.

I smiled when Dane came over and put his arm around me. I leaned into his hold and laid my head against his chest.

Even if Tate was still unsure about me, this moment was going to be one of my most favorite.

Tate turned to Millie when he heard the other dogs in the back. "There're more?"

"Four total." I laughed.

Tate smiled at me. "Four dogs?"

Millie giggled. "We all have our own puppy."

Tate set his puppy down and both kids took off to the backyard, puppy in tow.

"He's perfect, Dane," Hailey said as she came over and hugged him, nudging me out of the way.

I cleared my throat and went inside to start getting plates and things ready.

I heard the kids laughing in the backyard.

When Trevor walked in, I smiled a little. "Have you heard if Jason was able to get things delivered?"

I looked out the kitchen window and smiled.

"Not yet. I told him not to stress but Jason wanted it all to be perfect."

"I know. He's a good guy." I kept my eyes on the kids playing. "He's mine, Trev. I have a son. Can you believe it?"

"He looks exactly like Dane, except for his smile. That's all you. I've never seen Dane have that big of a smile on his face. He was so proud. He's going to be a great dad."

Millie and Tate came running into the house followed by the four puppies. They headed straight up the stairs. They slowed so the puppies could follow behind them.

"Millie is actually laughing and smiling. They're a good fit."

I nodded.

"Where are the kids?" Dane asked as he came into the kitchen. He was grinning.

I pointed to the stairs. "Running around upstairs with the dogs in tow." I laughed.

Hailey came in with Zach. "Sadie, can you get out a few extra plates? Tate said he really wanted to meet the boys, so my mom is bringing them over."

"Yeah, sure." I grabbed a few more and set them on the bar.

"Why don't you go see if he likes his new room?" Dane kissed my head and started grabbing glasses.

"Alone?" I whispered.

I was so afraid of rejection. Nothing hurt like when he told me he wanted me out of that visitation room. I couldn't bear to feel that again.

"Do you want me to go with you?"

I noticed Hailey was listening to everything we were saying to each other. *Don't get pissed, Sadie. She's just watching out for Dane.*

I shook my head. "No, I'll go."

I went upstairs and saw Millie, Tate, and the puppies sitting on the floor in Tate's room. I leaned against the door frame and smiled.

"Did you show him the whole house?" I asked Millie.

"Everything but Uncle Dane's room." She looked at Tate. "Your dad doesn't have anything in his room yet."

"Your Uncle Jason is taking care of that."

Tate looked at me. "Did you help fix my room up?"

"With a lot of help from your uncles and aunt." I smiled. "Do you like it?"

He scratched behind one of the dog's ears. We really needed to get them collars so we could tell them apart.

"It's amazing, thank you." He smiled at me and my heart melted.

His eyes went to the picture of him and his adoptive parents on his nightstand. He looked at me again.

"Thank you for putting that there. Millie told me it was your idea."

"You're welcome."

"Let's eat, pregnant lady is hungry!" Hailey said from downstairs.

We all started laughing.

"You kids go wash your hands, and I'll get the dogs back outside."

Chapter Eighteen

DANE

I leaned against the door frame as I watched my son sleep. *My son.* I smiled even larger when I saw the puppy wiggle next to him. I walked over and picked up the book he had been reading. I placed it on the end table next to the bed and covered him and the puppy up. I couldn't believe my son was there with Millie and me. I gently brushed a piece of hair out of his face before turning to leave the room. I stopped when I saw the picture of his adoptive parents. I picked it up and smiled softly.

"Thank you for looking out for him and loving him. I promise you, I'll do the same." I would be forever grateful to this couple for taking in my son and caring for him when I couldn't. A sadness filled me as the fact that I had lost so much time with my son hit me full force. I missed his first everything. I slowly sat down in the chair and looked toward the bed. I froze when I saw Tate watching me. I stood and walked over to him.

"I didn't mean to wake you up."

He smiled the most adorable sleepy smile. "It's okay."

I sat down on the bed next to him. "I'm going to take care of you. I promise."

"I know you will." His dog, who he named Boy, stretched and yawned making Tate laugh.

"You don't have to spoil me, you know that, right?"

"I know, that's just who I am. I grew up in a rough home so I tend to spoil but I also don't put up with disrespect or rudeness."

He nodded. He looked at the book on the end table. "Did you know Sadie put that book in my drawer? Or did you put it there?"

His voice sounded thick, like he had something stuck in his throat. As I studied his eyes, I could tell he was trying to hold back tears.

I moved so I could put my back to the bed and patted the spot next me. I wrapped an arm around him. "She did."

"Have you read it?" He wiped his eyes.

"No, I didn't even know she put it in there until earlier. You don't have to read it if you're not ready."

"She says a lot of bad words," he said with a little laugh.

I smiled a little. "Yeah she'll have to work on that." I kissed the top of his head.

"I like the book, but it makes me sad for her." He reached over me and grabbed it.

"You have a good heart, Tate."

He opened up to a page. "Your name is in it a lot."

He pointed the page and handed it to me.

> I felt him kick today. It was the weirdest fucking feeling in the world. But I loved it. My whole world felt like it was crumbling, but his little kick, just knowing he was in there alive and well, made things okay somehow. I immediately wanted to call Dane because he should be here. He should be able to feel how amazing this is, but I can't call him.

That was it. There was nothing else after that except water stains on the page that I figured were her tears.

I handed back the diary to him. Tears filled my eyes. "I missed so much."

"It's okay that you did. I understand her a little bit after reading some of this book but I'm still angry. Why didn't she fight for me?"

"I don't know. I've wondered the same thing. You'll have to ask her. But you have plenty of time to get all the answers you want. Right now, I have a question for you." I ruffled his hair. "Do you want to go to public school or homeschool like Millie?"

He scrunched his nose while he thought, another Sadie trait. "School. I want to make friends." He smiled. "I want to play baseball, too."

"Then tomorrow we will go register you."

"When does school start?"

"In two weeks. Once I get you registered we'll go get school clothes for you."

I kissed his head again. "Get some sleep. We'll talk more in the morning." I got out of bed and headed downstairs. I had an air mattress to sleep on but I would have to wear myself out more before I tried to sleep. At night when it was quiet and I wasn't busy was when my nightmares returned. I hoped they didn't tonight.

I SAT AT Hales' table with my head on my arms. "I tried talking Millie into public school since Tate is going. She almost had a panic attack." I sighed. "I'm going to take on more office work instead of working on site so I can focus on her schooling."

"I can help too. I'm home with Joshua."

She teared up. "I can't believe the twins start kindergarten." She wiped her eyes just as the twins came running into the kitchen. Joshua laughed from his high chair where he was eating Cheerios.

"Thanks. I know Trevor is pushing for me to be at the office more so it will make him happy."

"You tell her," Elliot said, shoving Jamison toward Hailey

"Tell me what?" She raised a brow at her boys.

"Joshua clogged the toilet!" Jamison said and Elliot smacked his own forehead and groaned.

"Joshua is in his highchair, stupid!"

Jamison made a freaked-out face. "Er, umm...there's a frog in the toilet. A big bullfrog."

Elliot looked completely guilty.

Jamison was holding his breath, trying not to laugh.

She opened her mouth to say something, but closed it. She looked completely confused. Hailey stared at them like, *what the hell*, for several moments. I could see her face getting red which meant she was about to explode.

I bit down on my lip to keep from laughing. Before Hales could blow up, I scooped them up and slung them over my shoulders.

"Let's go check out this toilet."

The boys laughed.

I went upstairs with both boys and shook my head as I saw Millie and Tate peering into the bathroom. "What's going on?"

They were laughing so hard.

"Elliot brought that bullfrog in his room two weeks ago," Jamison said, tattling on his brother.

I put the boys down and held onto the back of their shirts as they tried to make a run for it. "Show me."

Elliot rolled his eyes. "His name is Jerry, Jami-*son*," he said, accentuating the last part of his name.

"And now Jerry is dead because you freaked out because you thought you heard Mom coming down the hall! You can't stick a giant bullfrog down a toilet!" Jamison was angry.

I walked in the bathroom and looked at a drowned bullfrog in the toilet.

I shook my head and grabbed a trash can liner from under the sink. I used it to scoop out the bullfrog and tied it off. "Get some towels and clean up the water, you two."

I looked at Millie and Tate. "Can you two supervise them while I get rid of the bullfrog? I'll be right back."

I heard the front door open and looked at the time on my watch. "It sounds like your dad is home," I said with a raised eyebrow at the boys.

I heard Zach yell their names as I was making my way down the stairs. I met him halfway. "They're supposed to be cleaning up the water. Millie and

Tate are watching them until one of us could get back to them." I grinned. "Some poor teacher is going to have their hands full."

Zach groaned and went up the stairs.

I chuckled as I handed Hales the bag with the dead frog.

She sighed and laughed a little. "Can you watch Joshua while I go throw this out?"

I looked at Joshua in the highchair and laughed when he threw his sippy cup onto the floor and giggled. This was the game he liked to play with me. Throw something in the floor and Uncle Dane will pick it up.

I picked it up and handed it to him then kissed his head.

Chapter Nineteen

SADIE

I took the Zip-Loc bag of ice from Trevor and put it on my left eye. "Thanks."

Mom and I had gotten into a fight. A real one. The screaming turned into pulling hair, and pulling hair turned into throwing punches. When Dad walked in the door from work, he pulled us apart. I was done. So done with her. I had to leave since she wasn't going to. I looked at Jason as he came through the doorway with my suitcase.

"You guys really don't have to let me stay here." I had nowhere to go until the small guest house on Dane's property was finished, but I hated intruding on Jason and Trev. I could pull from savings and stay in a hotel or find a place to rent for the time being if I had to.

"It's not a big deal. We have the extra bedroom." Jason smiled at me. "Besides, I know for a fact Dane was planning on getting that little house done soon."

"I told him not to worry about it. I want him focusing on everything else right now." I pulled the ice from my eye. "How bad is it?"

Trevor made a face. "It looks pretty bad. Dane is going to flip. You know how protective he is." He rubbed the back of his neck and glanced at his watch. "Maybe you should tell him, that way it's not a shock to him."

"And say what? I acted like a child and punched my mom so she punched me back?" I felt like an idiot. I should've just left the house instead of adding fuel to Mom's fire. But she was asking to meet Tate, and I said no. Things just escalated from there.

"Just tell him that you and your mom got in a fight and you lost your temper. He will understand, but him seeing you with a black eye will worry him if he doesn't know what happened. You know his mind goes to bad stuff."

I set the ice down and called Dane.

"Hey," I said when he answered. "So, I probably can't go with you to sign Tate up for school tomorrow."

I heard him yawn. "Why not?"

"Did I wake you up?" I looked at the time and cursed when I saw it was midnight. "Shit, sorry, Dane."

"It's fine. I'm not asleep. I'm pacing."

"Oh. Why?"

"I don't sleep very well. I pace until I fall asleep." He yawned again. "Now, why aren't you coming tomorrow?"

"I have a black eye. Well, not yet, but it will be by morning." I was embarrassed and disappointed in myself. I was going to miss my son's sixth-grade registration because I had a damn black eye. But I couldn't go. It'd embarrass him. I couldn't let him be labeled as the kid with the mom with the black eye. I groaned and leaned back into the couch.

"First, why don't you do that contouring shit and cover it up with makeup, and two, why the fuck do you have a black eye?"

I smiled a little at how much he paid attention to how I did my makeup.

"I can try. And...I punched my mom in the face so she punched me back."

There was a moment of silence before he burst out laughing.

"Does she look worse than you?"

"Yeah."

"What did you guys fight about?"

"She wanted to meet Tate and I said no." I noticed Trev and Jason weren't in the room anymore. "It's her fault. All of this."

"Sadie," he said calmly. "Come home."

"Huh?"

"Come to the house. You can sleep on the air mattress."

"I'm at Jason and Trevor's. I'm okay."

"That doesn't change the fact that I want you here, but okay." He yawned again.

"Y-You want me there?"

"Yes. I figured you'd know that by now." I heard a puppy barking a little through the phone. "Shhh, Scout." I heard some shifting. "Scout and Juno-Bear are like my shadows."

"But what about Tate?"

He sighed. "I guess we should wait then. I swear I'm getting your little house done by the end of the week."

I laughed. "I'll really be fine. You have bigger things to focus on."

I closed my eyes. "So, I'll do that contouring shit and see you in the morning?"

"Yes. And be prepared for some questions from Tate. He's been reading your diary." I heard Dane let out a gasp of air then a groan. There was a loud pop, some scared puppy barking and a thud as if the phone hit the floor.

"You okay?"

He groaned again. "The dogs pounced on me then took a bite out of the air mattress."

I laughed. "Guess you'll be sleeping in the couch. When will your furniture be in?"

"Tomorrow, hopefully."

"I should probably go take a shower and get some sleep. But I don't want to stop talking to you."

"I don't want to stop talking to you, either, but you need sleep, Daisy."

"You need sleep too, baby." I yawned.

"I don't sleep much." He yawned. "No, you two can't sleep on the couch with me." I heard the puppies whine and Dane huff.

"Me either." I stared at the bag of ice that was now melted. "Can I ask something that's probably crazy?" I got up and threw the bag away.

I found my keys.

"Sure."

"Can I come…" I felt myself blushing. "Can I come over and see you? Even if it's just five minutes. I need your arms around me. I won't come in."

"Daisy, I've already invited you over." He chuckled.

"I know, but Tate…"

"Is in bed. I will just meet you outside. Okay?"

I couldn't stop smiling. "Okay. No laughing at my eye." I hurried out to my Rover. "I'll see you in ten minutes." I got in and cranked the engine.

"I'll be waiting outside."

I hung up, put on my seatbelt, and headed to his house.

WHEN I PULLED into the driveway, he was waiting for me on the front porch. Both puppies were on their leashes and wagging their tails.

"Where's Boy?" I asked as I walked toward him.

"Boy is in bed with Tate and Sassy is in bed with Millie."

I stopped in front of him and smiled appreciatively. No shirt and his sweats were…*yum.*

I bent down and pet the dogs. Juno-Bear, my new baby, licked my hand.

"I think we ended up with the two mischievous ones."

I stood and smiled. "How was he tonight? I know you said he started reading my journal. I left him a note to read it when he was ready. I don't want hide anything from him." Tears filled my eyes. "I've been such an emotional mess, and I don't know how to just feel okay."

He pulled me into his arms and put his chin in my head. "It'll take time. It's okay to not feel okay, Daisy."

Damn, his arms. His skin. The way he smells. I melted against him.

"Everything will work out." He kissed the top of my head.

"I know, and I'm trying to be patient, but it's hard."

"Nothing that's worth it is easy."

I smiled against his skin. "I know." I looked up at him so I could see his baby blues.

He moved hair from the side of my face where I had the black eye and tucked it behind my ear. "It doesn't look too bad."

"Liar."

He laughed. "I hate that you and your mom are fighting, but I'm proud of you for sticking up for our son. He's not ready to meet them."

I nodded and sadness weighed heavy on me. "I hate it, too, but I want to do everything right for him. I need him to trust me before I let him meet the ones who pushed for the adoption."

He kissed my forehead and nodded in understanding. "You need to go get some rest, Daisy."

"One second longer."

He kept his arms wrapped around me. "I love you, Daisy, and in time so will Tate."

"I know." I moved a little so I could see his face. "Thank you. For everything."

I wanted to kiss him. *So. Fucking. Bad.* But I knew us. We'd kiss, we wouldn't be able to stop, and we'd end up in my Rover. We weren't ready for that. We were getting a chance to make this work and to do that, we had to fall in love in reverse.

I looked at my hand that was over his heart and tattoo. I felt so small compared to him, but I loved how he towered over me and held me. I never felt safer than when in his arms.

I moved my hand and kissed the daisy tattoo. I backed away and smiled. "Goodnight."

He grinned. "'Night, Daisy."

I watched him go inside with the dogs before leaving.

Chapter Twenty

DANE

I braided Millie's hair while Tate bounced on his feet next to us. He was so excited to see his new school. Millie had been extra quiet this morning. Something was off. Once I finished her hair, I made her look at me.

"What's wrong, Munchkin?"

"I don't have to go to public school, do I?" she asked me quietly.

I shook my head. "No, you can still homeschool. I'm setting up a desk for you and you can decorate your own office at work."

She smiled a little, but it faded quickly. Tears were in her eyes as she looked away and pet Sassy.

"Millie, what's really wrong?"

"I had a bad dream."

I pulled her into my arms and kissed her head. "About Elliot?"

She nodded against my chest and started crying. It had been eight years since her dad had died but she still had nightmares about him being sick and dying. I thought with time she would forget some of it, but Millie didn't forget anything.

"And you died," she whispered.

"Hey, nothing is going to happen to me." Tate had stopped bouncing and was looking at Millie worriedly. I rubbed her back soothingly.

We had days like this. Days she would have panic attacks and not be able to leave my side. Even with therapy this hadn't changed.

"Do you want to go hang out with Aunt—"

She shook her head before I could even finish my sentence.

I continued to rub her back gently. The owls had disappeared four years ago, about the same time I came home. Losing that connection with her parents had devastated her. "Do we need to go to your mom and dad's home before we head to the school?"

She shook her head again and held onto me more tightly.

"Okay. Deep breaths, my munchkin. Everything will be okay. We'll go with Tate to register him then take the puppies to Uncle Zach's and drive him crazy while we let them play in the water and with the boys. Okay?"

She nodded but wasn't calming down. I was at a loss of what to do until Tate knelt down next to her and whispered something in her ear. I didn't have a damn clue what it was but she slowly started calming down. He smiled at her and she kept her eyes on him until she was able to get a little better control.

He grinned at her. "Hey, Millie, why is Peter Pan always flying?

She shrugged and smiled a little. "Why?"

"Because he Neverlands."

Millie giggled and I laughed. I loved that Tate and Millie hit it off. Not only was I getting to know my son, but Millie was getting a friend who could calm her down a lot faster than I could.

Sadie was meeting us at the school, but I hadn't heard from her this morning seeing how covering that black eye was going.

Tate looked at me. "Is my mom, I mean Sadie, coming soon?" He sounded really confused with himself. "I mean she is my mom, but I'm not calling her Mom."

"She's going to meet us at the school or she's supposed to."

He nodded and took Millie's hand. "Let's go see the dogs before we leave."

Millie nodded and wiped her eyes before following Tate out to the gated backyard.

I pulled out my phone as soon as they were out of earshot and called Sadie.

When she picked up she didn't answer right away. I heard something drop, her say her favorite F word, and then her sigh. "Hey. Sorry. I dropped my hair straightener." She cursed again. "On my foot."

"Did you burn yourself?" I smirked a little. She always had been clumsy.

"Thankfully, no." She laughed. "The problem is my long hair…My hand gets tired by the time I'm done. I was a second away from taking a scissors to it."

"Well, don't do that right now. We're about to leave the house. It will take us ten minutes longer to get to the school than you. Also, we are going to Zach's afterward. Do you want to come with us?"

"Sure, as long as Tate is okay with it. Is he excited?"

"He seems okay with it. He asked if you were going." I didn't tell her about the mom thing. I don't think Tate was ready for her to know yet. "He's very excited. Zach has a surprise for him once we get to the house. He got him a Stockbridge uniform for the games, and I've already talked to the traveling baseball team coach. I haven't told him yet. I thought maybe you would want to." I sighed. "Millie is having a bad day, though. So, if she doesn't talk to you, don't get upset." I looked toward the kitchen door as the kids came through with all the puppies on the leashes.

"Oh wow! That's great! And that sucks about Millie. Maybe we can take them out for lunch, too. I guess I'll see you soon. And you can sort of see my black eye, but it just looks like I did a shit job on my eyeshadow." She chuckled. "See you soon."

"Lunch sounds good. We'll see ya soon." I hung up the phone and turned to the kids. "Let's go." I took Scout and Sassy's leashes and we all headed to the school.

SADIE PULLED UP to the school when we did. She got out and came over to the truck and opened the door for the kids. She shut the door after they got out, and I noticed she had two small boxes her hands. She set them on the seat and then shut the door.

Sadie walked over to me and smiled at the school. "Can you believe our kid is going to school where we went?"

Millie grabbed my hand and held tightly, and I nodded. "It seems surreal."

Tate grabbed my other hand as Millie pressed herself against my side. I peered down at her and smiled, trying to hide my worry. I hated when she had days like this.

"You ready, Tate?" I asked with a smile as I glanced down at him. I grinned even broader when I saw that he was trying to mimic how I walked and how straight I stood.

"Wait!" Sadie was beaming. She took her phone from her back pocket and motioned for us to squish together. "Smile!" She took a picture. "Okay, now we can go in."

I chuckled as we headed inside. We made our way to the office, and I suddenly started to feel nervous. *My son was going to Stockbridge Middle School.* I smiled at the woman behind the desk.

"Dane! What are you doing here?" Tiffany asked a tad too excitedly. She had been in the year behind Sadie and me.

"I called Principal Jeffers. I'm here to register my son for sixth grade."

She turned to Tate who was standing next to me and smile. "Isn't he the spitting image of you! You're as cute as your daddy has always been."

Sadie had a pained smile on her face. The smile she made when she was fighting the urge to say something completely vulgar. Sadie never liked Tiffany. When we dated, Tiffany was always trying to break us up.

Tiffany looked at Sadie and then at me. "Wait, is he both of yours?" I could tell she was doing the math in her head and her eyes widened in shock.

I put my hand on Tate's shoulder. I raised my eyebrow at her. "Yes, now can you tell Principal Jeffers we are here," I said with a frown. This girl always got on my nerves.

Tiffany ignored Sadie and smiled at me. She nodded before leaving the front desk to go get the principal. I stared at Sadie with a raised eyebrow letting her know to calm down a bit. She should know that Tiffany only ever got on my nerves.

I gazed down at Tate and Millie. "So, Sadie is thinking about cutting her hair. What do you guys think about that? Good idea or bad idea?" I needed to give the kids something to focus on instead of the crazy secretary.

Millie looked up at Sadie and tilted her head to the side as she studied at her hair. She glanced at Tate waiting for him to answer first.

He blushed a little. "I think you should keep it. It's pretty."

Sadie smiled. "Then it stays."

Tate smiled. "Did it take you a long time to get it that long?"

Sadie shook her head. "My mom never let me cut my hair unless it went past my belly button. So, I've always had long hair. Today it just made me really, really angry."

He chuckled. "How can hair make you mad?"

Sadie laughed. "It's a girl thing."

Millie looked at Tate. "Do you know how it took forever for Uncle Dane to braid my hair this morning?"

Sadie looked at me and her expression turned soft, like she was going to melt into a big pile of mush right here in the office.

Tate nodded at Millie.

"That's why. It takes a long time to fix. If Uncle Dane does a complicated braid it takes forever." She smiled up at me. "But it's worth it."

I tugged on her braid. "Of course it is." I turned from the kids and focused on Principal Jeffers as he came out of his office, Tiffany following behind him.

"You four come on into my office. We'll talk about getting these kiddos signed up."

Millie's eyes widened and gaped at me in a panic.

"Just one. My son, Tate, will be going to school. Not Millie." I hated the tears that had started forming in her eyes. I put my hand gently around her shoulders as we followed Mr. Jeffers into his office.

Chapter Twenty-one

SADIE

I was proud of myself. I only mumbled one nasty thing and it was only loud enough for Tiffany to hear in passing. I'd never liked her. I was trying not to be petty, I mean we had been out of school for almost a decade, but that didn't change the fact that she was a snake in the grass and tried desperately to date Dane back in school.

Dane smiled at the kids as they played with the puppies in the little lake area that Zach had set up for the kids. The twins were laughing and playing with Millie, Tate, and the puppies. He turned his head to catch me watching him. "What?" he asked with a smile.

"What, I can't stare?" I smiled.

He blushed a little. "I guess you can." He grinned.

"He's perfect." I moved so I was closer to him and laced my fingers with his.

Hailey walked over to us. Her eyes went to our hands and I let go. Hales studied my eye for a second.

Hales motioned toward it. "What happened?"

"I got. . ." I frowned. I didn't want to tell her. She had barely said two words to me since being here and when she did speak, she was a bitch. I looked at the kids instead of finishing my sentence and then turned to Dane. "I'm going to go play with them."

I squealed when Tate splashed me. He was laughing so hard he could barely catch his breath. I picked him up, even though he was as big as me, and fell into the water with him. When we came up, I glanced over at Dane and Hailey. It seemed as though she was giving him an ass chewing.

Dane stood and went into the house. I could tell from the clenched fists and the reddening of his face that he was pissed.

Tate and Millie took notice that there was something wrong. I looked at them and the twins. Zach walked out with Joshua toddling behind him. Hailey rolled her eyes and walked toward the house.

I kissed the top of Tate's head and smiled at Millie and the twins before walking over to Zach.

"Should I leave?" He looked at my eye. I'm sure my makeup was washing off. "Me and my mom got in a fight."

"Nah, it's fine. Hales will get over it. She's just worried about Dane. I tried to explain to her that he's a big boy, but it didn't help any."

"They're best friends. I understand." I scrunched my nose. "He used to be my best friend." I didn't really mean for that to come out of my mouth. I hated how childish I sounded. He wasn't a box of crayons I was fighting over in kindergarten, but I felt my stupid self totally going there. "I feel like when we make progress, she makes us take like fifty steps back."

I stared at Zach who seemed completely torn. I knew I was putting him in a hard place. Hailey was his whole world, I shouldn't be talking to him about this.

"You know what? I'll leave. This isn't fair to you, and I don't want this drama around the kids." I smiled sheepishly and walked over to the kids and dogs and told them all bye. I twisted my wet hair to get some water out of it as I walked to the front of the house and to my Rover.

I got in my vehicle and took my keys out of the console. I cranked the engine and left. I was stupid for thinking I could be welcome at Zach and Hailey's house. I didn't want to go, but I also didn't want to not go and miss out on time with Tate, Dane, and Millie. I was at a loss for how to handle this. I would never try to come between Hailey and Dane, but it also wasn't fair for her to try to come between us. She wasn't giving me a chance to show her that I was serious about being here, being a mother, and learning to be exactly what Dane needed.

I HEADED DOWNSTAIRS to clear my head after the day I'd had. I didn't hear from Dane, but I didn't expect to. He needed to work out whatever was going on between Hailey and him.

I was in complete shock when I walked into the ballet room to practice a routine and saw Cooper and Alice waiting with big smiles and my camera bag. I started jumping up and down and screaming.

"Are you serious? What are you crazies doing here?" I ran over and pulled them into a group hug.

The day had gone to shit and after leaving Zach and Hailey's. I had planned on practicing a routine to teach my class, but now, two of my very best friends from school were there and with my baby.

We pulled apart and Cooper handed me my camera bag. "We thought we'd hand deliver this. Neither of us trusted the post office to get it here or the moving truck."

Alice was grinning. "Speaking of the moving truck, I got everything packed and it should all be here by the end of next week. The movers pick it up on Monday."

I jumped again. "I can't believe you two are here! I have so much to tell you!"

Cooper tilted his head. "What's up with the eye?"

I laughed. "That's part of what all I have to tell you. So, I guess you met Jason, my new boss?"

They both nodded and speak of the devil, Jason walked into the room.

"Jason, these are two of the best dancers in the entire world! And two of my very best friends." I squealed and hugged them both again.

Cooper smiled after we pulled apart again. "He knows. We called the studio when our plane got in to make sure you were going to be here when we got here. Jason knew we were coming since this morning."

Alice inspected the room. "This place is amazing!"

Jason smiled proudly. "Thanks, Dane built it. I'm sure you've heard all about him," he said, waggling his eyebrows at me.

I froze. I never told anyone in New York about Dane or my life in Stockbridge. Jason frowned a little but replaced it with a forced smile.

"Can we have a tour?" Alice asked.

I looked at Jason. "Is it okay if I show them around?"

"Sure. There are classes going in rooms three and five, but the rest are freed up. I have to go do some paperwork while I'm waiting for my next class."

I nodded and set my camera down near the stereo. I then took them around and showed them everything. When we were done, I took them upstairs to the apartment to show them my temporary home.

Alice sat on the couch and Cooper leaned against the arm of the couch.

"What's up with the black eye? Did you fall?" Cooper snickered.

I tried to laugh to play it off while I tried to come up with a lie, but failed. I ran my fingers through my hair to move it out of my face. I chewed on the inside of my cheek while I debated on whether or not to tell them my mom hit me.

Before I could get a single word out of my mouth, Dane walked into the apartment.

He stopped when he saw the two people in the room. "Umm, sorry. I didn't know you had company."

I smiled. "It's okay. I didn't know I would either. They surprised me." I pointed at Cooper. "This is Cooper" —I pointed at Alice— "and this is Alice. Both very good friends of mine I met at Juilliard." I looked at Dane and smiled. "And this is Dane."

Cooper pushed off the couch and held his hand out to Dane.

Dane took his hand and shook it. "Nice to meet you." He turned to face me. "I'll call you later. I don't want to interrupt."

Alice stood and smiled. "It's nice to meet you. And you're not interrupting."

I could tell Alice and Cooper were waiting for me to say exactly who Dane was to me. But, I didn't know. I mean, I knew, but I didn't know how to put it into words.

Dane watched my face and seemed confused by my silence. "I can't really stay. I just needed to talk to Sadie." He looked at me and smiled. "I wanted to invite you over for dinner and your friends are more than welcome to come too." He smiled at them. "I need to get back down to Millie. Our son is with Zach getting fitted for his uniform. They should—" He stopped talking when he saw the shocked expressions on their faces. He cleared his throat and left the apartment.

I looked at my friends whose mouths were on the floor. I took a deep breath, preparing to tell them everything.

Chapter Twenty-two

DANE

I handed Millie the glasses and Tate the plates as I opened the boxes of pizza. I had planned on fixing a nice dinner but I had an emergency at a site and just got back from work. I hadn't even had time to change out of my dirty work clothes. I had just enough time to wash my hands. I looked down at myself and shrugged. *Oh well.*

I heard a knock at the door.

I tugged Millie's braid and gave her a small smile.

Tate smiled. "Is that Sadie and her friends?"

"Yep." I peered down at myself again. "I should have made time to change. I'm a mess." I smiled and headed to the door. I opened it and grinned. "Hey. We had to order pizza. I had an emergency at work." I smiled at Sadie.

Sadie smiled and shrugged. "I love pizza."

Alice and Cooper were dressed like they were headed to a fancy restaurant, not my house for pizza. Cooper held a bottle of wine in his right hand.

Sadie saw my face and snickered. "I told them to dress casually and that you hate wine," she said quietly as we walked in.

Alice screamed when the dogs came running. She hid behind Cooper's back.

Sadie bent down and let them lick her in the face and pet them to calm them down.

"Actually, I don't allow alcohol in the house. Not around me or the kids. Sorry," I said apologetically before picking up two of the puppies. "I'll put them in the backyard."

Sadie scrunched her eyebrows in confusion. I used to drink some, but she didn't know I didn't anymore.

Cooper looked at the bottle. "I'll take it back out to Sadie's vehicle."

"Thank you." I headed toward the back of the house out the back door, and Juno and Boy followed me. I put Sassy and Scout down and they all started playing in the yard. I shut the door and went into the kitchen to wash my hands. I looked at Sadie and the kids as I came into the dining room.

"The kids set the table."

"They did a great job." She kissed my cheek. "Thank you for inviting them," she whispered.

Alice and Cooper came into the room.

"You're welcome. Any friends of yours are welcome here."

Millie moved so she was closer to me.

Sadie put her arm around Tate's shoulders and kissed the top of his head. "Guys, this is Tate. My son."

Tate smiled his little crooked grin.

Alice and Cooper looked at me, and then at him with strained smiles. This was obviously all news to them.

I winked at him, hoping to put him at ease.

"He looks just like Dane," Alice said with a smile to Sadie. She then looked at Tate. "I'm Al-ice," she said, saying it like she was talking to a deaf person.

Tate tilted his head and gawked at her. He turned to Sadie. "Is your friend special?"

I burst out laughing before I could stop myself. I coughed to try and cover it.

Sadie covered a laugh. "Alice, he can hear." Sadie smiled and shook her head.

Alice's face began to flush. "Sorry. I'm not used to children."

Alice and Cooper averted their attention to Millie.

I smiled and ruffled her curls. "This is Millie, my niece and Tate's cousin."

Cooper covered his heart in relief. "I thought you were going to tell us you had two kids."

Sadie gritted her teeth as she put her arm around Tate defensively. I could see she was embarrassed at how they were acting and slightly hurt.

Millie didn't smile. She moved closer to me.

Sadie kissed the top of Tate's head and smiled at Millie. She then looked at me apologetically. "Let's go eat." Her tone was dry.

"The dining room is this way." I led the way to the dining room and pulled out the chair for Millie, then for Sadie.

Sadie told me she always wanted a table like you'd see in an old farmhouse with all the mismatched chairs. She'd said she wanted a dining room fit for the Mad Hatter. So, that's what I got.

"We have soda, juice, milk and water," I said to Alice, Cooper, and Sadie.

Sadie sat down in her dark purple chair and looked mortified when she saw Alice and Cooper checking the chairs for stability.

"Guys, they're brand new. They were made to appear old." Sadie was red.

Alice furrowed her brow. "Oh. But why?"

Cooper shook his head and sat down.

Sadie was reaching her boiling point with them. I could see it in her eyes.

"To look like the table from *Alice in Wonderland*, of course," I answered.

Tate and Millie laughed.

Cooper looked at Sadie. "Remember when we did an *Alice in Wonderland* ballet and you were the Queen of Hearts?"

Sadie calmed down a little. It took her a minute, but she smiled. "I remember. You were the rabbit and Alice was behind the scenes co-producing."

Millie was listening intently to them.

"Millie loves ballet. She's pretty talented herself." I looked at her with pride in my eyes.

Alice smiled at Millie. "My favorite ballet is *Phantom of the Opera*. What's yours?"

She stared down at her plate instead of answering.

"Millie is shy. Her favorite ballet is *Swan Lake*."

Alice smiled and looked at Cooper "Cooper performed in that."

Millie was picking at her food instead of eating it. I leaned down next to her. "Do you want to go eat in your room?" I whispered to her.

She nodded. I gave her a smile when she kissed my cheek. She grabbed her plate and drink. Tate watched her go longingly, and I nodded to him. He quickly grabbed his stuff and followed after her.

Sadie fiddled with her napkin, she was bothered that they left. She looked at me. "Dane, we can leave."

I noticed Alice and Cooper staring at me.

"Millie doesn't like people much." I placed my hand on Sadie's where she had it resting on the table. "I thought she would be fine, but she's had a rough day. I'm sorry."

As a matter of fact, we'd all had a rough day.

Sadie nodded. "I understand. It's okay. Did you go into work?"

I looked down at my dirty clothes and laughed. "Yeah. There was an emergency." I rubbed my wrist absentmindedly hoping she didn't pay attention and notice my brace was gone. *Again.*

"What do you do for work?" Cooper asked after taking a drink of his water.

"I'm in construction." I smiled at him. I could have said I ran one of the nation's most successful and diverse construction companies in the nation, but I knew people like Alice and Cooper. They had money and liked to show it. I didn't.

"Oh. That's nice." Cooper grabbed another slice of pizza. He used paper towel to soak up the grease.

I took Sadie's hand in mine and laced my fingers with hers. I watched in confusion as he smashed layers of paper towel on the cheese and toppings to get it off.

"Sadie, have you been working out and stretching?" Alice asked her.

Sadie nodded. "Some. It's been a wild ride lately, so, I haven't been as diligent about it."

"You could always come exercise with me every morning," I teased her. I knew how much she loved sleeping in.

She laughed. "Yeah, but I'd be grumpy."

I chuckled. "But you'd have a nice view," I said as I wiggled my eyebrows at her. If she knew how much I actually worked out, she wouldn't even consider it. Ever since the Marines, my morning exercise was what set my day and it was nothing short of intense.

She laughed and playfully scrunched her nose. She smiled. "Challenge accepted."

"Okay, so this is serious?" Alice said with a confused laugh.

Sadie frowned. "What?"

I lost my smile.

"We all know how you like to joke with us. We're waiting for you to tell us you're kidding. A kid and a boyfriend who works construction?" Cooper replied in a snarky tone.

"One, my son isn't a joke," I snapped. "And two, what the hell is wrong with construction?"

Sadie slapped the table with her open hand. "Cooper!"

Cooper stood. "This is insane. Giving up the biggest promotion at Juilliard, a once-in-a-lifetime opportunity, for this? Bring your son with you! Don't give up on all you worked toward!"

I clenched my jaw. "For *this*? You mean, for me, a construction worker?"

Alice pulled down on Cooper's arm making him sit.

Cooper looked at me, slightly apologetic. "Sorry. Until today, I had no clue you existed. I'm just shocked."

Well, that hurt. But it was understandable. She tried to leave everything in Stockbridge behind. Including me. *Especially me.*

"We should go. Sadie, we can catch up tomorrow over brunch." Alice stood. "Let's call a cab," she said turning to Cooper.

Cooper stood and reached across the table to shake my hand. "Thank you and again, sorry. Sadie, we need to talk tomorrow."

They left the room and, when the front door shut, Sadie looked at me.

"Umm, shouldn't you tell them we don't have cabs?"

Sadie rolled her eyes. "I dare you to call Zach and have him pretend to be an Uber driver."

"He'd kill me, but it would be entertaining. And we'll just let them figure it out. I'm too angry to go out there and tell them right now."

She nodded and her face turned red. "Dane, I'm sorry. I wanted to tell them everything. But it was just easier to have a separate life there. It made coping with everything easier."

I brought her hand to my lips and kissed the back of it. "I understand, Daisy. You know I would give you the world if I could. I can only not give you one thing. I can't move from Stockbridge." I needed her to know that. "I can give you anything else you want but not that." I suddenly was feeling depressed. "I bet I could pay Zach to do the Uber thing." I looked away from her as I changed topics.

"Dane."

I looked at her. My stomach was in knots.

She ran her thumb across the scar on my chin and smiled. "I'm not going to ask you to move. I told you I'm here to stay, and I meant it."

We heard the door open, and then Cooper walked in.

"No cell service," he mumbled.

Sadie laughed and stood. "I'll take you to the hotel."

"It wouldn't have mattered. We don't have cabs here." I grinned. I really was not a big fan of this guy. What right did he have to say that I wasn't good enough? He didn't know a damn thing about me.

I stood. "You should tell the kids bye before you head out."

Sadie nodded and glared at Cooper. "Don't say a word while I'm not in here. You're just going to dig a deeper hole with me." She cut her eyes at him before heading down the hall.

I put my hands in my jeans and looked at Cooper. "I was going to call my brother to pick you up."

"That's okay. I'm sorry I was a dick. But in my defense, this is not the Sadie I know. I'm just in shock."

I shrugged. I was trying not to let his attitude bother me, but it was. "You never answered my question. What's wrong with construction?"

"Nothing is wrong with it for people like you."

I raised an eyebrow. "What do you mean, people like me?" I crossed my arms in front of my chest, and I was proud I didn't wince when my broken hand hit my arm. *I really need to wear my brace.*

"Sadie told me not to speak."

"Well, she's not here, and I want an answer."

He rubbed the back of his neck. "Ummm, how do I put this without sounding rude..." He thought. I don't think he was capable of not coming off rude. "Blue-collar."

"Blue-collar. Like working class. You're saying I'm not good enough because I work, and you think I don't have enough money to make her happy?" A part of me wanted to tell him that I probably had more money than he would ever see in his lifetime, but the bigger part hated talking about money, and I hated being judged by it. "I can give her a comfortable life."

He nodded. "I'm sure you can, but you have to understand that I don't know this Sadie. I know Sadie who became one of my best friends in New York. She dated one of the biggest—"

"Cooper, stop," Sadie said as she walked in. "And what he was about to say was one of the biggest douchebags on the planet. It would have never worked out, so don't even go there, Cooper. I love that you're trying to look out for me, but don't. I know what's best for me, and that's why I'm moving back here." Sadie kissed my cheek. "I'll call you later, okay?"

"All right. Be safe driving back. Watch out for deer." I kissed the top of her head.

As they were walking out, I heard Cooper talking to her about the other guy she dated. Sadie was pretending not to listen. I heard the front door close.

I sighed and shook my head as I headed toward my bathroom.

Chapter Twenty-three

SADIE

I moved into the splits and leaned forward. I hadn't really stretched like I should have been doing, so it hurt like hell. All I could think about was dinner the night before. I was so embarrassed. I knew bringing Cooper and Alice to Dane's was a bad idea. They are very outspoken and snooty as hell. They were good people, they just didn't live simply like people in Stockbridge. And in their defense, they had no idea that I had a life like this or that I preferred life this way. They're Juilliard brats, and I was one too for the past eight years. It sucked because now Dane had a bad impression of them, and those were two people I wanted to keep in my life. I talked to Dane for over an hour on the phone last night, and he said he was fine, but I knew better. You can't be fine after people treat you like you're trash.

Yesterday was a shit day. Tiffany making eyes at my man, Hailey coming between Dane and me again, and then my friends acting like rich assholes.

Jason came down the stairs and smiled at me as he saw me stretching. He glanced at his watch. "Why are you up so early? I usually don't see you until around eight or nine."

"Because I haven't been asleep yet," I said sitting up and moving my legs until I had the soles of my feet pressed together.

He sat down next to me and started stretching. "I thought maybe Dane had talked you into doing his insane workout with him."

"I'm too embarrassed to see him right now."

He stopped stretching and looked at me. "Dane is easy going. He'll be fine. I'm sure he'd like to see you. Although, you might want to wait until after the workout. Did he tell you what all he does?" he asked with a smile.

"I know he's easygoing, but it's me. I just feel bad about yesterday. And no, he didn't." I stood and moved my arms above my head and then pulled them behind my back.

He put his legs in front of him and grabbed his toes. "He runs for twelve miles, does a hundred sit-ups, push-ups, and chin-ups, then he lifts weights. It's insane. He gets it all done before the kids wake up. Of course, he's not supposed to be doing anything with his hand right now. But he's stubborn."

I pulled my left arm toward my right side and then did the opposite arm. "Yeah, he is. But I'm going to talk to him about it after brunch with my friends." I walked over to the stereo and turned on some music. I smiled at Jason. "Up for a dance battle?"

He laughed and stood. "Sure. It's a great way to warm up. And about those 'friends'..."

I rolled my eyes. "My friends are good people, they just aren't from around here. I'm going to talk to them today." I started the music. "All right, pretty boy, show me what you got."

I cranked the volume as "Down" by Marian Hill played loudly through the speakers.

I SENT DANE a SnapChat of me looking like a bat while I listened to Coop and Alice go on and on about what I was giving up. They even had a list of pros and cons.

Dane sent the Snap filter back, but it was of him, Tate, and Millie.

I sent back one of me with a frown and captioned it with: **#jealous**.

"Hey!" I snapped when Alice took my phone from me.

"Are you even listening to us?" She was now the one frowning.

I reached across the table and took one of Coop's fries. "No."

Coop raised a brow.

"What? You aren't going to eat them anyway. You're on that weird Paleo Diet bullshit."

"Maybe it's a cheat day." He took a bite of one and acted like it was painful to chew it.

I laughed.

Alice glared at Cooper. "You're supposed to be helping me, not playing nice right now!"

"Sadie, just tell us what you're thinking," Cooper said before taking a drink of his water.

I tried to reach for my phone again, but Alice put it in her designer purse.

I huffed. "I'm thinking that I have a son, the love of my life, and a family here. This is my home, always has been, but I ran from it."

"How can you consider Juilliard running away? Isn't that your dream?" Alice's face contorted in confusion.

I nodded. "It is. It was. But dreams change, Alice. I never thought I'd get a second chance to be a mother to my son. I never thought I'd figure out a way to work things out with Dane. But, I have the opportunity to do both, and I won't give it up for a prestigious dance school and flashy job title."

"Bring them with you. You were going to be the head dance instructor for the ballet department, Sadie. Do you realize how amazing that accomplishment is?" Cooper looked at me like I was turning away the world, but what he didn't realize was that the whole world, *my* whole world, was in Stockbridge. Juilliard meant nothing to me anymore. I wasn't even sad that I was leaving it behind.

"Do you realize how amazing of an accomplishment it will be when my son can look at me and actually love me? Do you realize how big of an accomplishment it will be if Dane and I work out? I have new goals. I know this isn't fair to you guys because I never told you anything about my life here or about my regrets. It was easier that way for me. But, now you know. I won't and will never consider taking Dane, Millie, and Tate away from the home they love. So, don't go there because it will always be an affirmative hell-fucking-no."

"And what about Ethan? What have you told him?" Cooper knew my feelings about his brother. It wasn't happening. *Ever.*

I didn't even reply. I wasn't wasting my energy.

"He told me he's called and texted you every day," Cooper said, but I wished he would just shut up.

But I also knew he'd keep on if I didn't give him some sort of response. "Your brother is the biggest jackass in the world, Cooper. Just because things were good for him, does not mean they were for me. My heart was never in it. I tried because I was using it as a test to see if I could feel something for someone like I did Dane. Anytime I ever dated anyone, it was me trying to move on, but you see I never stayed with anyone past a few months. Well, except your brother, but that was because I didn't want to hurt you by hurting his ego."

I held my hand across the table toward Alice. "Please give me my phone."

She handed it to me reluctantly.

"Can we just enjoy our time together? Your flight leaves in two hours. I want to still like the both of you when you leave."

They both sighed and laughed a little. I smiled when they nodded.

"And you need to be nice to Dane and get some lessons on interacting with kids." I raised both brows at them.

"We will. It's just different here. The people are different." Cooper put his arm around the back of Alice's chair as he looked at me.

I laughed. "Damn, you're such a rich turd." I rolled my eyes and threw a pickle off my burger at him.

He dodged it and laughed. "I honestly don't try to be."

I nodded. "I know." I smiled at them both. "Thank you for coming to see me. It was a great surprise."

"Of course. You're our girl. Now, tell us all about Dane. Leave nothing out." Alice was grinning and leaning forward on her elbows.

Chapter Twenty-four

DANE

I stood on the ladder and worked on the roof of Sadie's small house. I had some members of my team working with me, so hopefully we'd finish this thing within a week. After meeting Sadie's friends, I had this fear that she was going to decide to up and leave if she didn't have a nice place to stay. A place of her own. I finished up the section I was working on and came down the ladder when I heard Tate and Millie calling my name. I smiled at them as I walked over and sat on the steps in front of them.

"I'm ready for a lunch break. What do you guys want? I thought we could go out to eat then do whatever you two want to do." Tate started school in a week, and Millie and I both weren't ready for that. "We also need to go shopping for a desk for Millie to do her work on in my new office at work." Now that I was taking on more office work and management things, I would be helping her with her school work instead of Hales. With another new baby, she didn't need the added stress.

Tate looked at Millie and waited for her to say something. But she looked at him like she was waiting for him to say something.

Tate smiled and turned to me. "Can we go meet Millie's parents? I've heard all about them, but we should bring them flowers."

Tate was such a strong little man. He lost the only parents he ever knew, yet he was taking care of Millie and helping her cope with the loss of her parents that happened years ago.

"That sounds like a great idea." I grinned at him proudly.

Millie's smile instantly brightened.

"Can Sadie come?" he asked while picking at his shirt.

"Do you want her to come?"

He looked at me. "Do you?"

I smiled. "I'd like her to, but this day is about you and Millie."

"Let's call her and tell her to stop hanging out with those weird people."

I burst out laughing. "Sounds like a plan." I smiled. "You two go get ready and I'll call her."

They both headed toward the house in a rush while I dialed Sadie's number and slowly walked toward the house.

"Oh no! Calm down! Are you serious? I'm on my way!" she shouted. "Play along," she whispered. "Fevers suck. Tell him I will pick up something on the way home." I heard her telling Cooper and Alice bye.

"Umm, okay," I said with a chuckle.

"You called at the perfect time! Have I mentioned I love you? Thank you! Oh my gosh, those two were annoying the hell out of me. I love them to death, but damn." She huffed. "Sorry. You were really calling me. Is everything okay?"

I laughed. "Our son and niece wanted to invite you to take flowers to my brother and sister-in-law and in our son's words 'to get you away from those weird people.'"

She burst out laughing.

"I'd love to. And one day, I hope you guys all get along. They really are good people. On my nerves, but good people."

I heard her engine crank. "Want me to meet you at your house?"

"Yeah. We'll be waiting, Daisy love."

"I'll be there shortly. And did the kids really want to invite me or are you just trying to make me feel special?"

"They really wanted to invite you."

"That means a lot." I could tell by the way she was talking she was smiling huge.

"I love you. We'll see you in a bit."

I hung up the phone and went to change. After getting ready I sat on the couch waiting for Sadie to get there. I ran my hand over my jaw, noticing the stubble that was almost covering my scar. I really was ready to have the beard completely back. I took off my ball cap and put it on Tate's head when he sat next to me.

He froze when he reached out and touched the scar.

"Once the beard comes in all the way you won't be able to see it," I said self-consciously.

"What happened?"

Millie came over and sat on the other side of me.

"I joined the Marines shortly after I graduated high school. I had to go to war and…I ended up getting shot a few times," I answered as honestly I could without going into the gory details of what actually happened.

He scrunched his nose and his eyes as he stared at me. "Did it hurt?"

"Yes. A lot, actually. The ones of my chest still hurt from time to time."

"He rubs his chest when it's about to rain or get cold. The doctor couldn't get the bullet out that lodged in his breastplate," Millie added with a frown.

I snapped my head in her direction. "How do you know that?"

"I heard Aunt Hales and Uncle Zach talking about it when they came back from seeing you when you finally got shipped stateside."

"You've never talked to me about it."

"I don't like to. I almost lost you." She shivered a little.

I wrapped an arm around her and gave her a squeeze.

"It won't hurt anything still being in there, will it?" he asked.

I shook my head. "No, it won't hurt anything. It's just a part of me now." I smiled at him. "I'm fine, Tate. I promise."

"Uncle Dane needs someone to watch out for him." Millie grinned at Tate.

I burst out laughing. "I do not."

Millie rolled her eyes making me laugh harder. "Yes, you do."

"I'll watch out for you." He smiled.

I grinned. "Well, then between you and Millie, I'll be well looked after."

Millie giggled.

There was a knock at the door and I smiled at Tate. "You want to get it?"

He nodded excitedly and opened the door. Sadie smiled when he hugged her.

"Hey, Tater-bug!" She hugged him back and kissed the top of his head.

I stood up and came over to them with Millie.

"They want to get some flowers and go see Elliot and Sam." I kissed her forehead.

She walked all the way inside and Tate shut the door.

"That's a great idea!"

"Let's go eat, get some flowers, then take them to Sam and Elliot." I smiled at Sadie. "We also need to go get a desk for Millie." I looked down at my phone as it dinged.

> Trevor: How much do you love me?
>
> Me: What did you do?
>
> Trevor: We only had one applicant.
>
> Me: Who is it?
>
> Trevor: Dana

I frowned and glared at the phone.

> Me: Fuck that. No.
>
> Trevor: Well...You see what had happened was...
>
> Me: Trevor don't fuck with me.
>
> Trevor: She's pregnant, and Hailey came by and they got to talking...I was outnumbered.
>
> Me: You hired her?!
>
> Trevor: I'm sorry.
>
> Me: Fuck. Trev...

No response. I didn't realize I made a noise out loud until everyone looked at me oddly. I stuck my phone in my pocket. "Let's get something to eat, I'm starving," I said as I tried to get Sadie focused on something other than me. She knew something was wrong. I could tell by the way she raised her eyebrow at me.

"Who just texted you and made you make that murder face?" She was frowning big time.

I opened the door for Sadie and Millie. Once the kids were in, I smiled a little at Sadie. "Trevor did interviews for a secretary today. The only one who showed up I don't really like." I made another face. "I'll tell you more about her later."

I knew Sadie wanted all the details right then, but she didn't argue. She got into the truck and shut the door.

"What do you guys want to eat?" I asked after cranking the engine.

Sadie was pouting majorly. She shrugged and turned in her seat to look at the kids in the back. "What do you guys want?"

"Can we have Taco Bell?" Millie asked with a smile.

Tate grinned. "Can we? That sounds good!"

I nudged Sadie's arm with my elbow. "You okay with Taco Bell?" I grinned at her. She was so damn cute when she pouted. Once she nodded and turned to face the front, I started driving toward town. "Your little house should be finished by Friday," I said as I grabbed her hand in mine.

She smiled. "Awesome." She was being short which was never a good sign.

"I'll explain everything tonight. After the kids go to bed," I whispered. Millie and Tate were laughing about something in the back seat so I wasn't worried about them hearing.

"Sounds good." She gave my hand a squeeze. "And I need to talk to you about a few things, too."

This was going to be an interesting night. *Were we ready for all of this?* I sure hoped so because since Trevor hired Dana, she was going to need to be prepared.

Chapter Twenty-Five

SADIE

I woke up to Dane running his fingers through my hair. I looked beside me and realized I had fallen asleep in bed with Tate. Before falling asleep, I was reading my journal to him and answering any questions he had.

I smiled. "Sorry," I whispered as I sat up and set the journal on Tate's nightstand. I made sure Tate was covered and followed Dane out of the room.

"Why are you sorry, Daisy?" he asked as we sat down on the couch.

He yawned and wrapped an arm around me and my back was to him.

"I didn't mean to fall asleep. Thanks for waking me up."

He kissed the top of my head. "You want to stay here tonight? You can have my bed."

I smiled at him and nodded. "But I want you to sleep with me."

He played gently with my hair. "I'd like that."

I shifted a little until I was comfortable. "You go first with what you want to tell me."

"After I got back on my feet after I was injured, I dated this girl for a bit. She was the first person I dated after you." He started playing with my fingers. "It started out okay, or at least I thought it did, but I guess I wasn't really in a good place. I just survived something I shouldn't have and was a bit messed up. Anyway, that's beside the point." He stopped as he thought. "I just wasn't in the relationship as much as she was. I never could get over you. It pissed me off because I just wanted to be able to move on." I hated the hurt in his voice. He tried to hide it, but I still heard it. "I broke up with her after we almost had sex and I couldn't go through with it."

"And now she's working for your company? What the hell is Trevor's deal? He has to know this isn't okay."

He made a face. "Yeah, well you know Trev. He's too nice and easily persuaded. Hailey is friends with her and ended up helping convince him to give it to her."

I closed my eyes and groaned. "Fucking grrreeeat. Now her and Hailey will double team me. Does she still want to be with you?"

I was a jealous girlfriend. Always had been and it would never change. What was mine was mine.

"I don't know, and I don't care." He kissed my nose. "No worries."

I scrunched my nose.

"At least Millie's supposed to start going to work with me on Monday. That will help." He rubbed his beard, and I noticed the hair was almost covering his scar again.

I looked at our hands that held each other's tightly and at my legs that were draped over his. I loved this. When I caught him staring at me, I smiled. "Can we just forget about what I needed to talk about and just make out or something?"

He chuckled before kissing my lips softly. "No, I told you mine, so, it's your turn."

"Oooh, is this a game like I show you mine and you show me yours?"

"Something like that. Just not as fun."

I started slowly lifting my shirt so my belly button was showing. "You sure?" *Mission: Distract Dane.*

He stopped me from exposing more skin. "Sadie."

"It's not important."

"If it wasn't important, you wouldn't be trying to distract me." He leaned in and kissed me. "Would ya?"

I didn't really see any point in telling him about Ethan anymore. It honestly didn't matter. Earlier, I thought I should with the whole mention of Dana, but now I wasn't so sure. Ethan was a huge part of my life in New York, but we'd never be anything more than friends, so Dane had nothing to worry about. But, a little part of me knew I'd need to say something because knowing Ethan, he wasn't going to go down without a fight. Especially, when he caught wind of why I was really moving back here. I told Cooper and Alice not to say anything, but I also knew Cooper sucked at secrets when it came to his twin brother.

Dane tilted my chin up to look at him. "If you're not ready to tell me you don't have to. It can wait. No matter what, I'm not going anywhere."

"It's not that I'm not ready, it's a matter of does it really matter? I know you, and I just don't want you getting pissed off when there is no need. Yet, anyway."

He kissed me again. "Then don't tell me right now. I don't want to get pissed off tonight." He smiled against my lips.

I moved until I was in his lap and my legs were wrapped around his waist. I ran my fingers through his hair, messing it up a little, and smiled. "Have I said thank you lately?" I kissed him.

"You don't have to thank me, Daisy," he said as he kissed the side of my neck.

I nodded. "Yes, I do."

"And why is that?" he asked as he leaned back from me.

"For a second chance. Well, third chance. Er, I mean, fourth? What number is this?" I laughed.

"This would be number four and the last." He put his head against my shoulder. "I won't survive losing you again, Daisy."

"You won't."

He picked his head up and gazed back at me. He gently ran his fingers down my face. "I love you."

"Love you, too." I rubbed my nose against his.

He kissed me and wrapped his hand in my hair. "We should probably get to bed."

I moved off his lap and stood. I followed him to his room and stopped in the doorway when I heard Tate crying. I rushed toward his room and just as I made it in, he threw the framed picture of his adoptive parents at the wall. Before he could throw my journal, I wrapped my arms around him from behind and sat with him on the floor. He cried against my shoulder.

"They never told me! Why didn't they tell me about you and Dane?" he sobbed loudly.

I rubbed his back. "Because I told them not to. It's my fault, not theirs."

Dane and Millie both came into the room. They walked over to us and sat down, wrapping us in a hug. Millie whispered something into his ear we couldn't hear and kissed his cheek.

"Why don't we all go crawl into my huge bed? What do you think?" Dane said quietly to Tate. "We can all talk and get comfortable." He wiped Tate's tears gently. "We can talk about whatever you want."

Tate's body shook as he cried. He had calmed down some, but was still upset. He nodded and wiped his eyes. "Sorry. I had a nightmare and woke up. I'm just... I'm angry. I miss them, but I'm also so mad they never told me they weren't my real parents. I'm mad I found out like this."

I looked at Dane, unsure of how to respond. This was my fault. I wanted to fix it, but only time could do that. I focused back on Tate. I kissed his forehead and wiped away the tears he missed.

"Don't be angry with your adoptive parents. It's okay to be angry with me. Don't apologize, okay? Never feel like you have to keep all of your feelings in. You can talk to us, yell at me, or whatever you need to do to work through it."

Tate nodded.

Dane stood and picked him up, all of Tate's twelve-year-old self, and it didn't look like Dane had any trouble with it. Millie grabbed my hand.

"Tate, it's okay to be sad and angry," Millie said softly. "You have us to help you through it all. I promise."

We went into Dane's room, and I stopped when Tate picked his head up from Dane's shoulder and looked at me. His eyes went from hurt to anger and it was directed at me.

"I want you to leave," he said quietly, avoiding eye contact with me.

I felt like someone drop kicked me. I thought we had made so much progress and were past this. I reached up and touched his cheek and put on a brave face. I nodded, hugged Millie then Dane, and left before I lost it.

Chapter Twenty-six

DANE

After a night with little to no sleep, I was exhausted. Tate had stayed up talking to me for a while before drifting off to sleep. Once he was asleep, I had called Sadie to check on her. By the time I hung up with her, I was able to get a thirty-minute nap in before it was time to work out and get ready for work. I needed to go into work and find out if Trevor was a bigger idiot than I thought. I went to the front door and opened it when I heard a knock.

"Thanks for coming, Zach. I was going to call Sadie, but she didn't get a lot of sleep last night, and I'm not for sure Tate would want to stay with her."

"Bad night? Hailey told me Dana got hired. What the hell?"

I nodded. "Yeah. Her and Trevor are on my shit list. Anyway, I'll be at the office all day. As soon as the kids are awake, if they want to come up there they can. My workers shouldn't start on Sadie's place until nine."

"How are you handling everything, little bro?" he asked as he put a hand on my shoulder.

"Same way I always do. One day at a time. I know it will take time for Tate to work through his anger. I mean, Millie is still working through some of hers.

I just hope Sadie will continue to be patient and not push him too much. If she does, she may ruin any chance she has with him."

"And what about you? Will you choose Tate over Sadie if it comes down to it?"

I looked at him in shock. "What? Of course I will, Zach. He's my son. But it will all work out. I'm sure of it."

Zach smiled and gave me a small hug. "I was just checking. I'm proud of you. And Elliot would have been proud of you, too."

"Thanks. But this is all so hard."

"I know. Instead of Sadie moving out here to the small house, she could move into Elliot and Sam's place. That way she keeps a larger distance while Tate copes with everything."

I shook my head. "Quinn and Brink called and said that they're going to move in there until they decide to build their own place. They're trying to buy the land next to you guys, but you know how that goes."

Zach nodded. "Yeah. I was lucky to have this place because of my family."

"And I was lucky you sold me some of your land." I smiled at him. "I need to head to work. They're both asleep in my bed. That's where we all crashed after Tate's breakdown."

He nodded and headed to the couch. I checked on the kids one more time before heading to work.

WHEN I PULLED into the parking lot, I saw Trevor's car and Dana's SUV. I walked in and came to a complete stop when I saw her. Her dark hair had gotten longer. I looked at the dress she was wearing and the heels.

"You're way too overdressed for this job. Just come comfortable," I said with zero emotion. Anger was boiling inside.

Trevor was standing there next to her with a sheepish grin. "Dana lost her previous job due to the company filing for bankruptcy. She was without a job and she's pregnant."

Dana smiled. "I know it's weird, but I promise not to make things awkward. Strictly business. I swear."

I nodded and went down the hall. I unlocked my office door and went inside. I was furious. I rubbed my temples after sitting down. I couldn't believe this shit. I had enough to worry about.

Trevor came in and shut the door. "Sorry. I couldn't say no. She needs this job, Dane. And Hailey—"

I glared at him, making him shut up. "Just stop, Trev."

"Do you want me to go fire her?"

"You can't. We can't fire her without just cause or she could sue us. And with her being pregnant, she'd probably win."

He frowned and nodded. "Didn't think about that. Sorry."

I shrugged. "It is what it is, and I know she'll be good at her job. I just hope Sadie understands." I looked at him. "I should get to work, and I'm sure you have a shit load of stuff to do as well. You want to order in lunch today?"

"Yeah, sure. Just let me know what you want and I'll bring it to you. And is everything okay? I texted Sadie and she never replied. You two didn't have a fight, did you?"

"No, Tate had a bad night. He had a nightmare about his adoptive parents and got angry all over again. He wanted her to go home after that."

He shook his head. "Damn. Is she okay?"

"We talked a lot last night before she fell asleep, but she's heartbroken. I told her to give him time. She said she would. She's supposed to come over for dinner tonight." I yawned. "I didn't sleep at all last night."

Trevor stood and stretched. "Maybe you'll get some tonight." He chuckled. "I mean sleep."

I laughed. "Maybe."

"Maybe to which one?" He laughed some more.

I grinned mischievously. "Shouldn't you be getting back to work?"

"This is serious. How long has it been since you got some, man?"

I rolled my eyes and blushed some. "Does it matter?"

He shrugged, smiled, and left the office.

I shook my head as I chuckled a little and then got to work.

I RUBBED MY eyes as I finished up my last report. I glanced at the time and groaned. It was seven. Where the hell did the time go? I picked up my phone and called Hales.

"Hello?" I could hear the kids arguing in the background.

"Sorry it's so late. I got busy at work. Who's arguing? And can you ask my kiddos what they want for dinner?"

"The twins are fighting like usual. And I already fed all the kids."

"I owe you big time. I didn't realize how much I was behind from taking off. I will be there soon to get them. I'm so sorry, Hales."

"It's fine. It's what I'm here for. Why don't you let them stay and finish their movie? Go take Sadie out for dinner alone."

I looked at the phone oddly before putting it back to my ear. "Did you just tell me to go on a date with your mortal enemy?"

"It was Zach's idea. Not mine. Don't get too excited."

"All right. I will be by later. Oh, and what the hell were you thinking talking Trev into hiring Dana?"

She laughed. "She's going to be great, and why don't you just act like an adult and not be dramatic about it?"

"It's awkward."

"Only if you make it awkward. She's amazing and needed a job."

"I'm going to give it a chance."

"Thank you. Now go on your date before I change my mind." She laughed.

I smiled and hung up. I dialed Sadie's number.

"Hey, Daisy-Love."

"Hey, how is Tate today?" I hated how depressed she sounded.

"I don't know. I haven't gotten to see him. He's at Hales and Zach's. I lost track of time at work. I wanted to know if you wanted to go out to eat with me?"

She was quiet for a second. "Sure. We need to talk. Was Dana there?"

"Sadly, yes." I suddenly got knots in my stomach. "What's wrong, Sadie?" I stood up and grabbed my keys. I walked out of my office and locked the door. I turned and dropped my phone as Dana scared the shit out of me. "Why aren't you gone?" I snapped as I grabbed my phone off the floor. I cursed when I saw it was broken. I glared at her. I went to move past her when she grabbed my arm with her hand.

"Talk to me. We haven't seen each other in a while. And I was working late to organize everything. It's all a mess." She let go of my arm.

"I'm dating someone, Dana."

"I know, Dane. I'm here to work and nothing more. I swear."

I nodded and some of the tension left. "Lock up when you leave."

I walked out the front door and to the parking lot. I got in the truck and headed straight for the dance studio. As I pulled in, the Rover was starting to pull out. I watched as she stopped and parked again. I parked the truck and got out.

"Sorry. I dropped my damn phone and it broke," I said as she got out.

She couldn't make eye contact with me. She nodded.

I grabbed her chin and gently tilted her head up so I could see her eyes. "What's going on, Sadie?"

She took a step back. "Why didn't you text me or call me at all today? I was worried. I called and texted you."

"Because I got to work and locked myself in my office. I just stopped working. What's going on, Sadie? Are you seriously mad at me right now?"

She shook her head. "I'm irritated that I didn't hear from you all day knowing that your ex was there. I know you wouldn't do anything wrong, but still. You know how I am. But, that's not my problem tonight."

"Then what's the problem? Talk to me, Daisy."

"Maybe we shouldn't... Maybe we..." She was struggling to talk. She took a deep breath and let it out. "Maybe we shouldn't work on us right now."

I felt like the air had been knocked out of me. "Wh-what?"

She took another step back and wiped her eyes. "Tate doesn't want me around, Dane. And we have to do what's best for him."

"It will just take him time. He's going to have good days and bad. When I got back from the Marines, Millie wanted me some days and some days was angry with me because I left. It will just take time. Please, don't do this to me again. Don't leave me, Daisy."

She looked so torn. She took her phone out of her pocket and scrolled through what seemed to be text messages. She handed me the phone. It was a text from Hailey.

> Hailey: I talked to Tate. I didn't ask questions, he opened up to me. He told me he doesn't want to hate you but he does. He said he's trying. I asked how he felt about you and Dane getting back together and he said he didn't like it. Dane told Zach earlier that if it came down to it, he'd choose Tate over you. I thought you should know because I know how much you like honesty.

I handed her back her phone. I was going to kill Hales. "He just needs time, Sadie."

She held her phone and her hand shook a little. "Dane, I'm not angry for a second that you'd choose Tate over me. I expect that. But, he said he hates me. He said he doesn't want us together. And you have to choose him over me right now." Her voice shook and I knew she was trying to stay strong for me. She was doing her best not to crumble onto the pavement.

"What are you saying?" Tears filled my eyes.

She shook her head and looked down at the ground.

I nodded stiffly. "I guess I should go then."

"I'll stay at the studio. Stop building my place," she whispered. "Dane, this is killing me," she cried just as I walked away.

I couldn't answer her or look at her. I got in the truck and drove toward Zach and Hales. When I got there, I got out and went inside. I kissed both of the kids' heads before heading to Zach's workout room. He was wiping his forehead on a towel.

"Oh shit," he said when he saw the look on my face. He walked over to me. "Where is Sadie? Aren't you two supposed to be at dinner?"

I started wrapping my hands without talking to him. I was afraid that if I tried to speak, I would break down. He left the room and shut the door behind him. I started punching the bag as I played everything that happened that night in my mind.

Chapter Twenty-seven

SADIE

I stood in the parking lot of the studio, completely frozen. I couldn't move or feel. I was numb. Everything I wanted more than anything in this world, I couldn't have.

This was karma.

I deserved this.

I was a stupid girl for thinking this could all actually work out.

I couldn't make Tate accept me. I could just stay hopeful that he would one day. But what about Dane and me? Stars were finally aligning for us. I stared up at the sky and cursed the universe. This was payback for giving Tate away and breaking Dane's heart over and over again.

I turned toward the parking lot entrance as Trevor's GTO pulled in. When he got out, I noticed his usual attire of a suit was replaced with work clothes and he was filthy.

"What are you doing standing outside?" he asked as he walked over.

I shrugged. If I said what was going out loud it was like I was breathing life into what happened. Maybe if I stayed quiet, it would all go away.

He came closer. He took one look at my face, and I knew he knew. He grabbed my hand in his. "You want to go for a ride with me?"

I nodded.

He led me to his car and, after we both got in, he started driving toward the lake.

I put my hand on the door handle. "Trevor, turn around. If you're taking me to talk to him, don't."

"Will you trust me? I promise we're going somewhere quiet."

I sat back in the seat, but remained tense. "Maybe I should just go back to New York," I whispered.

"Is that what you really want to do?" He turned down a gravel road just before you get to Dane's driveway.

"No. It's not what I want. I want things to be okay, but as soon as I think they are, I find out my son still hates me." I wiped my eyes. I didn't want to let myself start crying more because I knew I was seconds away from a complete mental breakdown. "I'm going to fall apart. I can fuckin' feel it. "

"Sadie, Tate is twelve and has lost the only parents he knew. While dealing with the death of those he loved, he found out he was adopted. For a kid, he has held it together better than most adults would. He must get that from Dane," he said with a small smile.

"I know that, Trev." I pulled out my phone and read the text from Hailey to him. "Dane said himself he'd choose Tate over me. And right now, that's what he has to do."

"Hales is trying to protect her family. You can't take what she said and run with it. If Tate said all that, he could change his mind tomorrow. Again, he's twelve."

I nodded. "I know. But it hurts." I wiped my eyes. "I don't know what to do and walking away from the relationship felt like my only option right now. Dane needs to focus on our son."

"That has always been the problem. And yes, I know this time is different because Tate is involved. But with Dane's lack of sleep and all the stress, I don't think he will see it that way. He will see it as you're using Tate as an excuse to push him away again." He pulled into a grassy area with a small open shed. I saw an old car parked inside.

"I bought Jason a 1966 Mustang. Of course, it's a work in progress and a surprise."

"Why are you showing it to me?"

He grinned. "Showing? You're going to help me." He shut the car off and got out. I watched as he started up a generator and turned on some lights.

"Like old times," I said with a little smile after I got out.

My dad always kept old cars and Trev and I would help him fix them up. It was our thing when I wasn't busy dancing or performing with the glee club at school.

"That's what I thought. You could use something to get your mind off all the shit that's going on, and I could use help."

"Yeah, my head's all over the place right now. I haven't talked to my parents at all. Mom tried to text me, but I'm not ready to talk to her. Dad tried to call, but I know he's just going to talk to me about making up with Mom." I watched him pop the hood.

"I know this is hard, but giving up and running back to New York won't help anything. It's time to be the strong amazing woman I know and weather the storm."

"Okay, Hallmark card." I wiped my eyes and then pulled my hair into a ponytail. "I won't go back. I was being dramatic. But I don't know how to be strong and not pushy at the same time."

He chuckled a little. "Sadie, Tate sees you as the girl who gave him up and ran away. Show him the woman who wants him and will fight to win his trust and love. That's all he wants." He nudged me. "And you'll figure it out."

"I don't know…" I picked up a wrench. "Oh yeah, by the way, I should hit you with this for hiring Dana."

"Yeah. Sorry about that. But we need a secretary badly. And she was the only applicant."

I mumbled a few choice words under my breath. I wanted to say more about my jealousy issues, but that wasn't what mattered at the moment. "Should I go talk to him or wait?"

"Depends. What were the last things you said to each other and how did he react?" He leaned over the engine and started working on the engine.

I grabbed a flashlight and shined it where he was working.

"I told him not to finish the house and that it was killing me to put us on hold."

He groaned. "Wait until morning. Right now, he's probably punching the shit out of Zach's punching bag. Maybe he'll wear himself out and get some sleep." I handed Trevor a wrench. "I know he didn't sleep last night and hasn't been sleeping any lately. Let him get some rest so he can think straight."

I nodded. "Good idea. But, Trev...I don't know if being with him right now is the best thing, ya know? I don't want to ruin my relationship with Tate worse. But I also know I can't let a kid run the show. I just don't know how to balance all of this."

"You'll just have to figure it out as you go. I know it will be hard, but I have faith you'll get there. Just don't push Dane away. If you do, you won't like what happens. I can promise you that."

I thought about what he said, and he was right. All of this would be hard and there wasn't handbook for this. We'd figure it out as we go, and I damn sure didn't want to push Dane away. I sighed heavily and started helping Trevor.

"What am I supposed to do about Hailey? The only reason she felt the need to send me that text was to try to keep me away. I know she cares and is trying to protect Dane from getting hurt, but why can't she see that I'm trying?"

"After she sees him tonight, maybe she'll back off. If not, she's going to push him away."

I didn't say anything else. The last thing I wanted was for him and Hailey to have issues because of me. But, I wasn't going anywhere, so, she needed to get over it.

Chapter Twenty-eight

DANE

I wiped my face on the towel Hales brought to me after I finished boxing. "I need to get the kids home. Tate has his first day of school tomorrow." I started unwrapping my hands. They were numb from punching the bag so hard. I was so angry that I didn't take the time to put on gloves. I wasn't angry anymore. I was just... I guess the word is defeated. I couldn't even make myself stand up straight.

"I'm assuming my text caused issues." She sat down on the weight bench.

I cut my eyes at her. "You know it did. You did that on purpose just like you got Dana that job." I threw the bloodied wraps away. "I need to get my kids home." I started to walk past her, but she stood and grabbed my arm. I froze. I hung my head. "Hales, I just want to go home. I'm tired."

"I just want to protect you from her."

"I don't need protecting. I need my best friend to be supportive and that seems to be a stretch for you right now."

She didn't respond. Instead she looked hurt and walked out of the room. When I came out, she was telling Tate and Millie to get on their shoes.

I smiled a little at them. "Come on, kiddos. You both start school tomorrow."

Hailey hugged them both and left the living room.

I looked at Zach as he walked in and at Joshua who asleep on his shoulder.

"I'll see ya sometime tomorrow."

He nodded and gave the kids a sideways hug. He came over to me. "Hailey will come around, Dane. Just be patient with her. She's hormonal and in Momma Bear mode. Get some sleep tonight."

I nodded and went to the car with the kids. Once they were buckled in, I started home.

"Did you two have a good day?" I asked quietly.

Tate was studying me through the rearview mirror. "What's wrong?"

"I'm tired. I didn't get any sleep last night." I gave him a small smile.

"Are you mad at me?" he asked quietly.

I glanced Millie in the backseat and noticed she was already asleep.

I shook my head. "I could never be mad at you, Tate." I pulled down our driveway. "I don't want you to ever worry about telling me something. If you're not happy with something, I want you to tell me so we can talk about it. Okay?"

"Uncle Zach said you were angry. He wouldn't let me go in the workout room with you."

"I was angry about some things, but I wasn't angry with you." I parked in front of the house. I took my seat belt off, then patted the spot next to me. I smiled when he climbed over the seat and sat next to me. I wrapped an arm around his shoulders. "Tate, I want you to tell me what you want."

"What do you mean?" His eyebrows drew together as he took in what I said.

"Do you not like Sadie and me being together?" May as well come out and ask.

"I don't know."

"Tate, I won't be mad. I just want you to be honest with me and tell me how you're feeling. I can't help you or help you figure things out without knowing."

"Aunt Hales asked me about this, too. I don't know, Dane. I wish my parents wouldn't have died. I wish I would have known about you and Sadie sooner. But every time I get angry, I blame her. Some days I like her, and some days I don't because I remember she gave me away. I know she was young, but I'm young and if I had a kid, I'd never give them away."

"True, but if you had a kid, I would help you with that kid. Sadie had her parents pushing her in the wrong direction." I brushed some hair out of his face. "I know you don't know what you want, and I know how it feels to be angry. Just know that I love you, and I want you to always feel like you can talk to me. I don't want you bottling things up. Even if you think it'll make me angry, I still want you to talk to me about it." I ran a hand through my hair. "And I promise to talk to you about things. Deal?"

He nodded and thought for a moment. "Do you want to be with Sadie? Like, marry her?"

"Maybe one day. Right now, she has a lot of trust to gain back from me. I have to see that she's not going to run. I love her, Tate, but I love you, too."

"I need to tell her sorry." He looked down at his hands.

"Are you saying sorry because your feelings have changed or because you really feel sorry?"

"I feel bad."

I kissed his head. "You're an amazing kid, Tate. I know I have a long way to go to prove to you I'm going to be a good dad, but I'm proud you're my kid. And it's okay to love two dads and two moms. Loving Sadie and me won't ever change how you feel about your mom and dad."

"I miss them.' He turned and looked in the back seat at Millie. "You should get her inside. One time I fell asleep in the car and got a sore neck." He smiled at me a little. "Will you call Sadie and ask her to come over before I go to bed?"

"I will. And I swear Millie can sleep anywhere and not ever be sore." I kissed his head again. "Go get a shower and get in your pj's while I get Millie to bed and call Sadie."

He hugged me and got out of the truck.

I got out and got Millie out of the backseat. It took me a little bit to get Millie comfortable in bed. Once she was settled, I went to text Sadie but realized my phone was broken. I sighed before getting my iPad and texting her on it.

> Me: Tate wants you to come talk to him.
>
> Sadie: I'm covered in grease, but I can be there in a few minutes. He really wants me there or are you just saying that?
>
> Me: He wants you to come.
>
> Sadie: I'm at the shop by your house with Trev. I'll have him bring me over.
>
> Me: Okay

I put the iPad down and laid my head back. I rubbed my eyes and closed them. I just needed to close them for a second.

I JERKED AWAKE when someone touched my bruised knuckles. I blinked a few times and focused on Sadie. She smiled, her cheeks had grease smears. She sat next to me and kissed me.

"I'm sorry about earlier."

"We can talk about that after Tate goes to bed. He wants to talk to you."

She nodded, stood, and went toward his room.

I debated on if I should go with her. I trusted her with him alone, but I also knew his mind was in a bad place right now. Deciding it'd be best to be there just in case, I stood, stretched, and then went to his room.

When I stepped into the room, I was shocked. Sadie was crying and Tate was rubbing her back as he held her in a tight hug. She just kept apologizing over and over to him. I kept my focus on him, waiting to see if I needed to come in and help. I smiled a little at him. He smiled back as he started playing with her hair. He was listening to her apologies and gave me a thumbs up. I chuckled a little and left the room. That kid was more like me than was probably healthy.

I went downstairs and sat on the couch. I yawned and laid down with my arm behind my head. I laid there for a while before I heard footsteps coming down the stairs. I looked up at Sadie as she walked over to me. She sat down on the couch next to me.

"How did it go?" I sat up.

Sadie took one of my hands in hers and frowned at the bruises forming. "I just cried like a big ol' baby. I said I was sorry. A lot. I told him something that I don't know if he liked or not, but I had to tell him." She brought my knuckles to her lips and kissed them gently before putting our hands on her leg.

"What did you tell him?"

"That I'm in love with you and that no matter how mad he got at me, I was his mom and wouldn't stop trying to make things right with him. I told him the only way I'd stop is if I was dead."

I smiled at her and kissed her. "Thank you."

Her eyes went to my knuckles again. "What'd you do?"

"I beat the shit out of Zach's punching bag." I kissed her, again. "I'm going to run up and tell Tate goodnight."

"Do you mind if I take a shower and borrow some clothes? I'm gross. Trevor put me to work on that old Mustang."

I nodded and stood. "Go ahead. You know where everything is." I hurried up the stairs and went quietly into Tate's room.

I walked over to the bed and sat down. "Hey. I wanted to say goodnight."

He yawned and smiled sleepily. "'Night."

I kissed his head. "Get some sleep. You start school tomorrow."

His smile faded. "I hope they like me. I miss my old friends."

"They'll love you. And why don't we plan on the next long weekend we invite some of your friends here?"

He nodded. "That'd be cool." He glanced toward the door and then at me. "Will you let Sadie stay the night tonight? I don't want her going to her house and crying alone."

"Are you sure you'll be okay with me letting her stay? I know she'd like to help me take you to school."

He nodded.

I kissed his head. "Get some sleep, and tomorrow we'll make plans to let some friends of yours visit." I stood and headed back to the living room.

I went past the living room when I saw Sadie wasn't there. I went into my room and started undressing down into my boxers. I pulled back the covers and smiled when Sadie came out of the bathroom.

"Guess what?" I said with a smile.

She froze just as she was drying her hair with the towel. Her eyes were roaming every inch of my bare skin.

"What? You've seen me with less on." I grinned and wiggled my eyebrows.

Her eyes met mine, but I could tell she was struggling not to stare some more. "It's been awhile," she said with a bit of a struggle.

"Yeah. Eight years, two months, five days and…" I looked at the clock. "Thirty-two minutes." I moved my eyes back to her. "Tate asked me to let you spend the night. He didn't want you going home and crying alone." The sight of her in my clothes sent a wave of possessiveness through me. "Damn, you're gorgeous. I never understood why a girl as amazing as you would be interested in me."

She blushed a little. "I've always wondered why a guy like you would be interested in me." She laughed. "Dane, I would love to spend the night, but one of us will have to take the couch. If I get in that bed, those boxers will not be staying on. I promise they won't."

I sighed and started pouting. I went to my dresser, pulled out a shirt, and put it on. "I'll go."

When I started to walk past her, she moved in front of me and put her hand on my chest. Her breathing had picked up a little. I knew this part of Sadie like the back of my hand. She was losing control, and when she lost control, it was a Domino effect. We'd be in that bed with nothing on in a matter of seconds.

I covered her hand with my own. I leaned down and kissed her forehead. "Go to bed, Daisy-Love. You're right. We should behave."

She closed her eyes. "Why?" she whispered.

"I think you said something about doing things right this time and it seems that us sleeping together always makes things more complicated."

She gazed up at me. "Can we pretend I didn't say something so fuckin' stupid?"

"You have no idea how much I want to, but I don't want you regretting anything."

She kept her eyes on mine. She smiled a little and then took my Marines shirt off, leaving her in only my sweats hanging loosely off her hips. As much skin that was showing on her hips, there was no way she was wearing anything under those sweats.

"Damn," I whispered before I kissed her. I knotted my hand in her hair before pushing her against the bedroom door. I used my free hand to lock it before sliding it across the bare skin of her back. She cupped the back of my neck and pulled gently until my lips were on hers.

Chapter Twenty-nine

SADIE

I stretched and turned on my side, snuggling closer to Dane. It was still dark outside, so I knew we still had a little while before we had to get up, feed the kids, and take Tate to school. I texted Jason last night and he agreed to let me have the day off so I could be there to pick him up on his first day.

I loved the way Dane's bare skin felt against mine. I kissed his chest and smiled against his skin when he moved a little. He made a face in his sleep as his pain in the ass early alarm clock started going off. I laughed when he swatted at it to stop it.

He finally opened his eyes enough to turn it off. His sleep filled eyes landed on mine. "Morning."

I kissed him. "Morning."

He pulled me close. "I need to get up."

"You already are," I giggled.

He chuckled. "Not what I meant."

I smiled and kissed him again. "I know. I need to get up, too. I'll get dressed and go start breakfast."

"You cook? That's a scary thought."

I playfully shoved his shoulder. "Shut up. I know how to make pancakes."

He laughed. "Go on, sexy, before I don't allow you to. I need to go for my run."

"You know, I have a more fun way to exercise."

He grinned. "We can't. Millie wakes up early. And I really need to run." He sat up and started looking around for his boxers. I gently touched the scars on his back. "You don't want me to get lazy and flabby."

"Dane?" I furrowed my brows. "Do you still talk to your parents?"

He tensed some. "No. Why?"

I let my hand fall back onto the bed. "I was just wondering." The scars reminded me of them and I hoped his answer would be no. I didn't want them anywhere near Tate or Millie.

He found his boxers and quickly got up and dressed in some sweats. He leaned down and kissed me. "They try every once and awhile to come around. Usually when they need money." He grabbed some socks out of his drawer and a small box came out with it. He cursed and picked it up. I knew that box. It resembled the box he had given me the night he proposed, but surely, he didn't keep that ring all these years. He shoved the box back in his drawer before shutting it. He grabbed his running shoes and left the room.

I got out of bed and got dressed in a pair of his sweats and a shirt. I stared at his sock drawer. *Don't do it, Sadie. Don't look.* Oh hell, I knew damn well I couldn't talk myself out of looking. I opened his sock drawer and got the box. I opened it and my heart skipped a beat.

There *it* was.

He kept it.

That only meant one thing. He held onto hope for us. I knew Dane. He wouldn't give a ring he had intended for me to someone else. I smiled a little, put the box back in the drawer, and then headed to the kitchen to start breakfast.

I'D ENDED UP going into work to finish up practicing the new routine I was going to teach my teen girls for the upcoming recital. There were a few parts that weren't working, and I was determined to make it perfect. I had spent most of the morning staring at the time, anticipating three-fifteen when I could pick Tate up and hear all about his day. It was only eleven-thirty. I sighed, grabbed my purse, and headed out to my Rover.

I decided to swing by Subway to pick up lunch for Dane, Millie, and me. I didn't call him because I thought it'd be fun to surprise him. When I pulled into the parking lot, I frowned when I saw a car I didn't recognize. I knew it had to be Dana's. Up until now, I had forgotten his ex was working for him. I grabbed the food, locked my vehicle, and headed inside.

When I went in, a tall thin brunette was putting something in a filing cabinet. *Be nice, Sadie. She just works here.*

My smile became strained when she turned to me.

"Hello! How may I help you?" She smiled at me.

I held up the Subway bag in my hand. "I brought lunch for Millie and Dane." My smile completely faded. The girl was gorgeous.

"Oh, you must be Sadie! Trevor told me all about you." She pointed to a door. "Millie and Dane are in there working. Just go on in."

I nodded. "Thanks." I went past her desk and into the office. I smiled when Dane looked up from his computer at me. "Hey, baby."

Millie looked up from her notebook and smiled. I smiled and set the food on Dane's desk.

"I brought lunch."

Dane smiled brightly. "You're amazing. We were just talking about what we wanted for lunch." He stood and stretched. He came over and kissed my lips softly causing Millie to giggle.

"Uncle Dane, can I stop working?" she asked as she got up. Dane walked over and inspected all she had done on her pink laptop. Millie was such a girlie-girl.

He grinned. "Yes, ma'am. I guess you're done for the day. What do you want to do now?"

She grinned at me. "Can I come to the dance studio with you and practice until you get Tate?"

"Sure you can." I helped Dane move chairs around his desk so we could all sit down. I walked over to the mini fridge and got out three waters. I came back over to the desk and sat down. "I met Dana," I said quietly as I started getting Millie's sandwich out.

I shouldn't have said that. Whether I met her or not, it didn't matter. But I had a problem. I had jealousy issues, or maybe it was that I was just super possessive over what was mine. Either way, I couldn't stop the feeling that I wanted to go in there and fire her my damn self.

"Yeah. I have to admit, she's really organized everything. Trevor has a list that she's working off of." Dane took a bite of his sandwich.

"Can you lie to me and tell me she sucks?"

Millie tilted her head in confusion. "Why do you want Uncle Dane to lie to you? He tries not to lie."

Dane smiled at me. "I won't lie to you about anything, Sadie. That will get us nowhere. She does a good job organizing things and helping us run the business more smoothly, but I'm only interested in one woman, and that's you."

I looked at Millie. "You're right, I shouldn't ask Dane to lie." I laughed. "I have a problem." Dane when he laughed at my response. "It's not funny. It's a serious problem," I said, tossing a chip at him.

Millie kept her eyes on me. "What is your problem, Sadie?" She looked sincerely concerned.

"Dane and Dana dated, right?"

She nodded.

"I just don't like that she works here with him. It's a girl thing, I guess." I laughed and shrugged at my stupidity. One day, when Millie was interested in boys, she'd understand.

I could see that Millie was confused. "You don't have to worry about her. Dane never liked her that much anyway. He told me."

I laughed when Dane smiled. "Is that right?"

Millie giggled and nodded. She started eating again.

I looked at Dane. "Do you want me to meet you here with Millie around three o'clock so we can ride together to get Tate?"

"Sounds good. I should be here. If something changes, I'll call you." He frowned. "I forgot about needing to go get a new phone."

"Just call me from the office phone. Maybe we can go by and get you a new one after we pick up Tate. If you have time."

He was about to answer when the door opened and Dana was standing there.

"Sorry to interrupt, but Dane, you have a call from Mr. Miller and he said it's urgent."

Dane groaned at the phone on his desk that had a line blinking red.

I turned to Millie. "Let's take our food with us and head to the studio so he can work."

I stood and gathered our things quietly when he answered the phone. I kissed the top of his head before Millie and I left.

Chapter Thirty

DANE

I had a major migraine by the time I finished with Mr. Miller. The man was going to drive me insane by the time we finished his house. Earlier, I called Sadie from one of the worker's phones and told her I would just meet them at the school. I pulled in and parked next to the Rover. I turned the truck off and got out rubbing my forehead.

"Hey, my girls." I smiled at them.

Sadie raised a brow at me. "Bad day?"

"Horrible. Mr. Miller is driving me insane." I kissed both of their foreheads.

"Who is that?" she asked as we walked toward the front of the school.

"He's one of my clients that we are building a house for. He's mad because I'm not working on-site anymore." I rubbed the back of my neck. "So, now I have to go check things out before he'll pay for the work we've done. It's annoying."

Sadie laced her fingers with mine. "You're the best at what you do." She smiled at me and then looked at the double doors when the bell rang. "I hope the kids were nice to him."

Millie moved closer to me as the kids started filing out. "I'm sure they were. Tate's not weird," she said quietly.

I frowned at her. "Neither are you and even if you are a little unique, there's nothing wrong with that."

Sadie bounced on her feet a little. "There he is, and he's smiling," she said with a huge grin on her face. She let go of my hand and made her way through the crowd of kids before I could remind her Tate was in middle school and your mom coming to hug you in front of everyone was not cool. But there she was, hugging him and fixing his hair in front of a few boys that were walking with him.

Millie and I hung back and I smiled at Tate and shook my head. I mouthed *sorry,* making him grin a little. When they came over to us, one boy was still with him. This one was a mess, I could tell by the grin on his face.

"How was your first day, kiddo?" I smiled at my son before looking at the other boy. "And who is this?"

Millie was practically behind me at this point. The boy had smiled at her and asked her who she was, but she just hid herself more. I really needed to start working on her socialization skills. I stepped to the side and pushed her a little forward so she was more in front of me than behind. "This is Tate's cousin, Millie."

The dark-haired boy with bright blue eyes smiled. "I'm Chase Andrews." He smiled at me. "I know who you are, Mr. Shaw. My dad played baseball with you and he always said you should've gone pro."

I tilted my head to the side as I studied the boy. *Andrews.* "Is your dad Peter Andrews? He was a senior when I was in ninth grade."

He shook his head. "No, sir. My uncle is Peter. My dad is his twin brother, Jacob."

"Ah. Well, it's nice to meet you, Chase." I looked back at Tate. "How was your first day of school?"

Sadie was still smiling, she hadn't stopped since seeing him walk out the school doors.

"Good. Can Chase come over?"

"Not tonight. It's a school night, but maybe we can have him over this weekend."

Sadie scrunched her nose. "That's okay, right? He could just stay for a little bit."

I raised my eyebrow at her. "Not tonight. It's two more days until the weekend since school started on a Wednesday. That's soon enough." *Is she really contradicting me in front of the kids?* One, I'm sure he had homework; two, I needed to get Millie prepared for visitors; and three, Tate had baseball tryouts. "Plus, if you remember, Tate has baseball tryouts tonight."

Chase and Tate both avoided eye contact and seemed nervous. Sadie clenched her jaw but nodded.

Chase nodded. "Yeah, I forgot I had tryouts, too." He looked past us and smiled. "There's my mom. I'll see you at tryouts, Tate." They did this hand-shake thing and Chase walked past us.

My headache was a full-blown migraine now. I rubbed my head a little. "You guys want a snack before we head home?" I asked all three of them as they looked at me. Well, two. Millie was watching Chase as he got into his mom's car. When they drove back she looked back at me and shrugged. She walked over to Tate and hugged him.

"I missed you today." She smiled at him.

I looked at Sadie. Her arms were crossed and she was scowling at me. *Fun.* It seemed we would be having a fight later. Normally, it wouldn't bother me, and I might even enjoy it when we started making up, but right now my head was hurting too bad to even think about an argument.

We all walked to the parking lot. "Do you want to ride with me or Dane?" Sadie asked Tate.

"Can they ride with you? I'm worried about driving with them right now."

"What do you mean?" she asked sounding worried.

"I just have a bad headache. I'll be fine. I'd just rather not drive with the kids in the car."

She nodded and loaded the kids into her Rover. Once they were in, she came over to me and hugged me. "Why don't you go home and rest? I'll get Tate to tryouts and Millie can hang out with me."

"I'd love to, but I can't. I have to go check on some things about your house. That is, if you still want to live there."

She put her hands on her hips and cocked her head to one side. "Duh. Why wouldn't I? The moving truck comes in three days."

I kissed her. "Just making sure you hadn't changed your mind. Is there any furniture you'll need?" I opened my truck door. "Oh, and ask the kids what they want for dinner. I need to go grocery shopping so we don't eat out every night, but tonight is an eat out night."

"I can go to the grocery store for you tomorrow morning after we drop Tate off at school. And no, apparently Cooper and Alice bought some stuff. By the way, I found out in a text earlier they are coming down to help me move in. I told them I had plenty of help, but they wouldn't take no for answer. They really want to get to know you and Tate and make up for acting like snobs when they were here." She opened the door and handed Tate the keys. "Go ahead and start it up and turn on the air." He nodded and she shut the door and looked at me. "I'll bring dinner. You just go do what you need to do, and then go rest."

I nodded and kissed her. "Thank you, Daisy."

I watched them drive away before getting in my truck and calling Hales on the phone I borrowed from Trevor.

"Hey. Are you calling to tell me how horrible of a friend I am?"

"I'm sorry. I was angry, and I said things I regret. You know I love you, Hales." I groaned as I placed my head against the steering wheel.

"I love you more, and I know it's my fault. I'm just paranoid that Sadie is gonna screw up and you're going to go off the deep end. Anyway, what's up? You sound terrible."

"Do you have my shot that I have to take when my headache gets too bad?"

"I think so. I'll go check." I heard her say something to the boys. "You must not be wearing your glasses again, or, you're super stressed." I heard her digging around. "Yeah, it's here in the medicine cabinet. It's your last one, so you should probably call the doctor to get more called in."

"All right. Can you or Zach bring it to the house? And a little of both. I haven't been wearing my glasses, and I've been majorly stressed. Miller is driving me insane."

She groaned. "Are your guys still working on a house for that asshole? Hasn't it been like over a year now?" I heard Joshua repeat Hailey, but said, *ash-wole.* I laughed as Hailey was telling him don't say words like Mommy. "Where are you? Do you just want me to load the kids up and meet you?"

"I'm at the school, but I'm heading home." I started up the car, but ended up shutting it off

"Dane, don't drive. I know how bad these things get for you. I'll be up there shortly."

I didn't argue because she was right. After the Marines and getting hurt, my migraines were paralyzing.

"Where are Sadie and the kids?"

"They left. Tate has tryouts."

"She left you there knowing you're not feeling good?" she asked, sounding pissed.

"I played it off that it wasn't that bad. She doesn't know how they get, Hales."

She sighed. "Oh. Well, I'll be there in a second to pick you up."

"All right." I hung up and put the phone down. I groaned and ended up getting out of the truck and hurrying to some grass as I started throwing up. I hated these fucking things.

Chapter Thirty-one

SADIE

Y our dad is going to be so proud of you. Your aunt Hales was the pitcher and she can show you so much," I said to Tate as we headed to Dane's house. I looked at Millie in the rearview mirror. "And you, too. You actually said hi to some of the kids there. Super awesome, Millie." Of course, she whispered her hellos, but it was a step.

When we got to the house, I opened the door for Tate so he could carry the pizza boxes into the house. Millie walked with me into the house and then went to let the dogs out. I took the pizza boxes from Tate so he could help Millie.

I set the pizza down on the kitchen bar and walked around turning on lights. I stopped when I saw Dane asleep on the couch. I walked over and sat down next to him. I leaned down and kissed his forehead. He didn't even move. He was sound asleep.

I heard footsteps coming down the hall and froze when I saw Hailey with a laundry basket.

"Hey," she whispered. "He's out cold. He told me he didn't tell you how severe his migraines get. After he was injured he's had issues with them.

Certain things trigger them like stress and him not wearing his glasses when he's working on his computer for a long time."

I looked at Dane and then at her. "Should I take the kids somewhere else so it's quiet?"

She shook her head. "Nah, he'll sleep through anything with the meds he took. His doctor prescribes shots for him he can just do at home. I keep them at my place, though, because we don't—" she stopped talking and cleared her throat. "We just keep them there."

I stood after covering him with a throw blanket. "What do you mean you keep them at your place?"

She shrugged and started walking toward the laundry room.

"Hales," I demanded as I followed her.

"First of all, don't call me that. You have no right. My name is Hailey to you." I followed her into the laundry room. She set the laundry basket down. "And we keep all of his meds at our house because when he came back from the Marines where you pushed him to, he almost overdosed. He suffered terribly from some brutal PTSD and didn't even realize what he was doing. He's better now, but it took a year of strict therapy and other things to get him right, and Dana," she said quietly. She started folding Dane's jeans.

I scrunched my eyes. "Hailey, you have to stop blaming me. It's not fair."

She scoffed and rolled her eyes. "You weren't here to see it all. You didn't see him lying in a hospital bed and have doctors telling you his chances for survival were slim. When he left, it was because you pushed him over the edge. He lost Elliot and you all in the same year. Not to mention the fact that he proposed and you turned him down. Sadie, I don't owe you any explanation for why I don't like you or trust you. But hear me when I say, I will make you regret ever stepping foot back into his life if you screw this up. You have no idea how long it took him to get to where he is now."

I was pissed. Yeah, I totally deserved the cold shoulder, but I was trying.

"Don't give me that face. You know what you did, and yes, we all blame you for Dane losing his shit. And let's be honest, you wouldn't be here if it wasn't for Tate. You'd still be in New York living your dream while we all stayed here picking up the broken pieces of his heart."

I started to say something and she held up her hand.

"Save it, Sadie. I don't want to hear shit from you. Show me you're truly different and here to stay. Show me you're not here just to fuck up his life more and run off with Tate."

"I'm—"

"No. I don't want to hear your bullshit. Just show me. Show all of us."

I closed my mouth. I wanted to tell her to leave and that I could finish the laundry, but I knew she would probably ignore me. I needed to cry or scream. I didn't really know what I needed to do, but I had to get away from her.

I checked on the kids outside and then went to the kitchen to start getting out plates. It took every ounce of self-control I had not to march myself back into that laundry room and give her a piece of my mind. Well, and the fact that as badly as I didn't want to admit it, she was right.

I HAD JUST dozed off when I heard Dane move on the couch. I rubbed the sleep out of my eyes and sat up in the recliner.

"Hey," I whispered and smiled when his eyes found me. "How are you feeling?" I stood and walked over to him.

He sat up and stretched a little. "A little better. My head still hurts some. The couch is just making my neck and shoulders hurt." He gave me a small smile. "What time is it?"

"Nine-thirty." I got on the couch and moved until I was behind him. I started massaging his neck and shoulders. "Guess what?" I leaned down and kissed his neck.

"What?" he asked with a little bit of moan. He always loved my massages.

"Your son got pitcher."

"Really?" he asked excitedly. He grabbed his head. "I shouldn't have been so loud. Too loud." He dropped his hands. "I hate that I missed it."

I kissed his left temple gently. "Why don't you go soak in a hot bath, and I'll bring you some pizza? Then we can cuddle and go back to sleep."

"That sounds great." He stood and had to brace himself on the arm of the couch. "I hate these stupid things."

"While you were sleeping, I was googling how to help with migraines…" When he looked at me I smiled. "Orgasms are a natural cure."

He smirked. "Is that right?"

I nodded. "Yup." I stood and narrowed my eyes at him when I remembered I was supposed to be sort of mad at him. "By the way, don't ever downplay when you're not feeling good ever again." I moved until I was right in front of him. I put my index finger to his chest and looked at him as serious as I could. "Dane Shaw, I better not ever find out from someone else that you have to take shots or anything else that serious ever again."

He grabbed my hand and brought my fingertips to his lips. "I won't. I'll go to the eye doctor tomorrow and see if I need a new prescription. What all did Hales tell you about my shots and migraines? And what happened to testing out this theory on migraines?"

I hated replaying all she said to me because it pissed me off and it hurt like hell. She may be right, but not letting me speak at all was a bitch move. I shrugged and watched his lips kiss my fingertips.

His eyes locked on mine. "She told you about why she keeps the shots, didn't she?"

"She said a lot of things."

I could tell by the expression on his face he was getting angry. And him clenching his jaw was just going to make his migraine come back full force. "I didn't want you to hear about all that stuff from the past. And I swear I'm going to kill Hailey."

"She's just protecting you. You don't worry about it. This is between me and her. I'll handle it." I kissed him. "Just don't be pissed at me when I do. I know she's your best friend."

"Yes, she is, but you're the love of my life."

I kissed him again and my hands found the front of his jeans. "About that migraine." I needed to stop talking about Hailey and what all she told me. He was just getting all tense and that was the last thing he needed to do.

"Shouldn't we go to my room first?" he asked as he ran his finger down my face and then down my neck.

"Oh yeah, we have kids. Fuck." I giggled and grabbed his hand, leading him to his room.

Chapter Thirty-two

DANE

I adjusted my new glasses that I officially had to wear all the damn time. I was trying to get all my filing caught up when someone knocked at my office door. Millie went to get up, but I motioned for her to go back to working and went to answer the door myself. I opened it to see Dana standing there.

"Yeah?"

She held up a stack of files. "I got all of this organized. Can I put it in your filing cabinet?"

I moved back and let her in. "You may want to wait until I get my files all fixed." I waved at the mountain of paperwork I was trying to fix and re-file.

She set the folders down and put her hands on her hips. "Wow." She smiled at Millie. "How are you, munchkin'?"

Dana and Millie never got too extremely close, but Dana always tried. After a small wave, Millie turned back to her laptop and started working again. I sat down at my desk and put a few receipts into a folder.

I looked at Dana as she eyed the files again.

"Yeah, it's a disaster zone. But in my defense, I've just started working on the office instead of on sites."

She kicked off her heels and smiled. "Well, that's what you have me for. Are they all labeled?"

"Yes, but you don't have to help. I'm the idiot who didn't ever file anything." I stood and put a finished file back in the drawer.

"I'm done with all of my work out front. It's really no problem." She smiled when I looked at her. "Love the glasses, but I always have." She cleared her throat. "Sorry." She blushed as she grabbed a few files and walked over to the drawers.

"Dana, thanks for the compliment, but I'm really serious about Sadie. I always have been."

She laughed but kept her back to me as she worked. "I know that. What, a girl can't compliment you?"

"Not a girl I used to date, no. Plus, I'm one of your bosses now." And if my girlfriend found out, she'd kick your pregnant ass.

She came back over to get more files. "Tell me about her. I never let you before, but since she's back and you two are serious, I wanna know."

Millie stood. "Uncle Dane, I'm gonna go use the bathroom." She smiled a little at Dana and walked out.

I smiled as I thought about my Daisy. "Umm...well." I laughed as I thought about the best way to describe her. How did one describe Sadie Solis? "She's this mixture between a little bit of sunshine and little go fuck yourself."

She laughed. "She sounds fun."

"She is. She's amazing. She has so much passion and love in her. She and the kids mean the world to me."

"That's great. Really, I'm happy for you." She rubbed her little pooch before grabbing more files.

"Dana, can I ask you a question without you getting offended?" I finished putting all my papers into the files and stacked them neatly on my desk as I tried to think of the polite way to ask my question. Dammit, there really wasn't one.

"Dane, you've never offended me. Go for it." She turned to face me. "Who's the father, and is he going to help you?"

She chewed on the inside of her cheek and leaned her back against the wall. "Do you remember Darren Stevens? The guy that runs the YMCA?"

I nodded. "Isn't he married, though?"

She blushed. "Was. And I told him I didn't want his help. He's trying to work on his marriage, and I'm going to do the whole single mom thing. I never meant to be a homewrecker. I'm not that girl, but I had a moment of weakness." She got back to work when Millie came into the office.

I went to my desk and grabbed some files and was about to hand them over to Dana when Sadie walked into the office.

"What the actual fuck?" she snapped.

Millie giggled.

Sadie pointed at Millie. "Don't repeat the words that are about to come out of my mouth." Millie nodded and Sadie glared at Dana. "Why are you in here? With no fucking shoes on?" Sadie glared at me and if looks could kill, I'd be dead. Her attention went back to Dana and she started stomping in her direction.

I quickly set the files down and had to jump onto my desk and jump off to make it to her before she had Dana's neck in her hands. I put my hands on her shoulders and walked her out of the room.

Her teeth were clenched tight and she was fighting against me. It was so hard to take her seriously in her black leotard, black spandex shorts, bare feet, and her head full of hair in the cutest messy bun.

"Let me go, Dane!"

My Daisy was so tiny and adorable that you'd never think she was capable of throwing down. But when it came to me, she was always a little on the crazy side. Okay, a whole lot on the crazy side. No one fucks with Daisy.

"Why the fuck are you laughing? Dane, this isn't funny, let me go!"

I held her around the waist, trying so hard not to laugh. "Daisy, calm down. She was filing for me."

She huffed and looked at me with her jaw clenched. "Let me go. I'll be good."

I raised a brow. "Promise."

She nodded stiffly.

When I let her go, she made a beeline for the front. I chased after her but didn't make it in time. Dana was sitting in her chair staring at Sadie with wide eyes while Sadie dumped a jar of pens all over her desk.

I threw Sadie over my shoulder and carried her out while she yelled, "Look at his ass again, and I will fuck your whole world up, bitch!"

"Sadie, calm down," I said as I walked to the back of the building and went into one of our conference rooms.

"When I walked into your office she was looking at your ass, Dane! She wasn't just filing, she was checking you out! I know a ho when I see a ho!" She was fired up. Her messy bun had fallen out and now her long hair was a mess.

I set her down on a table and kissed her before she could say anything else. She wrapped her arms around my neck and relaxed a little while she kissed me back.

"I love you, Daisy," I said as I pulled back a little.

"If you love me, you'll fire her skank ass."

"Daisy, I can't. That's a lawsuit waiting to happen and she did nothing wrong. She was trying to help me get my files back in order. I haven't been in the office a lot and it's put some things behind."

"Dane, she was looking at your ass when I walked in."

I tucked her hair behind her ears gently. "I know. I heard you yell it at her." I sighed and kissed her nose. "Do you trust me?"

"Yes. But I don't trust her." She frowned.

"I'm not asking you to trust her but to trust me. I see her as my secretary only. And if it makes you feel better, I won't let her help me in my office anymore. Okay?"

She nodded and sighed heavily. "I was coming to tell you good news."

"What?" I asked as I adjusted my glasses.

Sadie smiled a little. She loved my glasses. "Take those off for a second."

I took them off and blinked my eyes to try and focus her.

"Yup. That's the problem." She motioned for me to put them back on. "You're too hot, Dane."

I laughed. "I have to wear them all the time now. Sorry. Now, what is your news, Daisy-Love?"

Her smile returned fully. "I talked to Alice earlier and we got to talking about Millie. With Alice's help, we can get scouts here."

"For Juilliard?"

She nodded. "I know she's young still, but she's good, Dane." She looked down at her feet and wiggled her toes. "I was so excited I forgot to put on shoes."

"This is something you need to talk to Millie about. I'm excited about her getting the opportunity, but she doesn't like people, Sadie. She has major panic attacks."

"I know. But she's different when she dances. It's like she forgets people are around." She started playing with the bottom of my shirt. "Dancing is her security blanket."

"True, but Juilliard is more than just dancing. She has to interact with people and go to classes. She had a panic attack when she thought I was going to make her go to public school. Just talk to her about it and see how she handles it. It may be something we work toward when she's older."

She looked a little disappointed but nodded. "I will." She glanced over her shoulder at the door and then at me. "Can you do me a favor?"

"What?" I kissed her nose.

"Lock the door."

I smiled and groaned. "We can't. Not with Millie out there alone. We need to get back. Plus, I can't leave here today until everything is done, and I'd love to spend time with my family tonight." I wrapped my arms around her.

She stuck her bottom lip out. I leaned down and tugged on her bottom lip with my teeth before kissing her again. I helped her off the table.

"Am I allowed to walk back in there with you?" She grabbed my hand.

"Of course."

She let go of my hand and started fixing her hair back into a messy bun as we walked in.

Dana froze and looked at Sadie with wide eyes again. Sadie hissed at her. My girlfriend actually hissed at Dana. Sadie smiled when I looked at her and skipped into my office.

"Sorry." I walked into my office and shut the door.

Chapter Thirty-three

SADIE

I looked at Brink when he walked into the room where I was practicing a routine with Jason. Jason looked worried, and I'm sure my face matched his.

"What's wrong?" I asked as I grabbed a towel and wiped sweat from my brow. I knew Brink and Quinn were in town this week, but him making a special trip had me worried.

I didn't want to tell Dane, but I kept having this dream that Tate would be taken away from me.

"Nothing is wrong," Brink said as he loosened his tie. "I found out who the anonymous letters are from."

This was something I had wanted to know since receiving them. I kept my eyes on him while I waited for his answer.

"His adoptive mother's sister."

My heart stopped. "Is she going to try to take him from us?"

He shook his head. "No. Quinn actually talked to her and asked her why she reached out to you and your parents. She said that her sister told her about you and she actually hired a private investigator to see if you were capable of being a mother. Once she saw you were, she sent the letters."

"Was Tate close to her?"

"Quinn said she only met him a few times because they lived so far apart."

I nodded and turned to Jason. "Can I leave so I can go talk to Dane?"

"Sure, sweetheart." He wiped some sweat off his forehead. "I'm worn out anyway."

I hugged Jason and kissed his cheek. He was becoming like a brother to me. "I love you, punkin'."

I put on my shoes and walked out with Brink. "You promise I don't have to worry about her fighting for him?"

"I promise. She wouldn't have sent those letters and let you see him if she was going to take him away. But she does want to still be a part of his life."

I was selfish. I didn't want to share him with anyone except the people that were in his life right now.

"I'll talk to Dane. Is she a good person?"

"As far as I can tell."

We stopped at my Rover. "Thanks for coming to tell me. You had me worried watching, you walk in like that."

He laughed. "Sorry. I was in the area and thought I might as well stop." He kissed my head. "I'm proud of you, Sadie. I know you probably don't hear that often enough, but I am. Oh, and I'm inviting everyone over for dinner tonight. Quinn and I aren't in town long, so, we want to see everyone."

"What time?"

"Seven."

I smiled. "We'll be there."

Once in my vehicle, I drove toward Dane's office. I promised myself I'd stay the hell away from that place for the rest of the week after my blow-up yesterday, but I needed to go talk to him about the letters and Tate's aunt before we picked Tate up from school. When I pulled in I saw Dane's truck was gone.

I put the Rover in park and called him.

"Hey, Daisy."

"Hey, baby. Where are you?"

"At home checking out your little house. And guess what? It's finished."

"Really?" I squealed.

"Yep. Everyone is cleaning up now and about to leave. We'll be able to start moving your stuff in as soon as it gets here."

"The movers told me it'd be Sunday. I was supposed to call them as soon as the house was finished, though." I put my Rover in drive and headed toward my new home.

"I hope you like it."

Dane hadn't let me see inside the little house since he started working on it.

"I'm sure I will. You could put me in a box as long as it was close to you."

He chuckled. "You should come see it."

"Already on my way."

"Really? Good. I've missed your sassy, sexy ass today."

I laughed. "You mean you're really not mad at me about yesterday? Did Dana show up for work today?"

"Yeah, she showed up." He chuckled. "And I was a little upset, but I know how jealous you get. It's a good thing I can pick you up. Can you imagine me losing it and you trying to stop me?"

I cringed at the thought. He'd fuck someone up. "No." I smirked. "Well, I bet she doesn't look at your ass again."

"I'm sure she doesn't." He chuckled.

I turned toward the lake. "So, I was coming to find you to tell you Brink came by the studio."

"Why?"

"He found out who sent the anonymous letters."

"I figured he would. Who sent it?"

"His adoptive aunt."

"Did he find out why?"

"Yeah. She wanted to reach out to me after hiring a private investigator to see if I was capable of being a mom. Once she saw I was, she reached out because she wanted him to go to me if possible. She had no idea about you, or I'm sure she would have reached out to you, too."

"She's not going to try and get him back, is she?" He sounded really worried.

"Brink said no, but that she still wants to be a part of his life somehow." I turned down our road. "I'm almost there."

"Okay. And we won't worry about it then. We will get her contact info and try to work out visits. I'll see ya in a bit, Daisy."

"Okay, baby." I hung up.

When I pulled into the driveway, I parked next to Dane's truck. I smiled when he opened my door for me.

He held his hand out to me and laced his fingers with mine as we walked to my little house. "Your back door connects to the fenced-in backyard so you can put Juno out with the other dogs."

"It's like a little cottage from a book! I'm in love!" I stopped walking and moved in front of him. "What happens when we move in together one day, though? What will we do with it?"

I would move in with him now if we both thought it would be healthy for Tate and Millie. But, we both had valid points of why we couldn't yet.

"It will be here for when the kids go off to school and want to come home and not stay in the main house with us."

We walked in, and I felt like I had walked into *Alice in Wonderland* with all the colors and how it was built. My dream.

Dane was watching my face closely as I took everything in. "Whatever you don't like I can change."

"Dane, you've been on my Pinterest!" My mouth fell open as I looked at the dark wood table and mismatched colorful chairs.

"I had a small one of my table made for you. And yes, I have been. I wanted it to be perfect."

"Dane," I said in awe, "it's perfect."

I started walking through the whole thing. I loved the open floor plan and that the living room, kitchen, and dining area were all open to each other. I went down the hall and saw that he had added a room for Tate. My heart exploded in my chest knowing how much he loved us both and how much he wanted us to be comfortable in both houses. Tate's room was a baseball lovers' dream. Again, Dane must've been looking at my kids' bedroom ideas on Pinterest.

I went to my room and smiled when I saw a vase of daisies in the middle of the floor. I told him not to buy a thing for my room because all my things would be here on the moving truck.

"Should I have let you do everything?" he asked. It adorable how nervous he was.

I wrapped my arms around his neck and jumped up. He caught me, and I wrapped my legs around his waist. I kissed him. "Baby, it's perfect. Thank you."

His hands cupped my ass. "You're welcome. I just want you to feel at home."

"I can't wait to show the kids."

"I may have to redecorate my place once they see it." He grinned before kissing me.

"While I have you here, I should probably tell you that Alice, Cooper, and Ethan will be coming with the moving truck. I found out this morning but wanted to tell you when I could see your face."

His smile faded. "Who's Ethan?"

I kissed him instead of answering.

He held onto me but moved away from my kiss. "Sadie."

"Cooper's twin brother."

He searched my face, his frown deepening. "You used to date him, didn't you?"

"For a year. We broke up last spring, which was my doing. It just wasn't working because some super-hot ginger kept fucking things up. I've never moved on, Dane. Ever."

He smiled a little before making a face and burying his face against my neck. "I'll be good," he muttered. "Do you want me to dress nicer while your friends are here?"

"Stop it."

He lifted his head to look at me. "Stop what?"

"You're not changing who you are for a second." I kissed his nose. "I've been avoiding Ethan's calls and texts. Cooper warned me that he was coming. Anything that is discussed, you'll be with me, okay?"

"All right. Do me a favor? Don't tell them I have a lot of money. I don't like people knowing." His smile slowly came back as he put me down. "I have something else for you."

"I won't. I mean, I didn't tell them a thing about you when I was there." I made a face when he raised a brow. "Sorry. Too soon for me to say shit like that?"

"Yes. Too soon." He grabbed my hand and lead me back to the table. He picked up a checkbook I hadn't noticed earlier. "I put your name on my account so if you need anything you can get it."

I shook my head adamantly. "No."

"Why not? You'll have Millie and Tate with you some, and I want to know you're okay. You don't have to use it. You can see it as for emergencies only if you want."

I put my hands on my hips and stared at him. "Fine."

His shoulders slumped. "What did I do?" He sat down in a chair.

"Nothing. You know how I am. I just don't... I don't like handouts. I know it's not a handout, but I'm really independent when it comes to shit like this. I've made it on my own for eight years. Accepting this house has been one of the hardest things for me to do."

"Oh. All right. I understand." He stood and kissed me. "I can take your name off the account."

I hurt his feelings. I could see it all over his face. "Don't take my name off."

"I don't want you uncomfortable, Sadie."

"I'll only be comfortable if you let me put your name on my account."

"Deal." He looked at his watch. "We should go get Tate and pick up Millie from Hales."

I grabbed the front of his t-shirt. "Hold up a second."

He put his hands on my hips and brought me closer to him. "Yes?"

I held a handful of the front his shirt as I smiled up at him. "Thank you from the bottom of my cold, jealous heart." *Dammit,* I loved his laugh, I smiled so big my nose scrunched up.

"There's nothing cold about you, Daisy-Love."

"Not even when bitch ass hoes are around?"

"Not even then."

I laughed and kissed him. "Let's go get the kiddos."

He picked me up and slung me over his shoulder. He laughed when I squealed.

"Mmmm, I really like this view." I slid my hands into his back pockets. "New jeans?"

"Yep. I had to buy a new pair when I ripped my last pair on a nail. And I like my view too."

I burst into laughter.

Chapter Thirty-four

DANE

I sat at the table as Hales cleaned the kitchen.

"You sure you don't want any help? I don't mind cleaning while you rest. And where's my stubborn ass brother?"

Joshua giggled. "Ash!"

I face-palmed. "Oops."

"He's being stubborn and working a night shift at Quinn's after baseball practice. He fired some chick." She started the dishwasher.

"He's always firing someone. I'll see if I need to help him out until he finds a new worker. He needs to be here helping you."

"It's fine, Dane. I got this. When we decided I'd be a stay-at-home-mom, I knew I'd be doing a lot. He helps. Trust me." She looked at the stove clock. "You coming to Brink and Quinn's for dinner tonight?"

I tilted my head to the side. "Brink's?"

"Yeah. He invited everyone over for dinner. Zach is gonna swing by as soon as he can leave. He told me he told Sadie to tell you." She lightly scratched her stomach. "I'm assuming she didn't tell you."

"I'm sure she forgot. We got distracted with her little house. It's finally finished." And by distracted, I mean we got distracted by making out and talking.

"Distracted?" She raised her brows at me. "Are you two being careful?"

I went to pop off something when I felt the blood drain from my face and felt sick to my stomach. *Fuck.* We hadn't been careful at all. Or at least I hadn't.

"Dane Shaw!" When I looked at her, her mouth was draped open.

I rubbed the back of my neck. "I forgot. I'm rusty at this whole thing."

She pointed to her stomach. "This is a product of Zach's so-called trusty method of 'pulling out'." She rolled her eyes. "And rusty? Seriously? You know how babies are made! How the hell do you forget condoms or at least attempting the pull-out method? Is she on birth control?"

"I don't know," I said sheepishly. "And I just kind of lose control around Sadie. Before recently it had been over eight years since I…ya know."

She sat down across from me at the table. "You have to find out if she's on birth control! What if this is her evil plan? You knock her up and—"

I glared at her. "Enough, Hales. Please." I grabbed her hand that was on the table. "Please trust me."

She sighed and nodded. "Okay. It's trusting her I have issues with. Dana told me she went all bat-shit crazy on her yesterday."

I smirked. "And I've seen you go just as bat shit crazy on exes of Zach's who have talked to him in Walmart."

Joshua giggled again. "Shit, shit, shit."

Sadie handed Joshua his sippy cup to get him to stop saying it. His toothless grin spread around the tip of it.

Hailey smirked and moved her hand from my hold. "I guess you're right. So, where is Sadie?"

"At work. Millie's at dance practice, so, she's going to bring her home after they're both done." I looked out the glass backdoor where Tate was playing with the twins.

"Tate's loving school and…he made pitcher, Hales."

"Are you serious? Did Zach coordinate that or was that all him?"

"All him." I grinned widely. "Seems like he got his dad's amazing baseball genes."

"Can I work with him? Please? This is God's way of making me sane, I know it is!" Poor Hailey got boys who love soccer and could give a rat's ass about baseball. Even Joshua says *yucky* when she tries to hand him a baseball.

I burst out laughing. "I don't see why not since you're the best pitcher in the family."

She was smiling the biggest I had seen in months.

"I've missed that smile. And I know Zach has as well." I smiled at her. "Are you two okay?"

"We're great. I mean, as great as we can be. Life is kind of busy and crazy right now. I eat, cry, sleep, or am pissed off all the time. This pregnancy is different than the others. I feel so blah." She ran her fingers through her messy blonde hair. "I feel bad for Zach. He's putting up with a lot. So, if he's acting weird, it's my fault."

I leaned forward. "He's acting weird because…well, he's hurt and confused. And you know Zach. He doesn't talk about anything until he has it all worked out in his head first."

Hailey suddenly looked worried. "What's going on?"

I picked up the sippy cup Joshua just dropped and handed it to him. "He thinks you're getting tired of him and that you don't want to spend the rest of your life with him. For someone who can be so cocky, he gets very insecure about you."

"Of course I want to spend the rest of my life with him." Tears began to well up in her eyes. "Dane, when did he talk to you?"

"A couple of days ago. I didn't know how to talk to you about it or if I should. But when I saw him this morning, he just seemed so depressed. He said you don't want to ever get married."

Tears filled her eyes. "He asked me to marry him about a month ago. I told him I didn't see the point when we already had kids and were living together. I was in one of my shit moods." She glanced at her phone that was on the table near her. "I'm such a monster lately." She picked up her phone. "I'm going to call him. I'll see you guys at Brink and Quinn's."

"Hales, he loves you. A lot."

She nodded. "And I love him more than anything. I just didn't see the point in marriage. But if he wants to marry me, then dammit, he can." She smiled a little and wiped her eyes when Joshua's bottom lip puckered out seeing his momma cry. "Mommy's okay." She kissed his head. "Thank you for telling me, Dane."

"You know I'd do anything for you two. You're my family."

I stood. "I'm going to head home with Tate."

"See you guys at Brink and Quinn's later." She stood and hugged me. "I'll call Zach and make him come home so we can talk about this."

I kissed the top of her head. "Good." I went outside and motioned for Tate. "Let's go home, kiddo."

He told his cousins bye and followed me to the truck.

"We're going to Brink and Quinn's house for dinner tonight."

"I know. Mom told me." His eyes widened when I looked at him. "I mean, Sadie. Sadie told me." He stared out the window.

I turned my focus back on the road and turned down our driveway. I patted the spot next to me. "Come here, kiddo."

He climbed into the front seat and put his seatbelt on.

I put an arm around his shoulders. "Tell me what's going on in your head, Tate."

"I don't know." He shrugged.

I parked and kissed the top of his head. "It's okay to be confused. Just know I love you, Tate. And I will always have your back." I gave him a smile. "You didn't tell me how school was."

He smiled. "It was good. Weird, though." He scrunched his nose like Sadie does. "A girl wrote me a letter."

We got out of the truck. "A girl wrote you a letter? What did it say?" I asked with a chuckle. "Is she cute?"

"She's okay." He dug in his jean pocket and handed it to me. It was all crinkled up, and I had to really work to get it flat enough to read it.

Tate,

*I think you are very cute. I'm glad you
are at my school now. I like baseball and
I know you do 2. My brother is the assis*

Sara Daniell

tant coach with your uncle so I will be at
games and stuff.
Love,
Koraline Jacobs

There were hearts drawn in pencil and colored in with red crayon. I smiled at him as he began to blush.

I handed him back the letter. "Well, aren't you the popular one," I teased as I ruffled his hair. "So, are you going to talk to her and stuff?"

He shrugged. "Probably not. Maybe. I don't know. I don't have time for girls, Dad."

I laughed. "Good choice. Just be her friend if you have time. Speaking of friends, this is the Labor Day weekend. Do you want to invite some friends from back home down here and invite Chase to hang out?" My heart was bursting with the fact he called me Dad. "And…I like that you called me Dad."

He laughed. "I didn't realize I did it until you said I did. I really like that you're my dad." We walked inside and the dogs came to greet us. He knelt down to pet them. "Don't tell Sadie I called her Mom, though."

My phone dinged.

> **Sadie: SHIT! I forgot to tell you dinner at Brink and Quinn's tonight at seven! I was talking to the kids about it earlier, and it just dawned on me I never told you. Sorry!! I'm finishing up here, and Millie and I will meet you at home.**

"I won't tell her. And I love that you're my son."

> **Dane: It's okay. Hailey told me. I will see you guys in a bit. Love you!**

I pet the dogs and let them out the back door so they could use the bathroom. "I think I may need to put in a doggie door, but by the time they are grown I don't think they will fit." Tate and I sat outside and watched the dogs run around and play. My son had called me dad. I felt like I was on top of the world. The dogs went to the gate and started barking. I scrunched my eyebrows as I heard someone pull in.

"Sadie and Millie shouldn't be home yet." I walked over to the fence and smiled when I saw Zach, but it faded when I saw the look on his face. "Tate, why don't you take the dogs inside." I opened the gate and stepped out to meet him halfway. Tate took the dogs in.

Zach came up to me. "I'm done! Finished! I hate that stupid place!"

"Calm down, Zach. What are you finished with?"

"Quinn's." He ran his hands through his hair. I noticed his hands were shaking.

"Someone else quit?"

"Yes. I don't want to sell that place because it has so many memories, but I don't think I can take it anymore. Not between that, coaching, and everything going on at home."

"Zach, when was the last time you got a good night's sleep?"

He shrugged and put his hands in his pockets. He stared out at the lake. "I don't know. Hales has been...very demanding lately. I feel like I'm losing my mind."

I put my hands on his shoulders. "Why don't you take a few days off. I'll take care of business at the pizza place."

His shoulders sagged. "You have enough on your plate."

"Yes, but you're at the end of your rope. Go home and spend time with your family. I'll go to the pizza place and handle things. Okay?"

"Thanks, Dane."

I put my hands on his shoulders. "Anytime. Now, go home and get some rest before dinner."

He nodded. "Speaking of dinner, is everything okay? Hailey told me it was really important I'm there tonight."

"Honestly, I don't know. I was just told to be there. Head home." I gave him a slight hug. "Everything will be all right."

He rubbed the back of his neck. "I'm seeing a doctor tomorrow. I'm talking to Hales about it when I get home."

"About what?"

"Getting a vasectomy. I don't think Hales wants any more kids after this."

"Probably not considering this has been the pregnancy from hell."

Zach laughed a little before walking to his truck and heading home.

Chapter Thirty-Five

SADIE

After getting ready, Millie and I drove to Quinn's Pizza to see if Dane and Tate were ready to go. Apparently, Zach reached his breaking point with the restaurant and Dane had to go fix whatever mess was going on. I parked on the street in front of Quinn's and Millie and I went in. The place was packed as usual. I found Dane teaching a waitress the proper way to fill a napkin dispenser. Tate was making eyes at the pretty waitress and it made me laugh.

I ruffled Tate's hair when we walked over. "Hey, Tater-bug."

He smiled and blushed when he realized I caught him. "Hey."

I looked at Dane. "Ready?"

"I can't leave yet."

"Dane," I said in a warning tone. "Don't make me go alone. Please. It would be like feeding me to the wolves. Hailey hates me right now, remember?"

He searched around the pizza place until he found a leggy blonde. "Tiff, can you handle things until I get back from dinner?"

She looked up from helping a different waitress and smiled. "Sure can. Go eat. I'll see ya soon, cutie pie."

Dane rolled his eyes. "Let's go. It'll have to be a quick dinner."

I felt heat rush to my face. The only thing that snapped me out of murder-mode was my son grabbing my hand. I glared at Dane. "She's lucky," I whispered in a harsh tone as we walked out.

"She calls everyone cutie pie and honey. She called Tate the same thing." Dane put his arm around my waist and walked us to the Rover. He kissed my cheek.

"She won't call everyone either of those things once I talk to her."

I watched Dane open the door to my vehicle for Tate and Millie.

"Be good. Zach can't afford to lose another manager. He's about to go insane as it is."

I groaned and kissed him. "Fine."

He grinned and slapped my ass before opening the driver door for me. Tate and Millie were laughing from the backseat. Once I was in, he walked around to the passenger side and got in. "You sure you don't mind bringing me back to work? I can drive my own truck if I need to."

"I'm sure we don't mind. Do we, kiddos?"

"Nope!" they said in unison.

I reached over and grabbed his hand as I drove. "It's super sweet of you to help Zach out, but I don't want you getting too stressed yourself."

"I'll try not to. It's just crazy right now for him. You should have seen him earlier today. I haven't seen him this undone in a long time."

"I guess I can help out if I need to as well." I smiled at Dane and continued to drive.

When we pulled up to Quinn and Brink's, my stomach had knots in it. They were staying in Coach's old house and there were so many memories here. I watched as the kids got out. After they were out and shut their doors, I looked at Dane.

"I am not responsible for anything that comes out of my mouth tonight. Just remember, if Hailey pops off some stupid shit, I will handle it." I glared at Hailey's huge space shuttle of an Expedition signifying she was already there. She probably had her gun loaded just waiting for me.

Dane kissed me. "Just remember there will be kids there as well."

He laced his fingers with mine as we walked inside.

Quinn was standing in the foyer and hugged me tightly as soon as she saw me.

"Hey!" She squeezed me again. "We're happy you're home to stay, Sadie."

"Thanks, me too."

I was a little shocked by her excitement but it was nice. We pulled apart and Dane found my hand again.

"Come on, everyone is already in the dining room waiting. Zach told me you all would be running late." Quinn smiled at the kids who were following right beside her.

We came in and sat down at the table that was set for a feast. Quinn never did anything small. It was always well-planned and perfect.

Dane put his arm on the back of my chair. "So, what's this dinner all about? Not that I don't mind eating with all of you, just wondering."

Brink handed us the casserole. Dane put some on his plate and offered some to the kids then to me. I put some on my plate and passed it to Hailey who was beside me. My eyes went straight to her left finger that had a huge rock on it. Was anyone else noticing this? Even Zach was acting like nothing was new.

Brink smiled. "Just wanted to spend time with my family while we're in town."

I nudged Dane's side and motioned with my eyes to Hailey's finger.

Dane's eyebrows shot up and he looked toward his brother who seemed more exhausted than I had ever seen him. Zach looked up from his food and over to the two of us.

"What?" he asked when we kept staring at him.

Hailey winked at Dane. She then handed Zach a roll with her left hand. Now everyone saw it and all eyes were on Zach waiting for him to notice.

"Thank you, tiger," he said as he took the roll from her. His hand froze as he saw the ring. "Ti-tiger?" his eyes went to hers. "Wh-why are you wearing that?"

"Because we're getting married. Next October. I already called my mom and told her to look at her calendar and find a wedding planner." Hailey was beaming. Their twins were grinning from ear to ear.

"But...you told me no," Zach said, his face showing his confusion.

Hailey cupped the side of his face. "And now I'm telling you yes."

Zach's face finally split into a smile. He covered her hand with his before leaning in and kissing her.

Dane whistled. "About time," he teased.

Millie giggled.

"So, Mom, you're going to have the same last name as us, right?" Jamison asked as he watched his parents pull apart.

Hailey laughed and nodded. "Yes."

Quinn squealed. "I can't wait to start planning with your mom! An October wedding will be perfect!"

"Congrats, you guys." I smiled and took a drink of water. I noticed Tate staring at me and then looking at Dane. "What is it?" I asked him quietly when everyone started eating.

"Nothing. Just thinking." He smiled a little and started eating.

As dinner lingered on, I listened to everyone talk and Quinn and Brink fill everyone in on their travels. I was enjoying listening to Quinn tell Dane about Ireland and how he should take the kids when Hailey got my attention.

I gave her a small smile. "Yeah?"

"You're not eating much. You feeling okay?" I noticed her eyes flicker to my stomach, and I frowned.

"I'm fine, why?"

She shrugged and took a bite of her food.

I kept my eyes on her. "Hailey, why would you ask that?"

"Are you on birth control?" she whispered.

My mouth fell open in shock. This girl has only said hateful things to me since being back and all of a sudden she feels like she can ask me a personal question? Her eyes went to my stomach again before she peeled them away and looked at her plate of food.

"I don't think that's any of your business," I whispered harshly. Thankfully, everyone was so engrossed in conversation no one was noticing what was happening.

"It will be if Dane gets you pregnant. Again."

I slammed my fork down. I'm sure she meant nothing by her response, but everything she said to me felt personal. "Excuse me?" I growled.

Everyone stopped talking and looked at me.

Hailey smiled. "It was just a question, Sadie. Calm down."

"Well, you can't ask me questions like that when you can't even say hi to me without gritting your teeth!" *Kids, Sadie. The kids are here and watching.* I inhaled deeply.

Dane put his hand gently on my thigh. "What question did she ask you?"

I shook my head as I exhaled. I didn't want to answer him or talk about this here. If I did, I would only get more pissed and make a fool of myself. I wouldn't ruin this dinner because Hailey was an idiot.

Dane's hand moved to my back and he started rubbing it gently. "Zach, why didn't you tell me how much of a mess the pizza place was in? I would have helped you a long time ago."

"You've been busy, and I thought I could get it worked out, but people just keep quitting on me. Or they're idiots, and I have to fire them."

I couldn't stop replaying what Hailey asked me. Did she think I was pregnant? I wasn't. For her information, I was on birth control. And if I wasn't and I did end up pregnant, that'd be none of her concern, either. If the kids weren't here, I would let her have it.

Stop thinking about it, Sadie.

Stop before you—

"Daisy-Love, are you ready to take me back to Quinn's?" Dane knew I was about to blow and he was trying to get us out of there before I did.

I thanked Quinn and Brink for dinner and left the table in a hurry. I felt an abundance of curse words about to roll off my tongue. We were just about in the clear, I was so proud of myself, but that all changed when I decided that I had had it. I turned on my heels and marched myself right back into the dining room.

"Let's get something straight, Hailey," I said, pointing my index finger in her direction. "I love Dane. I love him more than anything in this entire world. You can either accept that or disregard it and live in your bed of negativity. I don't give a flying fuck what you decide. All that matters to me is that I'm here and I'm trying my hardest to make life work for me here. I don't plan on going anywhere, so you can either accept it, be nice, or just stay the hell away from me!"

Zach stood so quickly his chair flew backward. He moved quickly so he was in-between me and Hales and Dane moved so he was in front of me.

"And don't ask me personal questions when you can't even say hi nicely!" I yelled from behind Dane.

"Dane," Zach said in a growl. Dane tensed at his brother's tone of voice.

"Zach, don't lose your temper on Sadie."

"Then tell her to watch her temper with Hales!"

"I will when Hales starts trying to be nice to Sadie! We've all made mistakes in the past. It's time for everyone to give Sadie another chance and to let go of the past."

Brink and Quinn gathered all the kids and took them out of the dining room.

Jason and Trevor walked in and stopped. "Sorry we're late," Trev said with hesitation to his voice. "Should we leave?"

"You could tell Zach to grow—" Dane stopped me from speaking by covering my mouth with his hand. He groaned as Zach's temper completely ignited and the next thing I knew Dane had taken a punch to the jaw.

Trevor and Jason jumped into action and held both of them back before a full-on knock-down-drag-out erupted. Next thing I knew, Trev was ushering Dane out of the house along with me and Tate and Millie.

Well, that went well.

Chapter Thirty-six

DANE

I held ice to my jaw and tinkered with my broken glasses. "I just got these
damn things." I sat in Zach's office looking over the books as Zach leaned
back in a chair watching me.

"Sorry. I'll pay for a new pair. I shouldn't have lost my temper."

I shrugged. "It's okay. I know you had some issues to work through."

He chuckled. "Yeah, but I didn't want to work through them against
your jaw."

"Yeah, I wish you wouldn't have, either. How's Hales?" I took a drink of
my soda and stared at my brother. It was three in the morning and we had just
finished all the books and caught his business stuff completely up. We were
both putting off going home to two angry women.

"Let's just say I'm seriously thinking about crashing at Brink's tonight. Or
should I say this morning." He ran his hands down his face. "I really am sorry,
man." He laughed a little. "Sorry, it's not funny but then again it kind of is. What
pissed Sadie off so bad anyway? I never heard Hailey say anything to her."

"Apparently, Hales asked her if she was pregnant."

Zach laughed. "That's what made her mad?"

"I think it was more her tone and the fact that her and Sadie have been butting heads so much lately. Sadie reached her boiling point." I took the ice off and looked at his books. "You're all caught up now. Oh, and do me a favor and don't tell Trevor I can handle books because then he'll want me doing ours." I grinned for a second before wincing. I rubbed my jaw and glanced down at my phone when it dinged.

> **Sadie:** Should I be worried that you're avoiding coming home?
> **Dane:** Zach and I just finished up. I'll be coming home soon.

"That's Sadie. I should head home and so should you."

> **Sadie:** It's 3 in the fucking morning.

I stood and stretched.

Zach stood as well. "Head home, bro. I'll talk to you later today."

I dialed Sadie's number as I walked out to my truck.

"Hey," she said stiffly.

"Hey. His books were a mess. We just finished up. I'm getting in my truck now."

"I believe you, but I also think you both were finding an excuse to stay away from me and Hailey."

I chuckled. "Maybe just a little."

"I don't find this funny."

"I have to find something funny about this. I'm the one who got the shit punched out of him." She didn't respond. "I love you, Daisy-Love."

"Don't Daisy-Love me right now. I'm pissed! Hailey had no right to ask what she did, and yeah you got hit, but then you just run off to go help Zach with some financial shit that could've waited. I needed you tonight."

"I went back to run the restaurant, which you knew I had to do, and Zach showed up to work on the books, so I stayed to help." I drove toward my house. I turned on the windshield wipers as it started to rain.

"Zach can handle his own shit. Oh wait, maybe he can't. Hailey took his balls from him." Sadie was in one of her moods. When Sadie was pissed the whole world would know it and she could hold grudges like it was her job.

"Zach's my brother and part of us being a family is we help each other out when needed."

She hung up on me.

I was trying really hard to remain calm but her hanging up on me pissed me off. I hit the steering wheel just before I turned down our road. When I pulled in and parked, Sadie was walking out with her purse over her shoulder.

"The kids are asleep," she mumbled as she unlocked her Rover.

I walked over to her. "Where are you going?"

"To the studio." She glared at me, opened her door, got in, and drove off.

I RUBBED MY head as I looked at my computer screen.

"Uncle Dane, are you okay?"

I smiled at Millie. "Just a little headache." I shut my laptop. "Let's go see Sadie."

We headed out to my truck, got in, and headed to the studio. I couldn't concentrate on a damn thing all day knowing she was mad at me. What she was mad about was in question, but the fact she was weighed on me.

When I got to the studio, I left Millie with Jason and found Sadie in the middle of a room dancing. She had no idea I was there, she was lost in the song "Rise Up" by Andra Day. I loved seeing her dance. I leaned against the door-frame and watched her.

My God, she's beautiful.

When the song came to an end, she stopped dancing. She looked in the large mirrors and saw my reflection.

"You're amazing."

She turned to face me.

"I've always loved watching you dance." I looked down at my boots. "My favorite was when you did the Nutcracker two years ago." I moved my focus back to her eyes.

Her expression softened a little. "You came?" She sat down on the floor and started stretching.

"I came to every winter performance for the past four years."

She moved both legs in front of her and pointed her toes. She bent all the way down to touch them. Her nose rested on her knees. When she sat up she looked at me with a raised brow.

"Is that supposed to make me not mad at you anymore?"

"No." I walked over to her and sat down next to her.

She smiled a little. "Oh, well it was working." She moved until she was in my lap and her legs were wrapped around my waist. She put her forehead to mine.

I wrapped my arms around her. "I love you, Daisy."

She kissed me. "You really came?" she whispered.

"Yes. I needed to see you. To know that you were doing okay."

"Why didn't you come find me when you came to New York?"

"I had been turned down by you and you ran away to New York. I...I wasn't strong enough to see you turn away from me again."

"Now that explains the random daisies I'd find on my windshield after those performances. I always thought it was strange seeing them in the dead of winter."

My face heated up. "I couldn't come see you and not bring you daisies."

She kissed me. "I decided I'm not mad at you anymore." She bit my bottom lip playfully.

"Oh, you're not?" I smiled and rubbed my nose against hers gently.

She shook her head and tilted it slightly as she looked at me. "Do me a favor, though. Don't ever step in front of me when I'm handling my shit again."

"I'll do my best."

She kissed me again. "I'm exhausted. We should go get Tate and go home. I'll cook something easy and then we can just be lazy."

She moved out of my lap and stood. She held her hand out to me. I took her hand and stood. "That sounds like a great plan. My head is hurting. It's not there yet. I took some Advil. Hopefully, I can get ahead of it and not have to have a shot."

She slipped on her shoes. "Let's hurry home then."

"Let's see if we can tear Millie away from dancing. Have you talked to her yet?"

She shook her head. "Not yet. I want to with you."

She grabbed her cellphone and purse and we headed to go find Millie.

Chapter Thirty-seven

SADIE

A fter dinner and getting the kids to bed, Dane took a shower and laid down. His headache only got worse. With no sleep, being punched in the jaw by Zach, and no glasses it was a recipe for a relapse of a migraine.

I didn't want to have to call Hailey, but that's who had his shots.

I put aside my pride and dialed her number.

I was smart and called from Dane's phone because there was no way she'd answer from my number.

"Hey, Dane," she said cheerfully.

"It's Sadie."

Silence.

"Hailey, I need one of Dane's shots and for you to come show me how to give it to him." I clenched my jaw. *"Please."* Who knew a single word could be so damn hard to say?

I looked over at Dane and saw him groan as he rolled to his side.

"I'll be over as soon as I get Joshua in bed."

I almost said thank you, but that would be pushing it. I hung up and laid down next to Dane. I started gently playing with his hair.

"Kill me now," he mumbled.

"Not gonna happen," I whispered. I hated seeing him like this. I wanted to take it all away from him. "Hailey will be here soon, baby."

"Where are the kids?" His voice was laced with pain and his eyes were shut tight.

"Sleeping. We read one of Millie's books until they dozed off." I kept running my fingers through his hair. "You're not going to work tomorrow."

"Agreed. I told Tate Chase could come over this weekend and we could invite some friends from back home over. I can't do that if I'm stuck in bed."

"Not to mention my friends and moving truck are coming Sunday."

I kissed his forehead.

"I changed my mind. I'm staying in bed all weekend." He opened his eyes for a second to give me a small smile but it didn't last long. His eyes closed tight again.

I heard the front door open and sat up. "That must be Hales or the dogs would be barking."

I got out of bed and met her in the living room.

I motioned for her to follow me.

We went in the bedroom and I saw how bothered she was that Dane was in pain. It was the first time since being back that I felt respect for her. She cared so damn much.

She sat on the bed next to Dane and looked at me.

"Come here. You're gonna do it."

"I hate needles and blood. What if I puke?"

She rolled her eyes. "Get over it."

My mouth was dry and just the thought of this made my stomach churn.

I walked over and watched her get the shot ready while she explained step by step what she was doing.

She moved the cover back so she could wipe Dane's arm off with an alcohol pad.

She handed me the shot. "Just squeeze his muscle like this and stick it in."

She stood but stayed close as I did what she said. I shocked myself when I was done and didn't get sick.

I kissed the spot where I gave it to him. "How bad was it?" I asked him quietly.

"Didn't even pinch."

Hailey took the used needle away from me and went into Dane's bathroom to throw it away.

Dane grabbed my hand as Hales came back into the room.

"He'll be out soon and probably sleep for twelve hours straight."

"I'll let Jason know I'm taking the day off tomorrow then."

I covered him back up and left the room with Hailey.

"Zach's going to go get him a new pair of glasses tomorrow."

"He doesn't have to. I can go pick them up if I need to."

I went into the kitchen and started cleaning up from dinner. I was shocked she didn't leave and followed me in.

Does she have a death wish?

She pulled out some other shots. "You should be the one in charge of these now." She held them out for me.

I set down the wash rag and took them. "Where should I keep them?"

"Somewhere the kids can't get into them. I don't think we have to worry about Dane anymore but it's better to be on the safe side."

I went to the medicine cabinet and put them in the box he kept meds in.

I gave her my best fake smile when I realized she still wasn't leaving .

She rubbed her stomach and played with a piece of lint on her shirt. "He's my best friend, Sadie. And you used to be too. You didn't just hurt Dane when you left."

"I've tried to say sorry, but you haven't given me a chance."

"I know. It's just hard. I'm watching him fall head over heels for you all over again, and I have this fear that it's going to end the same way except this time you'll not just leave him, you'll take Tate, too."

That was like a slap in the face. "Hailey, do you honestly think I'd leave my son and the man I love? I'm getting a second chance to make things right. I have no intentions of fucking that up."

Hailey looked at me and tears filled her eyes. "You left us without even saying bye." Her bottom lip started trembling.

My shoulders sagged. "I know. And I was wrong for that. But if I would've said bye I would have never left. But I had to leave, and I know you don't understand that, but I did. While I hate that I did, I love that I did all at the same time. I found myself and now I can be who I need to be for Dane."

We both turned when we heard a horrible sound coming from Dane's room.

Hailey made a face. "Sounds like the shot didn't kick in in time. He throws up when they get too bad."

"I'll go check on him." I adjusted Dane's t-shirt I was wearing. "Can we just call a truce? I miss you, Hales."

He smiled and wiped her eyes. "Yeah. We can call a truce. Just remember, I'm hormonal and mean to everyone."

I laughed and hugged her. "I love him, Hailey. I never stopped. It just took my stupid self a while to figure out what was important." I moved back from her. "I give you permission to kick my ass if I hurt him again."

She laughed. "And I will. Now, go take care of Dane."

I hugged her one more time before heading back to Dane's room.

Chapter Thirty-eight

DANE

I rolled over and buried my face against Sadie's neck. I had no desire to get out of the bed, but the loud noises from upstairs told me all the kids and puppies were awake. My headache had lasted for two days, and I finally woke up this morning without one, but I didn't want to get out of bed.

"I think the kids are awake," I groaned. We had Chase over and two of Tate's friends from back home. Millie had decided to stay with Hales and Zach, and to Zach's annoyance, I let her take Sassy with her.

Sadie stretched and then snuggled against me again. "I hear that. But as long as the house isn't burning down, there's no rush for us to get up just yet." He smiled at me. "Why am I moving into my house again? I've been staying the night for several nights now. I'm spoiled."

"You don't have to move out, but I know you will." I made a face. "You're into that whole independent thing."

She laughed. "Well, you know, I have to make sure I'm being an upstanding citizen. Can't go to hell for living and sleeping with a man out of wedlock." She laughed when I made a face. "Seriously, though, Tate is still weird about me being here like this right now."

I kissed her head and got out of bed when I heard knocking at the door. "I'm guessing they want food. And after being in bed the past few days, I need out of it."

She stuck her lip out. "All right. Let's go." She sat up in a hurry. "Shit! Today is Sunday! I forgot the moving truck and my friends are coming!"

I stopped putting my shirt on and got back into bed. I covered my head up with a blanket. "I changed my mind. My migraine's back."

There was a knock at the door again. "Can we make pancakes?" Tate asked.

"Yes, but that means you clean up the mess, too," Sadie said loud enough for them to hear. She then pulled the covers off me, laughing. "I don't think so."

"I guess if I must, but you owe me." I smiled and kissed her before getting out of bed, again. I ran a hand through my hair and down my beard that was finally covering my scar. "At least they won't be able to stare oddly at my scar this time."

She shrugged and started getting dressed. "Who cares if they do? It's a part of who you are and that's nothing to be embarrassed about."

I smiled at her and kissed her forehead before leaving the room. I came into the kitchen and smiled at the kids. "Morning, boys. Did you guys let the puppies outside?"

"Yes, sir. They're outside playing in the backyard," Chase said with a smile. I couldn't help but laugh as I saw he had flour in his hair. "You're already a mess." I walked out of the kitchen and went to the front door when I heard a knock. I opened it and laughed when Zach handed me Sassy on her leash.

"What's going on, bro?"

"I hate dogs," he said in a growl. "I only let it stay last night because of my niece, but she's gone shopping with Hales and Quinn."

Sassy licked my face and barked as the twins went running past us.

"Boys, you weren't supposed to leave the car!" Zach yelled after them.

I smiled at my brother. "Why don't you guys stay and have breakfast?"

"You making it?" he asked with a raised eyebrow.

"No, Tate and the boys are, and I'm sure they could use help from you. I'll go get Joshua out of the car."

Zach went past me with a smile, and I knew this was the plan all along. I laughed and went to his truck. I turned it off and got Joshua out of the back.

"Dwanie."

I sighed. "I can't believe your mom got you calling me that." I slung him over my shoulder, making him giggle, as I held onto Sassy's leash with my other hand. I was almost to the door when a nice cherry-red Expedition pulled up with a moving truck behind it. "Dammit, they're early."

"Damn-nit, damn-nit," Joshua said with a giggle.

"Don't repeat that." I walked inside and put Joshua down and let Sassy off her leash. They both headed toward the kitchen where all the racket was coming from. "Sadie!" I yelled out so she could hear me from wherever she was in the house.

She came down the hall into the kitchen pulling her hair into a pony-tail. "Hey."

"Your friends are here." I made a face and kissed her cheek. "I guess we should go out and meet them. I brought Joshua and Sassy in instead of greeting them."

She suddenly seemed nervous as she chewed on her fingernails. She went to the window and peeked out. "He really came," she whispered.

I walked over and looked outside. "Who really came?" I raised an eyebrow when I saw that everyone was dressed up. "Do they expect to be able to help us unload in suits?"

"I hired movers. I imagine they won't be doing any helping."

I saw Cooper and then a copycat of him get out of the expedition and look at my house. If I didn't know better, I would have thought Ryan Gosling had a twin and just showed up at my house. Sadie mentioned Cooper and Ethan were always mistaken as them and signed a lot of autographs to shit with people. They looked like rich pansy asses, if you asked me.

"Ah, that must be your ex, Ethan," Dane growled more than spoke.

Sadie moved away from the window. "Yeah." She kissed me. "Behave." It was cute how she thought she could ask that with how she acted around my exes.

I grinned. "I will behave as much as you did when meeting Dana."

"Again, she was checking out your ass."

"So, that means, if he checks you out, I get to attack him, right?" I smiled evilly. "This may be a great day after all."

She groaned and walked out of the house.

I chuckled to myself and followed her. I nodded toward Alice. "The dogs are locked up in the backyard. As long as you don't go there, you won't be attacked."

She laughed and to my shock, hugged me. "It's nice to see you again, Dane."

Cooper came over and shook my hand while Ethan pulled my girl into a hug.

"It's nice to see you both as well. Hopefully, this time we can all do a little better at getting to know one another." *Dane, be good. Don't go over there and punch him in the face. Be good. Be good.*

I walked over to them, and once he let go of *my girlfriend,* I wrapped an arm around her waist.

Sadie's body was tense. Ethan held his hand out to me. "You must be my competition," he said with a teasing smile. "Kidding. I'm Ethan, Cooper's twin and one of Sadie's best friends."

I shook his hand. "Dane."

He let go and took off his suit jacket and smiled at Sadie. "We didn't have time to change. We had a meeting with my dad before our flight." He glanced over his shoulder at the Expedition and then at Sadie. "We have the rental so we won't need a ride back to the airport."

Sadie nodded. "How long are the three of you staying? I know you said yesterday you weren't sure." she asked Alice.

"We haven't really decided. Ethan and Cooper got our hotel room for the whole week just in case. We all took vacation time to come here and hang out as long as we could with you."

Sadie gaped at Ethan. "You are not staying a week."

Alice laughed. "I'm kidding, Sadie. We are here for two days."

Ethan chuckled and nodded toward the truck. "The movers need your signature, Sades."

I walked over to the moving truck as Sadie signed the paper. "Hey, Daisy-Love, why don't you call Trevor and Jason and get them to come help."

"I will in a little while. It's still early, and I know they like to sleep in." She kissed me.

Zach walked over with a plate of pancakes and Joshua walking beside him. He took a bite as he stared at Sadie's friends. "Why the hell are they wearing suits and is that girl in a dress?"

Sadie laughed. "Because I'm sure they don't plan on lifting a finger. But seriously, they had a meeting before flying here."

"Ah." Zach took a bite of his food and gave me a humorous grin. I know he was thinking the same thing I was. "I'm gonna go back in with the kids and then I'll be out to help once everyone's done eating."

I climbed into the back of the truck after the movers opened it and grabbed a large box labeled kitchen. I looked at Zach. "Bro, stop eating and start helping."

Zach rolled his eyes. "I guess." He shoved the last bit of pancakes in his mouth and set the plate on the Expedition before taking the box I handed down. I picked up another box and jumped down. Between us and the moving crew, it wouldn't take too long to unload this truck. I walked into the house and smiled when I saw Sadie showing Alice, Cooper, and Ethan around. "Daisy-Love, I'm going to just start putting boxes down here if that's okay."

She nodded and smiled. "Thank you."

Ethan scoffed. "Dude, she paid people do to this. Why are you helping them?"

Zach set a box down. "Because he's not lazy or afraid of hard work."

"Zach, be nice." I looked down and smiled as Joshua waddled after his father as I picked up another box.

Ethan smiled at me. "Sadie tells me you had this place built for her."

I nodded. "Yes, I did. I designed based on Daisy's Pinterest page."

"Daisy?" Ethan snickered at Sadie and then at me. "Why the pet name?"

"We met for the first time in a field of daisies, and it's her favorite flower. She's been my Daisy since kindergarten."

Sadie smiled at me.

"Funny we never heard about you until recently."

"Ethan," Sadie growled.

"What? It's just funny that you've known this guy since you were a kid and you never said anything."

Alice saw the look on my face and elbowed Cooper for help.

Cooper smiled. "But now we know and we're happy for Sadie." He grabbed his brother's shoulder and gave him a little shove until they went outside.

I stiffened. "I'm going to grab more boxes." I kissed the top of Sadie's head, reminding myself to stay calm.

She cupped my face in her hands. "Remember, I love you, and Ethan is just trying to stir the pot. I'll talk to him and tell him to chill out." She kissed me. "Thank you for not breaking his face."

"Yet is the key word," I mumbled.

She sighed. "I know." She kissed me again. "Alice and I are gonna start unpacking."

I nodded and headed back to the truck.

Chapter Thirty-nine

SADIE

I picked at a piece of wood at the dinner table in my new house. All the kids were still over at Dane's place, so he thought it'd be best just for me to spend time alone with Ethan, Cooper, and Alice tonight. I wanted him here, but he was right. There were things that needed to be discussed without kids present.

I had just finished telling Ethan everything and was waiting for him to process it all.

"Are you kidding me, Sades?" Ethan took a drink of his high-dollar wine. "To me it sounds like this Dane guy and his family are calling all the shots. Have they given you any say at all?"

My mouth opened to speak but he cut me off.

"You said yourself, tell me if I'm wrong," he said looking at his brother and Alice then at me again, "that you told Dane about your son, then Dane's friend who is a lawyer got rights for Dane, Dane told you he would build you a house to keep you at arm's length, and you're just going along with it. This isn't the Sadie I know. The Sadie I know and adore would stand her ground. You are Tate's mother. You have as much say, if not more, than anyone else.

Yes, you did choose to give him up when you were a minor. A minor, Sadie. Not an adult who was capable of making decisions herself. I just can't wrap my head around you giving up being a dance instructor at Juilliard, the job you have been working toward since you stepped foot on campus. If Dane loved you so much, why isn't he packing his shit and moving there?"

"Because his family is here. He is Millie's legal guardian, and there is no way she could leave Stockbridge. I already explained this to you earlier."

He scoffed. "O-kay, so Dane is putting his niece, who has family here that is capable of taking care of her, over you? There's no compromise with him, don't you see that? You are just going along with everything. What happens when you wake up one day and realize all you let go because you let some redneck punk call all the shots?"

Juno was lying by my feet, and she growled at him before placing her head on my shoes.

I narrowed my eyes at him. "Yes, he's putting his niece before me, and I'd have it no other way! Dreams change, Ethan. And I love how you talk like you're some saint that I'd actually want to come back to in New York!"

"Okay, breathe, you two," Cooper said calmly.

"Redneck punk? Did you just insult my little brother?" We all looked up and saw Zach standing in the doorway. He looked at me. "Joshua left his blanket here."

I had it folded on the table. I picked it up and stood. "I need some air." I walked out with Zach and handed him the blanket. Tears were falling, and I was so pissed I was crying. I hated letting Ethan get to me like this.

"Don't tell Dane he said that. He doesn't need any more stress."

He wiped at my tears. "I can go kick his ass."

I laughed a little. "No. I'll handle it."

"I don't mind."

"Stop."

I walked to his truck and said hi to all my boys.

He chuckled. "I'm going to head home. Joshua won't go to sleep until he has his blanket."

"Mine!" Joshua squealed when he saw me. For some reason, Joshua had taken a liking to me and dubbed me with the name "mine".

"Goodnight, boys." I blew them all a kiss and shut the door. I waved at Zach after he got in and backed out.

I froze when I heard Ethan say my name from the door. When I turned, he walked over to me.

"Dammit, Sadie, I'm sorry. You know I pop off shit without thinking."

I wiped my eyes. "You have no right to talk about someone you don't know. If you knew Dane, you wouldn't have said that."

He reached out to wipe my tears, but I slapped his hand away.

"Don't touch me."

Anger and hurt flashed in his eyes. "Why are you always pushing me away?" he asked in a harsh tone.

"Because you have this hope that we'll be something and we never will. I don't know how to make that clear. I'd love to be friends with you, but you can't accept it."

He rubbed the back of his neck. His lips formed a hard line, and I knew he was losing his patience with me.

"You shouldn't have come here," I said quietly.

I heard the front door of Dane's house open. I looked toward it and saw him watching me closely. "Tate wanted to say goodnight."

"She'll be there in a second," Ethan grabbed my arm to stop me from walking.

Dane took a step toward us. "Let. Her. Go." His jaw was clenched.

Ethan hesitated but finally let go.

Smart move.

"Leave," I demanded.

"No, we have things to discuss."

"No, we don't. It's clear you don't and never will accept that this is my life now. There's no point in trying to be friends. You've made that clear." I walked off.

"Whatever, go run off to your little bitch ass boyfriend and play house! Fuckin' bitch."

Oh fuck!

Dane had him by the throat so quickly, I was shocked he could move that fast. He slammed him against my Rover.

"What did you call my Daisy?"

Cooper and Alice rushed out.

"Dane, let him go," Cooper pleaded.

I didn't care if he beat his ass. I was so pissed I was ready to pop some popcorn and watch.

"Not until he apologizes to Daisy."

"You should be the one apologizing to her," Ethan sneered. "Did you know she was given an instructor position at Juilliard? Head instructor. You didn't see the blood sweat and tears she put in to get it. But I saw it. I was there to doctor her blistered feet, motivate her and cheer her on, wipe her tears…"

Dane squeezed his throat a little tighter. "Apologize," he said in a growl.

"I'm sorry for calling her a bitch," Ethan said with a bit of a struggle. "I'm sorry, Sadie. You know I didn't mean it."

Dane let go of his throat but shoved him into the Rover before turning to me. "Are you okay, Daisy-Love?"

Was I okay? I wasn't really sure. I wasn't the girl that was supposed to have two guys fighting over her. It didn't feel as good as it looked in the movies. It sucked. I let out the breath I was holding and nodded.

I looked at Cooper. "Get him out of here and back to New York."

"Sadie—"

I cut my eyes at Ethan. "You ruined your welcome."

I hugged Cooper and Alice and walked toward Dane's house. When I made it to the porch, I stopped to wait for Dane.

"I just need a second to breathe before I go see Tate."

"I probably should apologize for losing my temper."

I sat on the swing. "Don't apologize." I noticed my hands were shaking.

He sat down next to me and covered my hands with one of his large ones.

I watched the Expedition leave. I hated my time was cut short with Alice and Cooper.

"I don't care about the job at Juilliard. It means nothing to me. Ethan didn't know that I threw myself into dance and getting that job to busy my mind from the constant battle it was in."

"I know dancing is important to you, Sadie. And I know the small country town life wasn't what you wanted."

"It wasn't when I was young. But it is now. I'm truly so happy here."

I turned toward the door when I heard it open. Tate was standing there with a sleepy smile. I patted the spot between me and Dane on the swing. Tate sat down and I played with his hair. My heart swelled when he laid his head on my shoulder. I looked at Dane and smiled.

"Are the boys already asleep?" Dane asked.

"No. They're talking about how cool my dad is. We saw you pin that guy to the Rover."

I laughed. "Your dad is the coolest."

Dane groaned. "Great. But he made Sadie cry and that isn't okay."

Tate laughed. "Can you teach me how to do that?"

"I don't know. Believe it or not I was holding him in a way that wouldn't cause him any damage. It was more to scare him than to hurt him. I don't want you thinking you can solve your problems like that. If I teach you self-defense, it will be only to protect yourself."

Tate nodded. "Okay."

I stood and held my hand out to Tate. "Come on. I'll walk you in."

Dane kissed Tate's head. "I'll be in in a bit."

I nodded and walked Tate inside.

Chapter Forty

DANE

I turned the desk light on as the room darkened. Tonight was my late night at work, and I wished I had gone home instead. I erased an area of the plans and frowned. I used my ruler and started measuring and drawing again. If Miller wanted to change his plans one more time I swear I was going to quit. This was fuckin' ridiculous. I leaned back in my chair as Trevor came into my office. He took the chair on the other side of my desk.

"How are the books looking?"

"Great. We're up from last year, but that's not why I'm in here."

"Are you here about Harvey?"

He nodded. "I'd like to send some crews down after the storm ends. I'm sure there is going to be a need for building crews to help clean up and rebuild. The storm is supposed to hit hard."

"I agree, but one of us will have to go with them. We can't just send our men down there alone."

"I know. I'm going to go."

I cocked an eyebrow at him. "Don't you usually send me down to do things like that?" I teased.

He laughed. "Yeah, normally, but Jason has family down there so he's going to be going as well. Besides, the kids are in school and Sadie would probably go crazy if you left her here."

"Probably. Let me know if you need me to go with you guys."

"I will. You realize that means you'll have to do the business meetings while I'm gone."

I made a face. "I guess that means I need to get my suit to the cleaners."

Trevor burst out laughing. "Hell no! Buy a new suit. Your other one is in scary bad shape."

"I hate shopping, but you're right." I groaned. "Sadie is going to freak when she realizes I will be up here alone all day with Dana."

"Maybe she won't notice. She's going to be busy running the dance studio while Jason is gone. If she accepts. If she doesn't, we'll have to hire someone to come in and run it. We'd both rather have Sadie do it."

"I'm sure she will. She loves working there." I rolled up the plans. "I'm going to take these home. I'm tired of being up here, and I want to see Sadie and the kids before they have to go to bed."

"How's Sadie liking her new place?"

"She likes it."

Trevor stood and stretched. "Why are you pouting?"

"I miss her being in my bed, but I understand why she wants her own place."

"I'm glad you do because I don't get it. If you two are all in this time, I don't see why you don't just get married and start your lives."

I put my hand in my pocket where I had the ring I had bought for Sadie so many years ago. "I'm scared shitless to ask."

"Why?" he asked as we walked out of my office and I locked it.

"I guess I'm scared of being told no again." I shrugged. "Plus, I won't ask her until Tate and Millie are okay with it. I'm not ready to have that conversation with them yet. Some days Tate is okay, but some days he isn't."

Trevor nodded. "I understand that." He went into his office and grabbed his stuff. After he came out, we locked up and headed out to the parking lot.

"So, I'm not being stupid?" I asked.

"Nah. I understand the whole not moving in thing when it comes to Tate. Giving it time won't kill anyone." He smiled. "I'm just happy to see you and Sadie together again. I'll see you later." He got into his car.

I got into my truck and pulled out onto the street. I pushed in Sadie's number and called her.

"Hey, baby. You headed home?"

"Yeah. I decided to finish up the work at home. I want to be able to tell the kids goodnight. I'm not for sure the Miller job is worth all this mess."

"The kids just got finished with their showers and are in pj's, watching a movie. They'll be excited you're coming home before they fall asleep."

"How was your day, Daisy?" I asked, smiling. *Damn, I love my family.* The feeling of going home to Sadie and the kids was the best feeling in the entire world.

"It was good. Had an interesting conversation with Jason. Apparently, him and Trev are going down to Texas to help with rebuilding after the hurricane hits. He said you knew, and usually you went. Anyway, he asked me to run the studio until he got back. Of course, I agreed."

"Yeah, the company usually helps with disaster areas."

"You're amazing, Dane. Now hurry home so I can see you."

"I should be home in about fifteen minutes. I'll see ya soon."

"Love you."

"Love you, too." I hung up and continued to drive toward home.

I looked in my rearview mirror as some asshole flashed their brights at me. I ignored it until the fourth time they did it. I pulled over to the side of the road and grabbed my gun from under my seat. I quickly loaded it. I was about to take the safety off when I saw Ethan in my side mirror. I opened my door and got out.

"Are you shittin' me? What do—" He swung and hit me in the jaw.

"You might have Sadie fooled, but you don't me!" He swung at me again.

I dodged his swing and grabbed his arm, twisting it until I had him pinned with his face against my truck.

"I really want to kick your ass, but that would upset Cooper and Alice which would upset Sadie. And Sadie knows who I am. You're the asshat who doesn't know a damn thing about me. You've judged me on appearances alone thinking I can't give Sadie everything you can."

"You can't. The only reason she's here is because you are holding her kid over her head!"

He let out a deep groan when I held him tighter.

"One, my son isn't a bargaining tool. And two, you don't know the real Sadie. I love her with everything I am."

"Then how can you take her away from Juilliard?"

"I didn't. She chose to stay. If Sadie didn't want to give up Juilliard, I would find a way to make it work the best I could."

Somehow, he got out of my hold and punched me in the jaw again.

I knew my control was slipping. "Ethan, leave now. I'm not someone to fuck with," I practically growled as I dodged another blow.

He kneed me in the gut.

The wind was knocked out of my lungs for a moment, and he used it to punch me in the face. I snapped. Before I could process what I was doing, I had uppercut the shit out of him, knocking him to the ground.

I pinned him with a knee to his chest and grabbed a handful of his shirt to hit him again, but I stopped. He was dazed, and if I hit him again, I could do real damage.

"Don't fuck with a Marine, jackass. Get in your damn car and go back to the hotel." I stood and walked back to my truck then I got in and headed home.

I picked up my phone and saw I had a missed call from Sadie. I called her back.

"Where are you?" she asked worriedly.

I wiped at the blood from a cut on my forehead. I guess the little shit had a ring on. "I need you to meet me outside with a wet rag and don't let the kids come out with you."

"What happened?"

"Ethan happened. You may want to call Cooper to get him to go check on him. He was out of it when I left him lying on the shoulder of the road."

Silence.

"Daisy?"

"I should've told you he didn't leave Stockbridge yet. He came to see me at the studio today. But he said he was getting ready to board a plane. I thought he was leaving."

"I'm only about five minutes away, Daisy. And this wasn't your fault. He was the one being an asshat. Call Cooper and let him know about his brother."

"I will."

"I'll be pulling in soon. I love you." I hung up and turned down my road.

Chapter Forty-one

SADIE

I paced the front porch while I waited for Dane to pull up. I was going to kill Ethan.

First, he showed up and talked to me at the studio when I made it clear he needed to just leave, and then he started a fight with Dane.

When I saw the headlights of Dane's truck coming down the driveway, I stopped pacing and headed out to meet him.

I had ice and a cool washcloth.

He parked, shut off his truck, and got out. He leaned against his truck and gave me a small smile or tried.

I stood on my tiptoes to wipe the blood from his forehead.

I handed him the ice and he put it to his jaw.

"I'm gonna kill him."

"I almost lost control on his ass. He's lucky I snapped out of it. I'm still concerned I broke his jaw."

"I don't care about his jaw. Are you okay?"

"Sore, but I'll live." I didn't realize I was rubbing my gut until Sadie lifted my shirt some.

"I'm fine. I just hate that the kids are going to see me like this."

"The kids are already asleep. They fell asleep waiting on you to get here."

He sighed sadly. "I hate working late."

"It's part of being CEO of a successful company." I moved the washcloth off his head. "Come in and take some Advil before you get another migraine."

He wrapped an arm around my waist as we went inside. He sat down on the couch and laid his head back.

I lifted his shirt to get a better look. I turned on the lamp next to the couch.

"It's not too bad." I ran my fingers through his hair. "I told Cooper to go check on Ethan."

"Good. And my stomach is fine. He only kneed me there once. My head is what he hit three times before I snapped." He grabbed my hand and kissed the back of it. "Can you get me the Advil and something to drink, please?"

I nodded, kissed him, and went into the kitchen. I got the meds and a glass of water. When I walked into the living room, I froze when I saw Alice. I never even heard a car pull up or the front door open.

"Ethan is at the ER. He's fine, but Cooper wanted to be sure." Alice looked apologetically at Dane. "I'm so sorry. We tried to stop him from leaving the hotel. We thought it'd be a good idea to take him down to the bar and let him calm down, but it just made things worse."

I gave Dane the Advil and water. He swallowed the pills and downed about half of the glass of water before turning to Alice.

"He's lucky I was able to get control, Alice. I could have done some serious damage to him."

She nodded and sat down in the recliner. She looked at me. "I told him not to go to the studio, either. He's just confused and hurting. I'm not taking sides, I'm just saying."

I sat beside Dane. "I know, but you know how he is, Alice. He doesn't listen to me if I'm saying something he doesn't want to hear. He disregards it and pushes me until I lose my cool. And now he messed with Dane."

Dane grabbed my hand in his. He gave it a small squeeze. "I'm going to go kiss the kids' heads. I'll be right back." He stood slowly, and it hurt my heart when I saw him wince.

"You guys were supposed to leave, Alice."

"We wanted to, but Ethan already paid for our flight back and to change it would've cost more."

I rolled my eyes. "He has the money."

"And he's a tightwad." She chuckled.

I ran my fingers through my hair and sighed. "I know I hurt him. I know I hurt you and Cooper by not being fully honest about who I am. Living a double life was hard. I didn't mean to hurt anyone, that wasn't my intentions."

It wasn't long before Dane was coming back down the stairs.

I smiled at him when he sat down. "Were they still sleeping?"

"Sadly, yes. I almost woke them back up, but I was good. Sassy and Boy about licked me to death before laying back down next to Millie and Tate, though."

I laughed and snuggled next to him. I looked at Alice. "You guys fly out tomorrow?"

She nodded. "Yeah. We were supposed to fly out today, but then Ethan acted like a damn fool after he came and talked to you. We missed the flight, which pissed him off more. Then he went to find Dane. Cooper was trying to get another rental to go find him since Ethan took off with the one we had."

I sighed. "So, he had to pay more anyway for a flight then."

Juno-Bear and Scout came over to us on the couch and put their paws up to try and climb up. They were already huge but so uncoordinated that they were having trouble. They both started whining at us.

"Yeah, he did. It's his own stupid fault. Anyway, I just wanted to stop by while I was out. I better go back to the ER and see if they are ready to leave yet." She stood and came over to the couch. She bent down to hug me. She then hugged Dane. "I'm happy to know she's happy here. One day, we'll get to visit and it not be drama filled. I swear Cooper and I are awesome people."

"You took care of my Daisy while she was in New York so you already have my devotion. And I was impressed with both of you when I saw you two dance."

She stood up straight and eyes widened. "What? When?"

"The past four years I've come to every winter performance." He shrugged. "I would have come to the others, but I was either overseas or on duty."

Alice gave me a huge smile. "Keep him."

I laughed and nodded. "Trust me, I am this time."

She told us bye and left the house.

I turned so I was facing Dane and kissed him. "Why don't you go get comfortable? We can go be lazy. I'll stay here tonight to keep an eye on you." I touched his jean pocket when I saw something sticking out. "What's that?" Before I could reach in to see what it was, he grabbed my hand to stop me.

I raised a brow. "Dane? What is it?"

"It's nothing," he said way too quickly. "I'll go get in some pj's." He kissed me and stood. I looked up at his face.

"Dane Shaw." I stood and reached for his pocket but he moved.

"Sadie, it's nothing for you to see. It's nothing bad, I promise."

I reached for his pocket again and laughed when he dodged me "I will tackle you if you don't show me."

"Daisy, be good. It's not for you to see."

I stuck out my bottom lip.

"That's not going to work this time." He hurried toward his room.

I chased after him. When I made it to his room and grabbed his jeans as soon as they hit the floor. I took off toward the bathroom, but before I could lock myself in, he grabbed me around my waist from behind. He tickled me until I dropped them.

He picked up the jeans and held onto them. "Be good." He walked over and put the jeans in the hamper. I couldn't see if he grabbed whatever it was out of his pocket or not.

"Fine if I can't see what you're hiding then you can't see any of this," I said, motioning to my breasts. I laughed when he frowned a little. I left the bathroom and went into his room. I dug around in his drawer to find a t-shirt.

"That's so unfair." He laid down in only his boxers and absentmindedly rubbed his jaw. "You like to shop, right?"

I found a shirt. "Mmm-hmm." I kept my back to him and slipped off my shirt and bra and put on his t-shirt. I slipped off my jeans and then picked up my clothes and put them in a pile next to the dresser.

"I need a suit for when Trevor and Jason go to Houston. I'll have to handle all the business meetings."

I climbed into bed with him. I traced the bullet scars on his chest. "When do you want to go?"

"I guess sometime this upcoming weekend. If you don't mind." He put his arm under his pillow behind his head and that's when I knew where whatever it was that had been in his pocket was under there.

I moved until I was sitting on top of him. I quickly slid my hand under the pillow and grabbed his hand. "Open it," I growled, making him laugh. He knew I wasn't strong enough to pry his hand open, but dammit, I'd try.

He frowned at me but released his grip and opened his hand. I reached into his hand and froze when I felt a ring. I let go of it and let it fall back into his palm.

"It's a ring," I said quietly, keeping my eyes on his. "Is it *the* ring?"

"Yes."

"Why were you keeping it in your pocket?"

"I took it to get it cleaned. And to talk to Trevor about it." He pulled his hand out from under his pillow and placed both of his on my thighs.

"And what did you say to Trevor?" I was cheesing.

He sighed dramatically. "Do you want the full truth?"

I nodded.

"I told him I wanted to ask you to marry me again, but I was scared shitless that you'd tell me no all over again. I, also, told him that before I would ever ask you I would have a talk with Millie and Tate first."

"Then I suggest you go have that talk with Millie and Tate as soon as possible."

He smiled at me. "Oh really?"

I leaned down and kissed him. "Yup."

He moved his hand up and under my shirt. "So, since I let you see what was in my pocket do I get to see now?"

"Only if you promise me something."

"And what's that?"

"You'll talk to Millie and Tate tomorrow. Because I so badly want to say yes."

"I promise. I'll talk to them as soon as I can tomorrow."

I squealed and kissed him. I laughed when he moved us until I was on my back and he was hovering over me.

"Oh, and one more thing," I said with a mischievous grin. He cocked an eyebrow at me and waited. "There better be daisies when you ask me."

He burst out laughing. "Have I ever forgotten to give you daisies when it was something important?"

I smiled. "Not once."

Chapter Forty-two

DANE

I walked into the office to check out Tate early. I needed to have a talk with my kiddos about Sadie. I was a nervous wreck. I had sent Sadie three vases of daisies to the studio and filled her little house with them for when she came home.

Tiffany smiled and motioned toward my glasses. "Nice. You here to check out that handsome boy of yours?"

"Yes, I am." I smiled a little and signed Tate out.

I stepped into the hall and leaned against the wall as I waited for him. When I saw him, I pushed off the wall and smiled.

"Hey, kiddo."

He grinned. "Hey, Dad. Everything okay?"

"Yep! I just need to have some time to talk to you and Millie, plus, I've missed seeing my kiddos this week." I hugged him. "Come on, mini-me. Millie has left it up to you where we go. She's just happy to get time with her guys." I chuckled. "At least, that's what she said."

"Where is she?"

"In the truck waiting on us. She's reading the fifth Harry Potter book and didn't want to put it down."

He took his backpack off before getting in the truck.

"Hey, Millie." He tugged on one of her curls.

She smiled at him as she looked up from the book. "Hey, Tate. How was school?"

"Good. I have some math homework I need help with later."

"Okie dokie." She smiled. "Where are we going?"

"It's up to you two." I glanced at them through the rearview mirror before heading out of the school parking lot. "It just needs to be somewhere we can talk."

"Park?" Tate asked.

"Sounds good." I smiled and turned toward the park. I turned on the music and we all sang along to Blake Shelton's "God Gave Me You" until I pulled into the parking area at the park. We got out and walked over to the picnic tables. I sat across from the kids.

"Okay. So…" I rubbed the back of my neck.

Millie cocked her head at me. "Are you nervous?"

"A little, yes."

"Why?" Tate asked.

I sighed and looked at them both. "Because it's hard for me to talk about certain things. Tate, Millie, I want to ask your permission to do something."

Tate stared at me and waited.

Millie looked at Tate before looking back at me.

"I would like to ask Sadie to marry me."

"Did you ask her dad?" Tate asked. "Aren't you supposed to ask the dad?"

I shook my head. "I'm asking the two people that mean the world to me, and at the moment, I'm not speaking to her parents."

Tate smiled a little. "Does this mean she'll be living with us?"

"Yes."

Tate leaned over and nudged Millie. "What do you think?"

"I think she makes Uncle Dane happy, and we both like her. Trust me, it could be worse. We could not like her. And if she marries him, you won't be scared she's going to decide to leave." She put her hand on his.

My Millie had come such a long way since Tate had come into our lives.

He blushed. He hadn't told me that he was afraid she'd leave.

He studied me for a moment before answering. "Okay. Ask her."

I covered their hands with my own. "It's okay to be scared, Tate. I'm scared too."

"She won't leave, though. She promised me."

"No, she won't."

"Did you get her a ring already?" Millie asked with a bright smile.

I pulled the box out of my jeans and placed it on the table in front of them. Millie opened it. "It's pretty."

"I was thinking that maybe you two wanted to pick out something for her as well. Something showing you're okay with her marrying me."

Tate was staring at the ring. "Can I take it out?"

"Sure."

I moved my hand off of his and Millie's. "Do you guys think I should pick out a different ring?"

He took it out and looked at it. A crooked grin spread across his face. "What if you get all of our names engraved in it? My adoptive dad did that for my adoptive mom."

I smiled. "That sounds like a great idea. Let's head to the jewelry store and see if they can get it done."

We all stood and headed back to my truck.

WE'D MADE IT home just as Sadie was getting out of her Rover. I saw the vases of daisies in her backseat. I couldn't wait until she saw all the ones that filled her house.

"Hey, Sadie," Millie said as she hurried over to her.

I walked over and kissed her.

She hugged me and couldn't stop smiling. She then hugged Millie.

"I see you got *some* of my flowers." I waited for her to focus on the fact I said *some*.

Tate came over to us and hugged her.

She kissed the top of his head. "Hey, Tater-bug. How was school?"

"Good." He bounced on his feet a little.

I grabbed two of the vases out of the backseat. "Tate, why don't you get the other one? Daisy-Love, can you go open your door for us?"

"Sure." She kissed my cheek and her and Millie headed to her house.

I winked at Tate, and we followed her. When she opened the front door, I waited for her to see all the many vases of flowers. I gently put the two vases down and Millie came back to stand next to me as Tate put his own vase down. I got down on one knee and waited for her to turn around. I pulled the ring box out of my pocket and opened it.

She turned and when she saw me on one knee, she lost it. She started crying but was smiling the whole time. She hurried over to me.

"I got your daisies and ring. Now, all I need is that yes."

Tate pulled out the box that held her necklace and opened it as Millie came to stand next to him.

"Yes!" She was a bawling-hot-mess of emotions.

I slipped the ring onto her finger, then stood and kissed her. I wiped her tears then moved behind her so the kids could give her their necklace.

"I love it!" she said, kneeling down when Tate motioned for her to. He moved her hair and Millie helped put it on.

She wrapped them both in a hug. "I love you both more than life itself."

"We love you, too," Millie said with a bright smile. "Can you move in with us now? I'm tired of being the only girl." She giggled.

Sadie laughed and nodded. "If it's okay with Tate."

Tate nodded. "I think it'll be okay, Mom."

Sadie froze. She looked at me and then at Tate.

I grinned. "It's probably for the best since I filled your house with flowers." I wrapped an arm around her and kissed the side of her head.

"He called me Mom," she whispered.

"I can hear you," Tate said with a chuckle. "And yeah, I did. It's time."

I watched Millie as she stared at her feet.

"What's wrong, Munchkin?"

She shrugged and forced a smile. "Nothing. Just...hungry."

Sadie walked over to her and knelt in front of her. "Wanna help me cook tonight?"

She nodded and Tate and I watched them walk off together. "Let's go let the dogs in." Maybe Sadie could get her to talk.

Chapter Forty-three

SADIE

After moving all the vases of daisies around so I could walk, Millie and I went to raid my kitchen for something to cook. Millie was sitting Indian-style on the bar watching me.

I held up a chocolate cake box. "We can have cake."

I smiled when she nodded. I set it in front of her.

I found a box of mac-n-cheese. "I know how much you love macaroni."

"It's my favorite. Dad used to cook it all the time for me."

She hopped off the island and grabbed a bowl out of the cabinet and started mixing the cake as I handed her the ingredients.

"While we're waiting for the boys to come back over, want to talk about whatever is bothering you?" I filled a pan with water and put it on the stove.

I stood near the sink, admiring the ring on my finger and smiled. *Finally, I'm marrying my best friend.*

She stirred the mix in the bowl. "Would...would it be okay to call you and Uncle Dane Mom and Dad? I know you're not but you're the closest thing I have. And Tate's like my brother more than my cousin, right?" She was so quiet when she spoke and she never once looked up from what she was doing.

I pulled my eyes from my hand and walked over to her, cupping her cheeks with my hands, I kissed her forehead.

"I'd be honored, Millie." I smiled down at her. "I know Dane would love it if you called him Dad, too. We love you so much."

A tear slipped down her cheek. "Really?" She smiled. "I love you guys, too."

I used my thumb to wipe her tears away.

I stuck my finger in the cake batter and licked it, making us both laugh when the boys came in.

"Mom, you gotta see the inside of your ring!" Tate said as he came over.

I held my left hand out and let him slide it off.

Millie set the cake mix down and pulled Dane out of the room.

Tate handed the ring back to me, and I smiled when I saw Dane, Millie, and Tate's names engraved inside.

"I love it!" I kissed the top of his head. "You three sure know how to make a girl feel special."

Tate was grinning. "You really love it all?"

I nodded as I put the ring back on. "So much."

Dane and Millie came back in and they both had red eyes like they had been crying.

"Well, Tate, Millie is going to be your sister instead of just your cousin. What do you think about having a sister?"

Millie played with one of her curls while she watched Tate.

"I thought she was already my sister." Tate smiled.

Millie grinned and hugged him. "Thank you."

I looked at Dane. He was smiling so big, and I swear he's never looked so sexy. I walked over to him and wrapped my arms around his neck.

"Family looks good on you."

"It looks good on you, too. Now, how soon can I get that last name of yours changed?" His dimples were completely visible.

"As soon as you want."

He looked at the kids then back at me. "Well, I have to buy a suit tomorrow. We could get you and the kids something to wear and go to the courthouse. Unless, you want a big wedding. If you do, we can do that."

"Should we talk to everyone before we do anything?"

Dane kissed me. "How about we go to the house and order pizza? We can invite everyone over to tell them."

"I'll bring cake and mac-n-cheese." I chuckled as I checked the boiling water.

He kissed me. "Sounds good." He pulled out his phone and motioned for Tate to follow him to the main house. Tate shrugged and they both walked out the door.

Millie blushed a little as she looked at all the flowers. "Mom, when did you know Dad was the guy for you?"

I thought back to all the years with Dane. "It's hard to pinpoint when I knew exactly. I've always loved him, but that love became more real in the ninth grade. I loved him but never really allowed him to love me back until now. I'm the happiest I've ever been. I don't know if that answers your question."

She pondered for a moment. "A little." Her face was the reddest I had ever seen before.

I opened the oven to check on the cake. "What are you not telling me?"

She shrugged and started playing with the bottom of her shirt.

"Do you not want to talk about it?" I couldn't help but smile. Millie had a crush.

She chewed on her lip nervously. "I...I like someone. But...he doesn't like me."

"Who? Is he at the dance studio?"

She shook her head. "No. It's...It's Chase," she whispered so low I had to move in closer to hear her speak.

I smiled bigger. "Aw, he's such a sweetie! How do you know he doesn't like you?"

"Because Tate is the only one who likes me. Everyone else thinks I'm weird."

"Did Chase say that?"

"No." She looked at me.

"Then you can't just assume that." I hugged her. "And how does Dane feel about you liking boys?"

Her cheeks were glowing from embarrassment. "I don't know. I've never liked anyone before."

"Well, as much as I'm sure you'd like to not tell him, I think you should. I want you and Tate both to come to me and your dad about anything. No judgement. I promise."

She made a face. "This should be fun."

I burst out laughing. "Yeah, for sure." I hugged her tight and kissed her head. "I love you, Millie."

Chapter Forty-four

DANE

I put the pizza on the table and looked around at the family as they all crowded around to get their food. I leaned closer to Sadie and kissed her head. "Why was Millie's face so red earlier?"

"She will have to tell you."

I opened my mouth to speak but not before Joshua came running over to Sadie screaming, "*Mine,*" excitedly. I couldn't help but laugh. That kid adored her and was the sweetest thing. I hugged Hales as she came over to me and smiled at Zach.

"So, why the sudden family time?" Zach asked.

Sadie picked up Joshua and was saying something to him to make him laugh. *That smile, though.* I swear every time that girl smiles I fall in love with her all over again.

I winked at Tate. "Do you want to tell everyone?"

He nodded. "Mom and Dad are getting married."

Trevor and Jason smiled real big. "When?" they asked together.

"Well, that's one reason we asked all of you here. We want to talk to everyone about that." I put my arm around Sadie's waist as I kept my eyes on

Hales, waiting for her reaction. She and Zach were looking at us both without showing a sign of what they were thinking.

Zach broke the awkwardness by finally walking over and hugging us both.

"Congrats. That's great! I'm shocked it's happened so soon, but I'm happy it did."

"Thanks. I need to talk to you before the night is up."

He nodded and walked back to Hailey's side. He looked down at her waiting for her to say something.

I grinned down at Sadie. "We're trying to decide whether to just go before a judge or have a wedding."

"Wedding," Hailey said quickly. When Sadie and I looked at her, she smiled. "Sorry. I was just in shock." She came over and hugged us both. "I know how much Sadie loves Halloween. We should have a Halloween wedding!"

Sadie laughed and looked at me. "That's next month."

"Girl, we can get it planned in no time," Jason said brightly.

I laughed and kissed the side of Sadie's head. "Why don't you all talk about it while I have a private word with my brother?"

She nodded, and Zach followed me to my home office. We walked in, and I shut the door behind us.

"I need to talk to you about Millie." I leaned against my desk and crossed my arms in front of my chest. I had no idea how Zach was going to take Millie calling me Dad and Sadie Mom.

"What's up? Getting cold feet already?" He laughed and sat down in the chair behind my desk. He swiveled it slowly side to side.

"Of course not, but Millie asked me a question today and I said yes. I'm afraid you'll be pissed at me, but she was feeling out of place. She just wants to fit somewhere." I rubbed the back of my neck.

"Just spit it out."

"She asked to call me and Sadie Mom and Dad. She's old enough to know we're not, and she still remembers Eliot and misses him."

Zach seemed a little confused but then smiled. "That's good, Dane. Really good. It shows she's healing."

"So, you're okay with her calling me Dad?"

"Yeah. Why wouldn't I be?"

"I don't know. I was just worried. So, looks like we're both getting married." I grinned.

"Sounds like you sooner than me, but Hales doesn't want to be pregnant and get married. Are you taking Sadie on a honeymoon? You two need some alone time. Hales and I can keep the kids."

"I don't know. I'll have to talk to her about it. I guess it depends on how long Trevor and Jason stay gone."

"Shit, I forgot about that." He furrowed his brow for a moment and then looked at me. "Is Sadie pregnant?"

"Shit, I hope not!"

He burst into laughter. "Hailey keeps having a dream she is. And now the sudden engagement…"

"Well, she needs to stop!" I ran a hand down my face. "That's a scary thought."

"You got her pregnant before," he teased.

I rolled my eyes. "Let's go back out there." I smiled at him. "Will you be my best man?"

"Hell yes." He cuffed my shoulder. "I'm really happy for you, Dane. You and Sadie deserve this."

"Thanks, Zach. That means a lot."

He nodded and let go of my shoulder before we headed out of the office.

I ADJUSTED THE tie Sadie picked out for me to try on with a suit. I fucking hated suits. I came out of the dressing room. I made a face as her and the kids looked at me.

"You look funny, Dad," Millie said as she looked up from her book.

Sadie came over to fix the tie. "He doesn't look funny. He looks handsome."

"He doesn't look like him, though." She glanced at my socked feet. "Are you going to wear dress shoes like Trevor wears?"

"Yup. He is," Sadie answered before I could. "And I like our normal Dane better, too." Sadie winked at me.

I smiled. "I have to look the part for the business meetings while Trev is gone."

"I like this one, but it'll need to be hemmed some. I can do it." Sadie laughed when I looked at her in disbelief. "What? I learned to sew in New York. I was tired of paying people to alter my dance outfits."

"Oh. That reminds me. Can you help Millie pick out a couple new dance outfits?"

She nodded. "Of course. But I know Trev and I are going to be placing an order soon for the recital. Do you mean just practice ones?"

"Yes. Mine are either getting too small or too worn out," Millie said as she closed her book and stood.

"Will Dad and Bubby wear a suit for the wedding?" She looked at Tate. She decided since she was calling me Dad and Sadie Mom, Tate needed a name, too. Bubby.

Tate looked at me. "Do we have to?"

Sadie shook her head. "Of course not. It's going to be a Halloween wedding. Anything goes. I don't care if you dress up in a costume." Sadie paled a little. She cursed several times. When her eyes met mine, they were full of terror. "I haven't told my parents. They're going to hear about it."

"Yeah, you know how this place is. Better tell them before it gets around town." I ruffled Tate's hair before going back to the dressing room to change. I grabbed the four suits Sadie liked the best and walked out.

"What do you kiddos want to go as to the wedding?" I asked.

"A ballerina princess," Millie said with a smile.

I looked at Tate.

"My dad." He cheesed.

I laughed. "So, some ripped blue jeans, Marines shirt, and boots?"

He nodded. "And the ball cap of yours Mom always wears."

Sadie adjusted my hat on her head. That was her baby.

"Good luck talking her into it," I said, tapping the bill making Sadie laugh.

"I might be able to let him borrow it," Sadie said with a wink.

We walked over to the shoe section and Sadie picked out two pairs of dress shoes that would match the new suits.

"Daisy, while I check out do you want to take Millie to the bookstore?"

Millie gave Sadie a bright smile. "Please! I'm out of new books to read."

Sadie grabbed her hand. "Of course! I need a new book, too."

Sadie and Millie walked off leaving me and Tate in the checkout line.

"After we finish here, do you want to go get a new video game or movie?" I pulled out my debit card as the cashier started ringing me up. The man looked me up and down.

"Sir, these are extremely expensive suits."

I narrowed my eyes some. "I realize that. Just ring them up."

He did as I told him. I thought I heard him mumble something about my appearance under his breath, but I ignored it. Once I had paid, we left the store.

"Where to, mini-me?"

"Can we go to Build-a-Bear? I want to make something for Millie."

"Sure. Don't tell anyone, but I secretly like that store."

He laughed. "Me too."

"Let's go make a bear for your sister." I cuffed his shoulder and we headed out.

Today was one of those days that would go at the top of the list as one of my favorites. Just spending simple time with my fiancée and kids was one of the best feelings in the entire world. *My family.* Things felt complete and whole.

Chapter Forty-Five

SADIE

I parked in the driveway of my parents' house. I hadn't talked to them in forever, and it was killing me. I hated fighting with them. I had a good reason to be upset, but I didn't want to be pissed anymore. I wanted to work things out. Not only that, they needed to hear from me that I was getting married.

The door opened and Dad stepped out. He smiled and held his arms open to me. I got out of my Rover and smiled when I made it into his arms. I loved the way he smelled, like pine and a shot of whiskey.

"Hey, Daddy," I whispered. I couldn't stay mad at him. I hated that he didn't talk to me after mine and Mom's fight. But I also understood why he didn't. He didn't like getting in the middle of things and preferred to let things simmer down before he said a word.

He kissed the top of my head. "I've missed you."

"I'm sorry I didn't talk to you. I've just been so angry with Mom and... you." I pulled away and looked up at him.

"I know, and I understand. Sadie, I wish I could go back and change things, but I can't. We were worried about you and already had marital problems. That year was pure hell, and we all made decisions we aren't proud of."

I nodded. "I know." I smiled a little. "Tate calls me Mom now. He's so amazing."

"I'm so happy for you, baby girl. How's he doing with Dane? How are you two doing being around each all the time?"

"Well, that's why I'm here. Where's Mom?"

"In the house."

We walked inside and he led me to the living room where Mom was sitting on the couch working on her computer.

"Look who's here," Dad said with a huge smile.

When Mom noticed me, tears filled her eyes. She shut her laptop and set it next to her on the couch. She stood and went to hug me but stopped. I smiled, broke the distance, and hugged her.

Dad spoke when we pulled apart. "I'm so glad you're here. Do you want to come back home and stay here until you can afford your own place?"

I shook my head and held my left hand out toward them.

"Dane asked you to marry him?" Mom asked in shock.

Dad's mouth fell open. "It's huge."

I looked at my ring and smiled. I let my hand fall to my side. I showed them my necklace from the kids. "Things are so perfect right now. We want to get married next month. A simple wedding on Halloween."

Mom laughed. "Of course. Halloween is your favorite."

"How are the kids handling all of this? I know Millie doesn't like many people." Dad watched me as we all sat down.

"Good. The kids are really excited. Millie actually asked to call me and Dane Mom and Dad."

His eyes widened. "Really? Wow."

"Do we get to meet Tate?" Mom asked.

I shook my head. "Not yet. I'm leaving that up to him."

"But we will see him at the wedding. Shouldn't you introduce us before then?"

Shit. She was right.

"I'll talk to him and figure out when."

Mom started to say something, but Dad stopped her. "Just let us know, Sadie. We don't want him being uncomfortable."

He put his hand over on Mom's. It was so good to see them working things out with each other.

"Thank you. That's all I need right now is for you guys to be patient and understanding. I don't want to go weeks without talking ever again. It's killing me."

"We don't want that either, and the last thing we want is to upset Tate." He squeezed Mom's hand.

"Right?"

Mom nodded in agreement.

"Thank you." I smiled.

"You're welcome, sweetie. How's Dane doing? His business still doing well?" Dad asked.

"Really good. Trev is about to go to Texas to help with rebuilding. Do you guys know Jason?"

"A little. He's the owner of the dance studio Dane and Trevor built, right?"

I nodded. "Trev and Jason are together. Jason has family down there so he's going too."

"So, no more Juilliard?" Mom asked.

I shrugged and smiled. "Nope. This is home. Everything that means the most to me is here in Stockbridge."

Mom smiled. "I'm proud of you, Sadie. And I'm sorry for everything."

I smiled bigger. "That means a lot." I looked at the time and stood. "I should go. Sorry I couldn't stay longer, but I have to run by the grocery store before I head home."

Dad stood and hugged me. "We'll see you soon, baby girl."

I hugged my parents and left feeling so much better. Working things out with my parents was so important to me. I knew we still had a long way to go, but this was a step.

I GOT OUT of the Rover with a smile and a bouquet of daisies for Dane. He was always buying them for me, but I never once got them for him. I smiled when I saw him sipping a glass of sweet tea on the front porch. Joyful tears filled my eyes. I was looking at a portrait of my life. The kids playing with the dogs, the setting of our home, and my baby grinning at me.

"Hey, Daisy-Love." Dane stood and walked over to me. He leaned down and kissed me. "Do you need me to get the groceries?"

I held the flowers out to him. I laughed when he noticed my watery eyes. "Happy tears. Sorry, I was having a moment."

He took the flowers before gently rubbing his thumb under my eyes to catch my tears. "You brought me flowers?"

"Yeah."

He kissed me. "Thank you."

I cupped the side of his face. "I love you, you know that, right?"

"I know. And I love you, too. You and the kids are my world, Daisy."

I smiled and let my hand fall back to my side. "So, my parents and I are okay-ish. Talking to them was a step in the right direction. I have to talk to Tate about meeting them before the wedding, though." We walked to the back of my Rover and I opened the back.

He started grabbing the bags. "Hales is inside. Be warned. She has a stack of wedding magazines."

"Hailey?" I asked in shock as I shut the back of my Rover. "She hates planning."

"Apparently, her hormones have changed that." We walked inside, and I saw Millie sitting on the couch next to Hailey browsing some magazines. Joshua came over to me and hugged my legs.

"Mine!" he said with a toothless grin.

I picked him up and kissed his cheek. I looked at Hailey. "Hales, it's gonna be a Halloween wedding. Not much planning needed."

"We still need to pick out a dress and decide what kind of decorations and food you want."

"Right this second?" I laughed.

"It's only a month away and there so much to decide," Hales said as she handed me a magazine once I sat down. Tate came running into the room with Chase behind him.

"Dad, we have practice in twenty minutes."

Dane nodded. "I know." He kissed me. "We'll be back."

"Okay. Be safe." I looked at Millie. "Can you help me by putting away groceries?"

She nodded and jumped to her feet.

I sat down next to Hailey with Joshua in my lap. I eyeballed the magazine in her lap. I already had an idea of what I sort of wanted. "I want a black dress. I want the wedding at night. Candles everywhere, the really tall, drippy wax ones. Oh, and daisies." I smiled. "Those are my only requests."

Hales sat back against the couch and grinned. "We can do that. Oh, do you want to hire one of those orchestras and play that gothic sounding music?"

"Hales, that's too much. It'd be beautiful, but pricey."

She shrugged and flipped through the magazine. "Dane can afford it."

How much money did my fiancé have? I knew he had a lot, but to pay for an orchestra? That was just insanity. I made a face. "Whether or not he can, I'd never ask him to do that. And it's only a months' notice."

"He told me whatever you wanted, you got." She grinned. "And if you pay enough you can get anything done in a short amount of time."

I thought about it. It really would be amazing, and I had connections. I could probably find a group to do it for little to nothing. "I could call in a favor to some classmates at Juilliard." I smiled.

"If you want. This is your big day, Sadie."

She was right. I'd only marry Dane once. This was huge. Dane and I were finally making us work. Me not being stupid and running anymore was worth a huge celebration.

"Well, let's get to planning then," I said as I started flipping through the magazines.

Chapter Forty-six

DANE

I leaned against the wall as I waited for Quinn, Brink, Alice, and Cooper to get off the plane. I was going to just buy them tickets to fly them in to surprise Sadie, but Brink and Quinn were coming back from New York and let them fly with them.

I pushed off the wall and smiled when I saw everyone walking over.

I held my hand out to Cooper. "It's good to see you again."

He shook it. "For sure, man. Congrats on the engagement."

Alice skipped over and hugged me. She kissed my cheek. "I told Cooper I was ready for my ring next."

I chuckled, then hugged Quinn and Brink as they walked over.

"How was the plane ride?" I asked, looking at the group as I started walking.

"Excellent," Cooper said. "It was nice getting to know Brink and Quinn. We had no idea we had such cool people living close to us.

Quinn smiled. "I love Alice. I swear she's my long-lost sister."

"Two Quinn's together. Scary," I teased.

Quinn laughed and shoved my shoulder a little. Brink smiled a little. "We split our time between there and here. And who do you think Dane stayed with when he came to see Sadie dance?"

Alice grinned at me. "I still melt every time I hear you came to see her perform."

I blushed.

Brink cuffed my shoulder. "Have you guys decided on a honeymoon yet?"

I shook my head. "She won't tell me where she wants to go." I looked at Alice. "Do you have any ideas?"

Alice squealed. "Yes! Guatemala. She told me her mom's parents are from there. She's always wanted to see where her roots are."

"Not a very honeymoon place," Brink added as we all piled into my truck.

I shrugged. "If it's where she wants to go, then we'll go."

"Maybe she'd like Barcelona. Remember when we went?" Quinn asked Brink. "It was perfect and full of Spanish culture."

I cranked the engine and started driving toward home.

"Spain was nice. But Italy was my favorite." Brink raised his eyebrows at Quinn.

I rolled my eyes. "I shouldn't have started this conversation."

Brink laughed. "Well, it was amazing."

I looked over at Cooper in the passenger seat. "Sadie still has no idea you guys are coming. She's been so busy with planning the wedding and running the dance studio, I thought she could use some help, and I know she misses you guys a lot.

"Alice and I would love to help her out. Anything we can do, we're here. It's nice when you're the son of a board member at Juilliard. You can leave whenever you want and stay gone as long as you need."

"Thanks."

I PLAYED WITH Sadie's hair as she laid with her head on my chest. "Did you like my surprise?"

She traced the tattoo over my heart with kisses. "Very much," she whispered against my skin. "And it worked out perfectly that I'm here and Alice and Cooper can stay in my house."

"Sadie, where do you want to go for our honeymoon?"

She propped herself up on her elbows and looked at me. "We don't have to go anywhere."

I scrunched my eyebrows together as I returned her stare. "You sure? We could always make it a family trip if you don't want to leave the kids."

"I really don't want to leave them right now. One day, but everything is changing so much for them. I don't want to leave them just yet. Let's plan a trip for the summer when they are done with school. I'd love for them to come with us, too."

I ran a finger gently down her cheek. "Millie has been asking to go somewhere."

"Where?"

"Universal studios, to Harry Potter world."

"That'd be amazing!"

I kissed her. "I agree." I yawned. "Two more weeks, and you'll be Sadie Shaw."

"I'm the luckiest girl in the world." She smiled. Her mouth fell into a slight grin and her expression turned thoughtful for a moment. "Dane?"

"Yeah?"

"Can we adopt Millie?"

Another, *fall-in-love-with-Daisy-all-over-again*, moment.

"We can talk to her about it. I think she's old enough to make the decision herself."

"If she wants to, can we make it official on our wedding day?"

"I think that'd be perfect." I kissed her nose. "Oh, by the way, Hales told me I need to have a talk with you about my current financial situation."

"She did?"

"She said it's something a significant other should know, and I should tell you before I gave you my wedding present."

"O-kay."

I moved away from her and opened the drawer to the end table next to my side of the bed. "The men in our family are big about buying one specific gift for our loves. Elliot bought Sam her home, Zach bought Hales a beach house in Gulf Shores, and I bought you this." I handed over an envelope with a picture and deed of a townhouse in New York.

She sat up and opened it. When she realized what it was, her mouth fell open.

"Shut up! Are you serious?"

"I know how much you love New York. Now we have a place to go when we visit."

She tackled me, making me fall back into the bed. "Thank you!"

I laughed and wrapped my arms around her. "I'm glad you like it." I tucked her hair behind her ears once we settled back into bed. "Now, between the money Elliot left me, what I've made from investments Zach had suggested, and the money I've made from the business, we're millionaires."

She smiled. "Okay. Cool." Money was something that never fazed Sadie. Of course, she liked it, but she was always like me. Simple.

I laughed. "None of us talk about money. We're happy with working and living the simple life. I swear I'll drive my truck until it blows up."

"And my Rover stays. Forever."

"I know. I know. I swear we'll end up spending a fortune on it keeping it alive, but I feel the same about Coach's truck. I'm keeping it for Millie."

She yawned. "Tomorrow, let's take the kids to get donuts and go tell Coach Elliot and Sam the good news. They're the only ones we haven't told we're engaged." She kissed me and snuggled against me under the covers.

"I have a meeting at eight with Mr. Miller, then we can go." I yawned again. Scout and Juno came over to the bed and climbed in. They laid down at our feet. "I'm ready for Trev to be back."

"Me too. And Jason. Jason has become like my brother. They are so good together."

"They are. And Jason is amazing with Millie. He's really pushed her."

"She's amazing. I worked for years to have the talent she already has." Her eyes started getting heavy.

I kissed the top of her head. "Get some sleep."

She moved her hand up my chest until her hand found mine. She let out a small content sigh. I ran my free hand up and down her spine until she drifted off to sleep. I yawned for the millionth time and started drifting off to sleep. I was almost there when I heard a soft knock on the bedroom door. I watched as it opened, and Tate poked his head in. I smiled sleepily.

"Everything okay?"

"Nightmare." He walked in quietly. "Can I sleep with you guys?" He smiled at Sadie. "She's pretty when she sleeps."

I patted the spot on the other side of me. "She's pretty all the time. Get in, son." I held the covers up and he crawled in next to me. Boy jumped up on the bed with Juno and Scout. It wasn't even a minute later when Millie was poking her head in. I waved her over and she crawled in next to Sadie. When Sassy jumped up, I chuckled a little.

"Good thing I have a big bed."

Both kids giggled.

Chapter Forty-seven

SADIE

I woke up to someone opening the curtains in the room. Dane stayed the night at Hales' and Zach's house. Hailey, Alice, and Quinn insisted it was bad luck to stay the night together. I squinted my eyes when the sun peeked in and stretched. I smiled at Millie.

"You're up early."

Dane and I had talked to Millie about adopting her and making her officially ours. She said yes and we all cried. She had been talking about it non-stop since we asked her. She told me last night before bed that she didn't think she'd be able to sleep she was so excited. Quinn and Brink had the adoption papers ready, and during our vows, Dane and I had separate vows to Millie and Tate. Then we'd all sign. It was going to be perfect.

She bounced on her feet a little. "The dogs wanted to go outside." I loved the smile on her face. I patted the spot next to me on the bed. She climbed in and laid down. I tucked some of her wild curls behind her ears.

"Mom, why does Alice say she wants to see me dance?" Millie asked.

"Are you talking about what she said last night at dinner?"

She nodded.

"She works at Juilliard." I smiled.

"The dance school you went to?"

I nodded and furrowed my brow. "Have you ever heard of Juilliard?"

"Only what Dad told me. He said it's the best dance school in the country."

"It is. I've told Alice and Cooper how amazing you are."

She blushed. "I'm not that amazing."

"Millie, you're the best I've seen." I ran my fingers through her hair. "I'm serious."

"Do you think... Do you really think I'd be able to go one day? I mean, if I learn how to be around people better, that is."

"For sure."

She smiled brightly. "I want to teach little kids to dance like you teach them at Jason's studio."

I was about to reply but Alice, Hales, and Quinn came piling into the room talking about hair, makeup, breakfast, and all the other million things we needed to do. I pulled the comforter over mine and Millie's heads and we giggled. The comforter was pulled back and three very persistent girls stared at us.

"The wedding isn't until sunset. We have plenty of time," I groaned.

"It takes hours to get ready!" Quinn said in a panic. "We're already behind."

"I miss my boys," I said in a pout. "Can I see them for just a bit?"

"Nope. Now, we have appointments to get our hair done and nails. We don't want to be late." Quinn placed her hands on her hips and tapped her foot impatiently.

I got out of bed and went to reach for my phone, but Alice snatched it away.

"Hey!" I snapped.

Alice laughed and handed it to Hailey. "No talking to him until tonight."

"Get up and get going, girlies. We made breakfast." Quinn ruffled Millie's curls then left the room.

"Aunt Quinn bought me a dress to wear tonight." She scrunched her nose. "She said I can't wear my ballerina outfit to the wedding."

"Did she now? Well, guess what? I'm the bride, and what I say goes. You can wear whatever you want."

"If what you say goes, Mom, why don't you have your phone?" She grinned real big at me.

I burst out laughing. "Okay, so Quinn is being a bossy pants and when she's in this mode, we all tend to listen. She's scary."

Millie laughed. "Yep. Real scary."

The door opened again, and Quinn poked her head in. She snapped her fingers. "Chop! Chop! Breakfast is getting cold. Come on, girls, we have a lot to do today!"

I moved until Millie could climb on my back. She wrapped her arms around my neck and her legs around my waist.

Quinn smiled at us. "You won't be able to do that much longer. She's getting too big."

I laughed as we followed Quinn out of the room. "I know. I wish I could make her and Tate both stop growing for just a little while. Since we got Tate, he's already grown like two inches. He's going to be tall like his daddy."

We came into the kitchen, and I bent down a little to let Millie off my back. "What are Dane and Tate doing?" I asked as I picked up a piece of bacon.

Hailey and Alice were pouring orange juice in all the glasses at the table.

"That's not for you to know," Hales said with a sly grin.

Millie giggled and started fixing her plate.

Quinn sat down. "Alice, you and Cooper need to come have dinner with us one night when we all get back to New York."

"For sure!" Alice said as she took a seat. "I think Cooper and Brink have a serious bromance forming."

I heard the front door open and smiled when Jason came in. "Morning, girls! I came to bring all you beauties to get your nails done."

I smiled around a fork full of pancakes. "How's Dane and Tate?" I asked after swallowing.

"I don't know. I came straight here while Trevor headed over there."

I huffed and took another bite.

"Why don't you just call and ask?" he asked as he came up behind me and put his hands on my shoulders.

I narrowed my eyes at Alice, Hales, and Quinn. They all laughed.

"We aren't letting her talk to him. Since they've gotten back together, they've been inseparable. This is the fun about a wedding. No contact or get to see each other until she's walking down the aisle." Hailey was cheesing.

"Since when did you start liking all of this kind of stuff?" I laughed.

"I'm telling you, with the pregnancy, I'm this new person. I feel like a real girl."

We all laughed.

"Maybe you're having a girl," Quinn said with a humorous smile.

Hailey blushed a little and nodded. "I can't keep quiet any longer. It is a girl. Zach and I were going to do this huge gender reveal party, but then my mother got involved and annoyed me so I said forget it. You know how Zach is, he hates big stuff with a lot of people."

All of our mouths fell open.

Hailey laughed. "I know! Crazy, right? For a while there I thought Zach would never get his girl. We picked out a name and everything."

"What is it?" Millie asked as she bounced in her chair.

"We're naming her after Zach and Elliot's late grandmother, Nora Elaine."

"That's beautiful," Quinn said with a bright smile."

Hailey nodded. "I agree. I just hope she likes to play baseball since my boys seem to hate it."

"Are you two done after this?" I asked.

Hailey shrugged after taking a drink. "Who knows?"

Everyone laughed and started eating.

Jason kissed the top of my head. "Hurry up, beautiful. We got stuff to do."

"Yes, sir." I shoveled the rest of my food down.

Holy-fucking-shit-balls.

I'm getting married!

Chapter Forty-eight

DANE

I took in the scene around the entire yard. Since waking up this morning, the same huge grin remained plastered on my face. I was getting married to my Daisy-Love today.

The yard was set up in a gothic wedding style. Tall candles were on the tables, dark red roses and daisies were everywhere. The sun was starting to set, making the lit candles and old lanterns really stand out. I smiled at the Build-a-Bears at our dinner table that Tate and I had made for our girls. Sadie and mine were in wedding attire, Tate's was in a cowboy outfit, and Millie's was dressed like a ballerina. I smiled when Tate came over to me.

"I thought you were going to wear Sadie's ball cap." I adjusted his white cowboy hat.

"Don't tell her, but can't find it."

My eyes widened. "Oh, no. Where did you last have it?"

"I was wearing it when I was fishing at the lake with Millie." He thought for a moment. "I climbed a tree and I remember it falling off. Millie and I looked everywhere, but we can't find it. We had the dogs with us, and I think one of them may have taken it somewhere."

"Let's go see if we can find it."

"It's almost time for the wedding, Dad. We can look later."

I gave him a hug. "Don't be so sad. We'll find it."

He nodded and put his hands in his jean pockets. "Are you excited?"

"Very. Are you? This affects you as much as it does me."

His crooked grin appeared. "Yeah. Millie told me a few days ago that this was going to be the best day of her life. Mom told me the same thing." His smile grew bigger. "I miss my other parents a lot, but I'm okay, Dad. I really do believe things happen for a reason. I'm a lucky kid. I lost them, but I have you, Mom, and my sister. I just have a lot to be thankful for."

I hugged him again. "I'm lucky, too. I have an amazing son who gave me a family. All of this is because of you, Tate."

He scrunched his nose. "Really? How?"

I knelt down in front him. "You gave me a son that I adore, a daughter who is finally becoming truly happy again, and a wife who, because of you, came home."

Tears filled his eyes and his smile returned. I rubbed my thumbs gently under his eyes to catch the tears. "You are the best thing to happen to us, and I thank God every day for you."

He hugged me tightly. "I love you, Dad."

"I love you, too, son."

When he pulled back I stood. I smiled as guest started showing up. Our wedding wasn't going to be packed, but with the people that meant the most to us.

"Hey, Tate!" Chase said as his parents and he showed up. I shook Mr. and Mrs. Andrews' hands.

"Where's Millie?" Chase asked, looking around.

"Yes, where is she?" Mr. Andrews's asked with a smile. "We'd like to meet the girl Chase talks about all the time."

Chase's face turned red. "Dad!"

Tate cupped his hand beside his mouth and leaned in close to me. "He has a big crush on her."

Tate laughed when Chase shoved his shoulder. "Dude!"

Quinn came rushing over in red stiletto heels. She was such a pro in walking in those things, there was no doubt she'd be able to run a marathon in them. And win.

I laughed. "Son, why don't you go show them to their seats?"

He nodded and led them away.

"Sadie's parents are here. They just got done seeing her and she wanted me to let you know since they haven't met Tate yet."

I rubbed the back of my neck. "Does she want me to introduce them to him?"

"No. She just wanted me to warn you. She almost came out here with them herself, but Hailey and Alice are keeping her locked away."

Just then, I saw her parents. I hadn't seen them since finding out about Tate. Knots formed in my stomach.

I frowned. "About that. I haven't talked to her all day because of you."

Quinn laughed. "Just wait until you see her. It'll be worth not seeing or talking to her all day."

When Sadie's parents saw me, they looked ashamed of themselves, as they should.

She patted my shoulder. "I'll leave you to talk to them. I have to go make sure everything is ready." She adjusted my tie and kissed my cheek. "I'm so happy for you, Dane." She smiled at the orchestra that was all seated and ready to start playing. "This wedding is going to be perfect."

She walked off and Mr. and Mrs. Solis came over. I held my hand out to them. "Mr. and Mrs. Solis."

They both shook it. Mrs. Solis started looking around. It was clear that she was looking for my son.

"After everything settles down after the wedding, we'd love to have everyone over. Sadie mentioned she wished we could've found the time to meet Tate before the wedding, but sadly it never worked out." Mr. Solis smiled a little. "We're very proud of you and our daughter."

"Thank you." I scanned the yard. "Wait here. I'll be right back." I walked off and found Tate with Chase. I motioned for him to come to me.

"Sadie's parents just showed up."

"Oh." He stared down at his boots.

"They'd like to meet you. You don't have to talk to them if you don't want to, but I'd like to introduce you to them so they don't corner you later."

He looked up at me and nodded.

I put my hand to his back and led him to them. I wrapped my arm around his shoulders. "This is our son, Tate. Tate, these are your mom's parents."

Tate moved so he was pressed against my side.

Her parents introduced themselves. He said hi so quietly I almost thought he said nothing at all. He had made it clear to Sadie and me that the ones he was truly mad at were them. He didn't forgive easily, and I didn't blame him. I was the same way.

"Why don't you go back and hang out with Chase? We'll be starting soon." I handed him Sadie's wedding band. "You want to hold this for me?"

He nodded and put in his pocket. He told her parents bye and hurried off.

"He's adorable, Dane," Mrs. Solis said quietly. She wiped at her eyes.

Mr. Solis looked at me while he rubbed circles on her back. "We truly are sorry, Dane. We pushed Sadie to give him up."

"He's a great kid. And I know. She told me, and Tate knows that as well. It's going to take him time to want to be around you guys."

They both nodded.

Mr. Solis kissed the top of Mrs. Solis's head. "We're going to find our seats. Welcome to the family, Dane." He shook my hand. Sadie's mom hugged me, kissed my cheek, and they both walked off.

Zach, Jason, and Trevor walked over.

Zach cuffed my shoulder. "You ready, little bro?"

I nodded. "More than ready. I've been waiting for this day since the ninth grade."

We walked to the front of the aisle and Tate joined us. "You ready, son?"

He grinned and nodded.

I looked toward the back of the house as the music started. Millie came out first. She was stunning. I squeezed Tate's shoulder to get him to look up at me then motioned for him to look at Chase. He chuckled at Tate who was using someone's phone to take a picture of her.

I shook my head. I was going to have to keep an eye on him. I looked back toward the doors when the music changed. My heart sped up and tears filled my eyes. My Daisy-Love stepped out and I was completely and utterly at a loss for words.

My Daisy was absolutely breathtaking.

Damn.

Alice and Hailey helped fix her dress. Long, see-through black-lace sleeves went down her arms, and the black bodice was fitted tightly down to her hips where the bottom of the dress fluffed out in a giant swirl of sparkly black tulle. Her hair was all down and slightly curled. But what made me grin the biggest was my ball cap on her head.

Tate grinned up at me when I looked at him. "I didn't really lose it, Dad. I told her she needed to wear it today. I was kidding with you about losing it."

I chuckled as my eyes found Sadie again. When she started to walk, I noticed her black Converse peeking out from the bottom of her dress. She was pure perfection. I couldn't stop myself from meeting her halfway. I pulled her close to me, knotted my fingers in her hair, and kissed her.

Sadie's family, friends from Juilliard, and my work crew all were clapping and laughing.

"Well, I guess this means they do," the pastor said with a chuckle.

I pulled back from her a little. "Sorry. I couldn't help myself," I said, keeping my eyes on hers. "You're gorgeous, Daisy-Love."

She tugged gently on my tie. "You clean up nice yourself." She pulled a little harder on the tie until my lips found hers again.

"Okay, okay, save that for later," Zach said as he laughed.

Sadie stuck her tongue out at Zach as we made our way back to the front of the aisle that was a bed of daisy petals.

"They really outdid themselves on decorating. It's amazing," Sadie whispered.

I leaned close to her. "You should see our bedroom." I smiled at her. "Look at the table." I pointed to a table that had the bears Tate and I made on it.

Her smile grew. She squeezed my hand before looking at the pastor. "Let's do this thing," she said with the sexiest grin. "We've been waiting our whole lives for this." She motioned for Tate and Millie to come stand in front of us. With her free hand, she played with one of Millie's curls while the Pastor talked.

We promised ourselves to each other and to our kids. And just like that, life for me had changed. My Daisy became mine. All the years of waiting, all the doubt and heartache led to this perfect moment. *Forever*, we promised, and forever it would finally be.

Lightning Source UK Ltd.
Milton Keynes UK
UKHW01n1957100918
328674UK00001B/4/P